CUBAN BLUFF

By the same author

Spy! (with Richard Deacon)
MI5: British Security Service Operations 1909–45
MI6: British Secret Intelligence Service Operations 1909–45
A Matter of Trust: MI5 1945–72
Unreliable Witness: Espionage Myths of World War II
The Branch: A History of the Metropolitan Police Special Branch
GARBO (with Juan Pujol)
GCHQ: The Secret Wireless War 1900–86
The Friends: Britain's Postwar Secret Intelligence Service
  Operations
Games of Intelligence

FICTION
The Blue List

NIGEL WEST

CUBAN BLUFF

Crown Publishers, Inc.
New York

Published by Crown Publishers, Inc., 201 East 50th Street, New York, New York 10022. Member of the Crown Publishing Group.

Originally published in Great Britain by Martin Seeker & Warburg Limited, in 1990 in different form.

CROWN is a trademark of Crown Publishers, Inc.

Manufactured in the United States of America

Library of Congress Cataloging-in-Publication Data

West, Nigel.
    Cuban bluff / Nigel West. — 1st ed.
      p.   cm.
    1. Cuban Missile Crisis, Oct. 1962—Fiction. I. Title.
PR6073.E765C8 1991
823′.914—dc20   91-15577
                                                    CIP

ISBN 0-517-58538-3

10   9   8   7   6   5   4   3   2   1

First American Edition

This strange and still scarcely explicable affair ... There are so many questions which still remain unanswered. Why did the Russians risk so much? What was their ultimate purpose? Why did they withdraw? Why did they not retaliate at other, but equally sensitive, points?

HAROLD MACMILLAN IN HIS FOREWORD TO *Thirteen Days*

In the weeks before the Cuban missile crisis of 1962 two special security classifications were introduced for certain categories of top secret documents. ELITE was the code name given to the West's political back channels, and PSALM was the designated code word for the intelligence product.

Those who were actively involved behind the scenes, as the world was on the threshold of nuclear confrontation, became known as the Psalmists. This is their story.

Cuban Bluff

Helsinki, Finland;
Friday, 22 December 1961

Frank Friberg muttered a low curse as the doorbell sounded. He was perched precariously at the top of rickety folding steps, attempting to put a tinsel star at the top of the Christmas tree. He had promised his wife to finish the decorations before they left for the theater. Awkwardly, Friberg stretched his arm to check his watch. It was six-twenty, and the performance was due to start at seven. They would be cutting it close, and they were not expecting anyone.

"Can you get it," called his wife from upstairs. "I'm not quite ready yet."

Friberg suppressed another oath and clambered cautiously down the steps, leaving the line of electric fairy lights dangling from a branch. Unlike other American diplomats of his rank, there was no live-in staff in the Friberg household. A maid worked every morning, and she occasionally helped out if there was a dinner party, but their life-style was unostentatious, as befitted the CIA station chief in Helsinki. And whereas some of his colleagues lived in great state, entertaining political leaders and cultivating leading figures from the local military or the intelligence agencies, Friberg's role was deliberately low-key. Although not officially recognized as Soviet bloc, Finland was sufficiently close to the Soviet Union geographically, politically, and economically to make the country potentially hostile territory for the U.S. clandestine service. Accordingly, Friberg exercised a degree of caution before opening his door. He checked the peephole that had been inserted into the woodwork by the embassy's security office, and took a moment to register the little group huddled against the bitter cold on his porch. A short, bespectacled man in his mid-thirties stood there,

1

with a rather stout but handsome woman beside him, a small baby in her arms.

Friberg swung the door open instantly. This was no weather to be out in the snow; anyway, he thought he recognized the man, although he could not put a name to the face for a few moments. As he gestured to the couple to come in, his mind raced over the updated REDTOP order-of-battle cards he had studied the previous month. A Soviet, no doubt about it, thought Friberg. And a relatively new arrival at the embassy. He racked his brains. He'd arrived about three months ago, in a second secretary slot vacated by a confirmed First Chief Directorate officer. Could this guy be KGB, too? Then a name came to him. Klimov ... Anatoli Mikhailovich ... flagged as a possible intelligence officer.

Friberg watched as his visitors shook the snow off their coats in the hall and pushed the door shut, fitting it snugly into its rein-forced steel frame. A dozen questions came to Friberg. He thought it likely that the man trying to balance his fur hat on the shelf over the steam radiator was a sophisticated adversary, a member of the elite within Moscow Center's own elite. After all, he rea-soned, he had filled the spot left by Igor Tasoev, a man positively identified by the Agency's Counterintelligence Staff as a First Chief Directorate bagman. And in their typically plodding, bureaucratic way, the Soviets found it administratively easier to reserve particu-lar positions in their overseas missions for the KGB. Thus it was a veritable certainty that the TASS correspondent was military intelligence, a GRU operative, and Strelnikov's replacement was a KGB "K" Line case officer, just like his predecessor, and in all probability held the same rank, that of major.

"Good evening," Friberg welcomed nonchalantly, in English. "What can I do for you?" Out of the corner of his eye he could see his wife looking through the staircase railings, curious to see their unexpected callers.

The Russian spoke in a poor English accent as he unbuttoned his coat. His voice was labored, and he spoke in quick short bursts, as though he knew and had rehearsed what he had wanted to say but actually articulating the right words was more difficult than he had imagined.

"Am Golitsyn, Anatoli Mikhailovich." He held his hand out to his companion. "My wife, Svetlana, and daughter. Request political asylum. Live in America."

Friberg looked at all three silently. The man was short and wiry, his eyes full of determination. His wife, by contrast, seemed oblivious to the gravity of what had been said on her behalf, concerned only about the child that stirred slightly in her sleep. She had fine features, her hair swept up under her hat, but she was preoccupied by the baby that was slowly adjusting to the warmth of the house.

Friberg's instinctive reaction was one of caution. Have I been chosen at random, simply as an American envoy, or does he know my true role? Is he on the level, or is this a crude attempt at a provocation to create an embarrassing diplomatic incident? There had been several such episodes in the past, particularly in Vienna and Berlin, but never in Helsinki. This was almost home turf for the KGB, and the local *rezidentura* generally behaved in a way intended to avoid exacerbating relations with the Finns.

"Let me get this straight," said Friberg. "You're a Soviet citizen and you are seeking asylum in the United States."

The Russian nodded impatiently. He pointed to Friberg. "CIA." Then he pointed to himself. "KGB. *Kontra Razvyedka.*"

"Holy shit," muttered Friberg. "A hot one." Those two magic Russian words, virtually unknown outside the intelligence lexicon, meant Klimov or Golitsyn, whatever he called himself, was indeed "K" Line. Not just First Chief Directorate, but the super-secret counterintelligence department. The outfit that recruited and ran agents. Friberg knew from all the Soviet bloc lectures he had attended in Washington what the implications were. No vague talk of tradecraft and support logistics. This was it! Personal experience ... names, dates, and places. Full order-of-battle, not just of a single *rezidentura*, but of others in Scandinavia, and perhaps farther afield.

Golitsyn continued in his fractured English, becoming increasingly insistent. "Asylum to the United States. Have information, good information."

3

"Does anyone know you're here?" asked Friberg. Golitsyn looked puzzled. "When will your absence be noticed?"

"Embassy closed for vacation," responded Golitsyn. "Go now to the United States. I am major in KGB."

Friberg smiled. It always amused him that for an officially atheistic society, its overseas representatives always seemed willing to observe the local religious holidays. The idea of the Soviet mission closing for the annual celebration of the birth of Christ amused him. What would Lenin have said? Friberg dismissed the thought and returned to the business at hand. With the embassy closed, the pressure was eased. He had some breathing space before the search parties were scouring the city. "So you're KGB. Very well. Then you will understand there are a couple of questions I have to put to you ... to establish your credentials." Golitsyn nodded, apparently anxious to please. He must have known that Friberg would not be able to take him at face value and would need to check his bona fides.

"The first is one I am obliged to ask of anyone in your position seeking asylum. It's simply this: Do you know of any plans to launch a surprise attack against the United States of America?" The absurd formality of the inquiry amused Golitsyn and served to break the growing tension in the room.

"No," he laughed. "No attack."

Friberg had been keen to dispose of that little rite, a duty required of every CIA officer in his situation, and perhaps a reflection of the international atmosphere of the day. Having disposed of it, he could turn to the $64,000 question, which might confirm Golitsyn's claimed status.

"Who is the *rezident* in Helsinki?" Friberg knew the correct answer, but there was no reason to suppose that the Soviets had realized the Agency had positively nailed him.

"Colonel Zhenikhov," replied Golitsyn. "Real son of bitch, yes?"

"If you say so, Major," replied Friberg evenly, anxious not to betray his feelings, for he knew that his Soviet counterpart was indeed the good colonel. And he was a bastard, too, he thought.

Friberg was convinced. Telling his guests to sit down and make themselves comfortable, he started to put a well-oiled machine into action. He telephoned his deputy, Philip Whitehead, at his apartment on the Puolaharja, and used a prearranged signal to bring him over. It was automatically assumed that the line was tapped.

"Phil, it's Frank. I can't make the card game. Can you deal me out?"

Whitehead paused while the apparently casual remark had its impact. "No sweat. I'll take care of it right away."

Each station had its own procedure for handling emergencies over open telephone lines. Conversations were kept to a minimum, and every effort was made to have it sound natural, whatever the circumstances, avoiding any clue to relative seniority. Talk of poker, in Friberg's station, meant only one thing: a "walk-in." Over on the other side of Helsinki, Whitehead abandoned the book he was reading to his twins, kissed his understanding wife goodnight, and drove his Volvo across the city to the U.S. embassy building on Itainen Puistotie.

Whitehead parked his car in the space reserved for embassy staff and made his way to the side door. He identified himself to the Marine Corps guard on duty and took the elevator to the third floor, where he went through the same procedure again with the armed marine in the glass booth before letting himself into the secure complex of offices that accommodated the CIA station. It was a long corridor, and he went straight to the duty room where Gwen Knucke was hunched over one of the Agency's new electric typewriters. She was surprised to see him, but his manner dissuaded her from asking questions.

"Gwen, I'll have a cable for Washington in a couple of minutes. Can you give me a hand when I'm through enciphering it?"

Hardly waiting for her response, Whitehead ducked back into the corridor and made his way to his windowless office. His message would be short and to the point, no more than "REDTOP Westport bound," but only he could encrypt it. Only he had access to the codebook, which he kept in his combination wall safe. Having completed the cable, and double-checked it for errors, Whitehead returned the slim booklet of one time cipher groups to the first shelf. This was a tedious task that only he was authorized to perform, and he hated it. Finally satisfied that the cable was free of all mistakes, he added a prefix with the two special code words used to alert the Soviet Bloc Division duty officer and the Counter-intelligence Staff. Whitehead then returned to Gwen, who would act as the station's communications officer, and passed the message, slugged FLASH, to her. The need for absolute security precluded any accompanying small talk. A flash priority needed no explanation. Gwen was sufficiently professional to put the routine traffic to one side and access the secure teletype channel when she saw the code word classification Whitehead had selected. Once transferred onto a perforated tape, the text was fed into the transceiver, which inserted the groups of letters into the continuous chatter of high-frequency traffic that linked the embassy's roof to the relay station at RAF Croughton near Banbury in Oxfordshire. From there, the cable was boosted under the Atlantic by secure land line to the Agency's operations room in its new headquarters at Langley, Virginia, just outside Washington. The particular prefixes to the text would ensure prompt delivery to its two intended recipients.

Whitehead waited to see the tape shredded by Gwen and consigned to the burnbag, and then made an unusual request.

"Gwen, I need access to the classified compartment. Would you be kind enough to sign me out a sidearm?" All the station's weaponry, apart from the handgun in the station chief's personal safe, was kept in a steel locker, the key to which was in the custody of the current duty officer. The Agency's bureaucratic rules required an officer drawing a weapon to sign out the hardware and have the transaction witnessed by the duty officer. Gwen unlocked the steel cabinet behind her desk and watched silently as Whitehead extracted a buff envelope. Inside, she knew, was a .38 Smith & Wesson police special without any serial numbers and a dozen rounds of ammunition. Whitehead signed the necessary entry in the duty officer's withdrawal book and hurried back to his car. He had been in the building for less than fifteen minutes.

Whitehead placed the bulky envelope in his car's glove compartment, leaving the flap open so the revolver inside could be retrieved easily, and guided his car through the empty streets, checking the rearview mirror every few seconds. He was taking the standard countersurveillance precautions, and he wondered if the chief of station really had hooked a fish. Either that, or it was another exercise. There had already been two in the eleven months he had been posted to this cold, quiet, windswept town. More likely, he thought, a Soviet provocation. The possible benefits to Moscow were considerable: positive identification of CIA personnel *en poste*, an indication of relative ranks and an opportunity to study communications procedures, the location of a safehouse or two, and perhaps a row that would drag in the ambassador and the State Department. Certainly the Soviets were monitoring the station's signals from their huge antenna array near Tallinn, just a few miles away due south, across the Baltic, in the hope of recovering some useful data for the GRU's traffic analysts.

Whitehead made two more turns, just to test a new pair of headlights in his mirror, and then, reasonably satisfied he was not under hostile surveillance, turned north for his chief's home on Grasantie. He cruised past number fourteen a couple of times to examine for opposition presence. Even if this was a drill, he told himself, someone from the inspector general's office might well be lurking in the shadows, marking him down for failing to go through the whole routine. That had happened on his previous assignment, in Bonn, when he had been assigned to an operation known within the intelligence community as a "gangplank pitch." One of the local Novosti correspondents had been recalled to Moscow at the end of his routine tour and the chief of station had delegated Whitehead to do the honors. The usual procedure was an apparently innocent encounter only moments before the target left the host country, at which he was offered the opportunity to supply the Agency with information via a neutral address in a third country. The exercise had gone quite smoothly, but Whitehead had been criticized for having left his apartment and going straight to the rendezvous without taking any antisurveillance precautions. It subsequently turned out that the "Novosti correspondent" was really another CIA officer playing the role to test Whitehead, but he had learned his lesson. Despite the cold Whitehead flushed with embarrassment as he remembered the episode. This time he would go by the book.

Langley, Virginia;
24 December 1961, Christmas Eve

Leo McGee pushed his thick, black-rimmed glasses up onto his snowy white hair and rubbed his eyes. He had been scanning the batch of cables that lay on his desk and he was anxious not to miss anything. Reading in poor light, together with his passion for making tapestries, had ruined his eyesight so that although he was not yet fifty-five he was heavily dependent upon the heavy lenses that so tired him. But as exhausted as he was, and even on Christmas Eve, and a Sunday at that, he would not have wanted to be anywhere else. He was a dedicated intelligencer, and he had before him what he recognized to be a once-in-a-lifetime opportunity. The first hours after a REDTOP defection were critical, and the decisions taken by the CI Staff, of which he was a member, would be the subject of continuous review in the months to come. Sitting opposite him, reclining in the standard U.S. government issue office easy chair, available for GS-9 grades and above, was Scott Miler, ten years younger and another CI veteran. Unlike McGee, his immediate superior, who had gravitated into the CIA from a glorious war in the Office of Strategic Services, spent mainly in the Mediterranean theater, Miler was a former FBI special agent. Although he had lived in the States all his adult life, Miler's Scottish origins occasionally surfaced in his Highland brogue. This usually happened when Miler was excited, and this was just such a moment. Both men knew the importance of receiving a Soviet of Golitsyn's caliber.

"His designated code name is STONE and he says he holds the rank of major, First Chief Directorate. He was flown out yesterday, on an embassy courier flight, having been holed up in one of Friberg's safehouses, and now he's under interrogation at Westport."

Miler smiled in approval. Westport was the CIA's main defector reception and debriefing center, located in a large country mansion at Niederrad on the outskirts of Frankfurt, within easy reach of the huge CIA base in the town. Security was tight in order to protect both the defectors and the operational personnel posted there. Once isolated at Westport, a false defector would learn little to disadvantage the Agency. Precautions were taken to prevent a "client" from discovering his or her exact location, and the staff habitually adopted cover names to conceal their true identities.

"There were no diplomatic repercussions with the Finns, so either the Soviets haven't noticed they're a man short, or they have their own reasons for keeping quiet."

"Any clues to his meal ticket?" asked Miler. Every defector had to work his passage and justify his existence by supplying information.

"Only the Helsinki *rezidentura*. It looks authentic so far. We have a complete order-of-battle, dating back to 1947, and a very handy list of KGB agents who have infiltrated the Social Democrats. It's mainly political."

"Motivation?" Miler knew from experience that this was the key. Was the defector a committed idealist determined to undermine the Soviet system by betraying as much as possible, or a mere opportunist desperate to improve his financial standing? Miler had seen all kinds, from a spontaneous line-crosser in Berlin who had grabbed a chance to live in the West with his mistress to a mercenary in Vienna who had spun out his tale for months so as to milk the Agency for a lucrative consultancy post.

"Hard to say. He's brought his family, and says he's been memorizing files for two years. However, it seems our man had a row with the *rezident*, Zhenikhov, over how one of their star political assets should be handled. He backed the deputy *rezident*, Sergei Vladimirov, and Ambassador Zhakarov against Zhenikhov and reported him to Moscow Center. It turned out that Zhenikhov had more friends at court than the ambassador, and his future began to look rather bleak."

"Any previous?"

"Yeah. If he really is Golitsyn, and not Klimov, then he was flagged in Vienna six years ago. Piotr Deriabin identified him then as a First Chief Directorate type. Tricky wife, loner, possible misfit. Could be our man."

"I'm not sure I like the recommendation," murmured Miler.

McGee attempted to reassure his colleague. "Don't worry. That's just Deriabin. All prejudice, no heart. He didn't have anything good to say about *any* of his colleagues. He hated them all, but Golitsyn rather less than the rest. Felt sorry for him, I think. Let's hope he's wrong about the wife."

Miler remembered Deriabin all too well. A short, swarthy Russian who had come across in Austria. His defection had prompted several arrests and suicides in the Federal Republic where he had been running a network inside NATO. A man with an encyclopedic memory, he had been put on the payroll as an adviser and had been with the Agency ever since.

"A picture is coming over the wire from Germany so Deriabin can confirm his identity. He can fly over to Europe and do a visual if necessary."

"How has he fared on the polygraph?" Miler asked cautiously. It was standard procedure for all "clients" to be "fluttered." Not everyone accepted the device as an accurate gauge of someone's veracity, but as a psychological tool it was invaluable. The false defectors, or "plants," made every excuse to avoid having to submit to it, convinced it would expose them. But for every measure in the counterintelligence business, there was a countermeasure. That was the essential enigma at the heart of the intelligence conundrum, and what made the occupation so attractive to McGee and Miler.

"STONE has performed oddly," continued McGee. "He won't deal with anyone who speaks Russian, so we have to converse in German and his really lousy English. It could be a novel way of neutralizing the polygraph. He's very sensitive about having any Russian-speakers near his family."

"What do the tapes show?" asked Miler.

"The audio recordings?"

Miler nodded. He knew the value of what those in the business euphemistically called "technical coverage."

"The safehouse was wired, of course," McGee explained. "And so was the car in Frankfurt. So far, nothing suspicious. They probably realize Westport is miked, so we would expect the tapes there to be clean. But the safehouse conversations are all kosher. They must have talked this over between themselves already. She is very compliant, contrary to Deriabin's recollection. He seems confident, self-assured, but not overassertive with her. He doesn't take much notice of the baby."

"Are they man and wife?" Miler was probing at every possible soft spot in Golitsyn's story. Quite often KGB personnel considered by Moscow Center to be at risk were posted abroad with a female colleague acting as the spouse while the real wife stayed at home in the Soviet Union.

"No reason to think otherwise," said McGee confidently.

"Has the psychiatrist done his preliminary yet?"

McGee tapped one of the files on his desk. "The learned doctor tells us this guy is a smart professional, high in self-esteem, and conscious of rank." He glanced down at the documents for a moment. "This language sensitivity has more to do with self-preservation, you'll be pleased to hear, than a phobia or a manifestation of paranoia." McGee yawned and shook his head to clear it. "He also likes dealing with those in authority and not their minions, which is a reflection of his heightened sense of self-importance. In short, not quite mister popularity, or a team player, but definitely a worthwhile catch."

Miler seemed to be satisfied as he began to share McGee's excitement. "So now all we need is the meal ticket. Did he say anything to Frank?"

McGee shook his head. "Only that we shouldn't even contemplate sending him back to be run in place. He says he has plenty, but the deal is that we get nothing sexy until he's in the U.S. Westport doesn't count," added Miler, stroking his chin thoughtfully. Both men were now concentrating on the critical issue of how to extract the maximum information from their catch.

"How do you feel about that, Leo?" Miler gave him a searching glance as he asked the question.

"I'm sympathetic; it's the kind of demand I'd make if I was in his shoes, but there is a principle here. He turned up, out of the blue, at Frank's house—that was calculated. He brought his family—that was also part of it. And he's making a point. He's virtually unknown to us, and so far he has been an expensive investment for zero return. A safehouse blown in Helsinki, an air force flight to Frankfurt, and the potential for trouble with the Finns. And now the Westport treatment. We're entitled to put a price on all that." McGee wanted his pound of flesh and he emphasized the point by digging his ruler into the blotting pad on his desk.

"But he's not been uncooperative?" Miler had a slightly puzzled expression on his face.

"Not really, but the doc measures him as a prima donna. If we encourage him, the price will just escalate. Since he's a walk-in with no background, we have to set the terms. And we want more than a few dopey Finnish politicians who we have always known were in the Soviets' pocket. What happens if we bring him Stateside, and he reneges on the deal? He probably knows we can't threaten to ship him home. We'd never get another defector again, quite apart from the legalities. The KGB would love it."

"But you're satisfied he's not a plant," Miler said as he got up, stretched, and gazed out the window across the Langley woods.

"It's early days, but from the order-of-battle material he looks on the level. We just have to show him we're in the driver's seat." McGee rubbed his tired, aching eyes and yawned.

"Has he made any other demands?" Miler asked suddenly.

"Not yet. If he's as professional as the doc says, he'll know that resettlement is a quid pro quo, and the ante has gone up recently."

Miler knew what McGee was referring to. Eighteen months earlier a middle-ranking officer of the Polish *Sluzba Bezpieczenstwa* had turned up unexpectedly in West Berlin. Michal Goleniewski's defection had enabled the British to arrest a whole network of illegals operating under deep cover. So far six people had been convicted of espionage in England, one in Sweden, three in Germany, and one in Israel. He had also implicated an American diplomat who had been the victim of a classic honeytrap in Warsaw.

The Goleniewski defection had been in the big league, and had put the Pole on a par with Gouzenko in Canada back in 1945, and the Petrovs in Australia in 1954. These had been the professionals who had allowed the West a few brief glimpses into the Soviet intelligence apparatus and exposed the espionage networks that had been nurtured with such care over so many years. Miler and McGee knew that this new defector, STONE, would have to prove every bit as valuable if he was to be accommodated in the same way: a new identity, U.S. citizenship, a pension for life, and protection for his family. It had to be a fair exchange, and STONE would have to make the investment worthwhile. McGee and Miler wanted the clues to the identities of KGB moles who had burrowed deep into Western governments. A First Chief Directorate officer of Golitsyn's rank could be expected to know a great deal, and it was their task to get him to share that knowledge. If they succeeded, McGee and Miler would be marked for big futures in the Agency. If they screwed up, they would finish their careers in the limbo reserved for intelligence officers who, like Cressida, trusted a "guest" from the other side. Like in any large organization, success had many parents, but failure was an orphan. One mistake on the way and the Agency would orphan them.

Whitehall; London;
Thursday, 15 March 1962

The anteroom was wood-paneled and high-ceilinged, with three long windows facing southwest; sunshine flooded in, and although Tom Waters welcomed the bright light on this otherwise cheerless spring day, he still felt uncomfortable. This was Whitehall and, in particular, that holy of holies, the Cabinet Office, where Britain's secret servants toiled unseen by the taxpayer. Tall and physically fit though he was, he felt curiously vulnerable in these unaccustomed surroundings. For him, it was not unlike waiting outside the headmaster's study as a schoolboy, wondering which of the many rule infractions had been spotted. The close-cropped hair at the back of his neck, thinner than it had been twenty-five years earlier, bristled at the thought.

The weather was too cold, and he would much rather have been back in Cyprus than enduring long this painful wait outside the government's inner sanctum, the Joint Intelligence Committee. Part of his discomfort was not knowing exactly why he was there. Of course, orders had much to do with it. He had been called in from his little office at the Signal Relay Station, atop Mount Olympus in the Troodos Mountains, to a brief interview with the base commander at Episkopi, in Britain's Sovereign Base Area of Cyprus. He had been given three days' notice of his flight back to RAF Brize Norton, and then another short session, an interview with his line manager at Benhall, on the outskirts of Cheltenham. That was the chain of events that had brought him from a dry, dusty Mediterranean climate to the noisy humidity of Whitehall.

There was rather more to it all than an inexplicable summons home for Waters, for he was no ordinary civil servant, and his

supposedly temporary prefabricated office buildings at Eastcote in the suburbs of northwest London not far from Waters's digs in Pinner. GCHQ's home had started life as a satellite for Bletchley Park, but after the war all the main sections had moved down from the Buckinghamshire market town into the anonymity of a suburban estate conveniently close to the South Harrow tube station. There, shielded from prying eyes, specialists in Block D matched the transmissions to the movements of Russian shipping reported by the Naval Intelligence Division of the Admiralty and every two weeks distributed assessments to those government departments that had a need for such knowledge. Among those on the circulation list were the originating intercept stations, where it was hoped that individual operators would benefit from the additional data about the vessels that the other interested intelligence agencies supplied: the names of the skippers and senior crew; those aboard suspected of being intelligence personnel; the cargo and its destination.

Waters's memorandum, which had started the flap in the first place, traced the known movements of two Soviet ships in particular, the *Omsk* and the *Poltava*. His attention had been drawn to them when, some three weeks ago, he had noticed a change in their routine. Whereas the crew was usually quite casual when it came to wireless operator chitchat, of the kind all signalers engaged in from time to time, a new discipline had been imposed. On just a few ships, and these two in particular, there had been a distinct change in routine.

There were also other oddities about their voyages. According to the shipping manifests that by international convention had to be declared when a vessel went through the Dardanelles, their destinations were North African ports, Algiers being especially favored. Yet the voyages were rather long for Mediterranean journeys, and none of the regular reporting agencies in Algiers had spotted either ship. So why the subterfuge? Equally suspicious was the complete radio silence imposed during much of the time and the curious timing of the Black Sea transits, which had both ships passing close to land only at night. What did the Russians have to hide? This had been the issue raised by Waters, and it had brought him posthaste from his billet in Cyprus to the Joint Intelligence Committee's regular Thursday morning conference in the rear of the Cabinet Office off Great George Street.

At that moment the door at the end of the anteroom opened and a tall, middle-aged bespectacled man wearing a severely conservative pin-striped suit strode confidently across the parquet floor. With the sun glancing off his bald head, it momentarily appeared to Waters as if his old headmaster was summoning the errant schoolboy into his study.

"Mr. Waters?" he asked, his attitude more welcoming than any teacher intent on chastising a delinquent child. "So good of you to come. I'm Hugh Stephenson, the chairman. Please come in and give us your briefing. I'm so sorry to have kept you waiting. Please forgive me for not introducing everyone."

Waters followed Sir Hugh Stephenson into the long, oak-paneled conference room. He made his way to the end of a long, highly polished oval table around which there were about a dozen men, their eyes all concentrated on him. He wondered about their identities, but had been forewarned about this unusual convention. The composition of the JIC was another of the State's secrets. Waters took the empty seat beside the chairman's and waited for a few moments while Stephenson made some introductory remarks.

For a moment, Waters felt a pang of self-doubt. He recalled the excitement he had felt as he had sat perspiring lightly in the warm Mediterranean air, night after night, hunched over his Marconi receiving equipment, logging each Soviet signal and watching the mosquitos burn up on his lamp. Had he been right to draw attention to what he had believed then to be a strange change in the Russian routine? Had there been an element of exaggeration in his report? Had anything really significant happened at all and, if so, did it justify traipsing all the way back to London? Did it warrant consideration by this group of expectant faces before him? Some of his colleagues at Pergamos, with whom he had exchanged notes, had been unimpressed. It was all negative evidence, they had said. Proof of nothing. No reason for making waves. Well, for better or worse, now he was committed.

Although Waters was not to know it at the time, Sir Hugh Southern Stephenson, GBE KCMG CIE CVO, was one of the anonymous men of the British intelligence hierarchy, but his background was strictly Foreign Office. For the past two years he had been chairing the main JIC in London; previously, he had run the regional sub-committee in the British Middle East Office in Cairo. Officially, he was listed at the Foreign Office, simply but somewhat disingenuously, as a Deputy Under-Secretary of State, one of those three-year stints in London that invariably heralded an ambassadorship in a Grade One post.

Of those seated around the table, Waters recognized only one person, his boss, Sir Clive Loehnis. Quite unlike Stephenson, Loehnis had spent much of his life in the intelligence world. The son of a London barrister, he had effectively enjoyed two separate careers, the first as a naval officer, the second as a cryptographer. He had been educated at the Royal Naval Colleges at Osborne, Dartmouth, and Greenwich and had retired with the rank of lieu-tenant-commander in 1935. Three years later, he had been tempted back to the Admiralty's Signal Division, and in 1942 had transferred to Bletchley Park, where he had participated in the extraordinary cryptographic success achieved against enemy ciphers. Ten years later, he had been appointed deputy to GCHQ's director, Sir Eric Jones, and he had taken over the reins upon the latter's retirement in 1960.

The others around the table represented the remainder of Britain's intelligence establishment. The director-general of the Security Service, Sir Roger Hollis, was on one of his many overseas inspections, so his place had been filled by his deputy, Graham Mitchell, a tall, athletic-looking man wearing slightly tinted glasses. One of his former colleagues in MI5, Sir Dick White, sat opposite him as the chief of the Secret Intelligence Service. Prematurely gray, he possessed the self-assured air of an academic. Beside him was a slightly older man, Vice Admiral Sir Norman Denning, director of Naval Intelligence. Born of humble yeoman stock in Hampshire, Denning and his two older brothers, Reginald and Tom, had all achieved great distinction, and had all been knighted. Tom had received a peerage and was recognized as one of the great judges of his generation, while Reginald, the eldest, had fought in two world wars as an infantry officer and survived to reach the rank of lieutenant-general.

Slumped in his chair farther along was the director of the Joint Intelligence Bureau at the Ministry of Defence, Major-General Sir Kenneth Strong, accompanied by two younger men, evidently both army officers, sitting on either side. The RAF was represented by a former fighter pilot, the assistant chief of the air staff, Air Vice Marshal Alick Foord-Kelcey, and directly opposite him was his War Office counterpart, the director of Military Intelligence, Major-General Marshall Oswald, once an intelligence officer with the famous desert rats in North Africa. The group was completed by the smaller, more rotund figure of Archie Roosevelt, the CIA's popular station chief in London. Most recently the head of the CIA's station in Madrid, Archie was Theodore Roosevelt's grandson and a cousin of FDR. He was also a gifted Arabist, having served in Lebanon and Turkey as station chief before his move to the Western Europe Division.

Together, this group collated intelligence from all the many and varied sources available to Her Majesty's government and advised the Cabinet's inner circle, the Overseas and Defence Sub-Committee, of current developments. This was the high-powered gathering that Stephenson proceeded to address.

"Gentlemen, we now come to item seven on our agenda and call upon one of Clive's staff to brief you on certain events in the Eastern Mediterranean. You should have before you three graphs, the significance of which Mr. Waters here will explain." He nodded at Waters. "Over to you."

"Thank you, Sir Hugh," began Waters a little uncertainly, running a hand through his hair as he wondered if his baggy old suit and soft-collared shirt was entirely appropriate in the assembled company. "Perhaps I should start with the three graphs mentioned by the chairman. The first is a schematic presentation of Soviet merchant marine signal traffic during the past two years. The second represents the number of merchant transits from the Black Sea, with a shaded graph showing those vessels originating from Odessa. Two conclusions can be drawn from these statistics: a perceptible increase in non-naval Soviet marine activity, and a corresponding reduction in signal traffic."

At this point the DNI, Admiral Denning, intervened. "Am I correct in assuming that under normal circumstances we would expect to see the reverse occur?"

"Yes, sir," replied Waters. "Even though we know most of the wireless operators are Red Navy, they have precious little signal discipline and over the years we have become used to their minor indiscretions in clear, and the usual preamble chatter. In theory, the more Soviet ships around, the greater the single sideband traffic. However, as the graphs demonstrate, the exact opposite has happened. Even the ship-to-ship transmissions have ceased. The only traffic we're getting is minimal ship-to-shore. In effect, we are losing a few ships altogether. After they have left the Aegean, we have no idea where they have gone."

"Is this phenomenon unique to the Black Sea traffic or is it more general?" asked Dick White in a soft-spoken voice. Waters would have been amused to have known that his mental picture of White as an academic was perceptive; before his entry into the world of intelligence White had been a teacher in a private boys school, Whitgift School in Croydon, Surrey.

"It would appear to be limited to our region," replied Waters. "Nothing seems to have altered at Murmansk or Vladivostok. I've checked our intercept records for the northern sectors and there's no change. I've also asked the Americans if they've noticed anything from their intercept facilities in Japan. It's business as usual. Nor has it affected the regular Red Navy. As you can see from the third graph, Soviet naval movements have conformed to their established pattern and their signals are just as profuse as ever. This episode is isolated to the Eastern Mediterranean, and limited to just a few units of the Soviet merchant fleet."

He took a deep breath and plunged on. "When the anomaly first materialized I conducted a tracing exercise on several Soviet ships, and I have identified two that have adopted this, er, idiosyncratic behavior, the *Poltava* and the *Omsk*. Both are fast, modern, oceangoing freighters."

Waters looked down at the long polished table and thought carefully before he resumed speaking. "There would not appear to be any obvious trading motive for the escalation in shipping, and we cannot be certain where it is going. The radio silence prevents us from taking fixes on the ships once they have cleared the Cyprus area. It is highly likely that it is headed out into the Atlantic, but if so the ships are transiting the Gibraltar NATO choke point at night."

Waters had expected more discussion of his remarks, but none followed. He received only a nod from Stephenson to indicate that his presence was no longer required, and a smile of appreciation from Loehnis, to reassure him that he had acquitted himself adequately. Hesitantly, he made his way back to the anteroom, wondering if his audience had fully grasped the import of his discovery. He had known from the beginning that the Soviets were up to something. The evidence was compelling, but what did it all mean? The unexpected imposition of radio silence by a naval unit had been recorded in the textbooks since the Battle of Dogger Bank in World War I and had invariably heralded a surprise initiative. But in a merchant fleet? It was very odd, and it meant something. And at this stage of the cold war, uncertainty was highly dangerous. Once Waters had left the room and closed the heavy, oak-paneled door behind him, Stephenson opened up the discussion. The DNI spoke first.

"We will take a closer look at these two vessels and check on their movements in the past." He knew that the Admiralty kept a comprehensive record of every Soviet vessel, and could cross reference to every port visited. "We'll also tighten up at Gibraltar and run some night patrols to check for Soviet transits. We'll soon find out what they're up to." His confidence was founded in the top secret Sound Surveillance System, known by the acronym of SOSUS, which listened to all marine traffic through a line of hydrophones stretched across the ocean floor at the Straits. Denning made a note to check the SOSUS product, which was known as CAESAR to those cleared for access to it.

Stephenson turned to Roosevelt. "Any comments on what you've heard, Archie?" he asked.

"This is news to me," he remarked, with a little skepticism, as he wiped his mustache. "I'll run a trace on these two suspect Soviets and let you know at next week's meeting. If Waters is still worried about his vanishing freighters we can always get the Sixth Fleet to keep an eye on them the next time they appear." Clearly he was unimpressed; he had other matters on his mind. With that the meeting broke up.

Both Roosevelt's limousine and White's more discreet Rover were parked in Horse Guards Parade, their respective drivers chatting to each other. As they saw their masters approach, they both extinguished their cigarettes and returned to their vehicles. But the two intelligence officers were engaged in deep conversation, and together they walked past the cars and took a stroll in St. James's Park. Both men were worried not so much about what Waters had told them, but about a subject that had been dealt with a little earlier by the JIC. Such was their anxiety and the sensitivity of their remarks that they had no wish to share it with their JIC colleagues even though they had all been cleared to NATO's Cosmic security level.

Despite their different backgrounds—Roosevelt from the American East Coast establishment, White from more humble origins—they had much in common. White had gone on scholarship to two universities in the United States and was a great admirer of most things American. For his part, Roosevelt had done much to strengthen the special relationship that existed between the intelligence services of the two countries.

The subject of their discussion was the Soviet spy protected by the code names ARNIKA and RUPEE. Very few people realized that both names referred to the same source, a Soviet GRU officer, and arguably the best spy ever run jointly in Moscow by the CIA and SIS. To most recipients, ARNIKA was a highly placed agent inside the Soviet missile program who had direct access to an astonishing quantity of strategic data, while RUPEE appeared to be a defector with a detailed knowledge of the Soviet military intelligence service. Over the past two years, since April 1960, when both came on line simultaneously, ARNIKA and RUPEE had been circulated to a huge number of government officials on both sides of the Atlantic. Everyone on the distribution list for one or the other product had been obliged to go through a special code word security screening, and few suspected that the information from each code name originated with the same person, a forty-two-year-old lieutenant colonel, married with a daughter, an apartment on a desirable block overlooking the Moscow River, and a penchant for expensive mistresses and call girls. Oleg Vladimirovich Penkovsky was no ordinary spy, and no ordinary defector, which was why Roosevelt and White were locked in intense conversation that Thursday morning.

In the view of White and Roosevelt, Oleg Penkovsky was easily the most important Soviet ever to volunteer to spy for the West. Quite apart from his own senior rank and his status as a trusted member of the elite GRU, he was close to many influential Russians, including Marshal Sergei S. Varentsov, the man in charge of all Soviet missile defenses. But best of all, Penkovsky was apparently motivated by an overwhelming ideological hatred of the Communist system that had killed his father, Vladimir Florianovich, once a senior officer in the czar's army, killed while fighting for the White Army during the civil war. He suspected that it was only a matter of time before his own meteoric career, first as a graduate from the Frunze Military Academy specializing in artillery, and then as an intelligence officer, would be ruined if the apparatchiks ever uncovered his father's true record as an anti-Soviet. In order to qualify for the coveted Frunze intake he had been obliged to conceal his father's past, an omission that was also a serious criminal offense. Indeed, the more promotions he received, the greater the likelihood he would be exposed by jealous subordinates or suspicious Party hacks. Instead of waiting for the inevitable, Penkovsky had opted to take his own revenge on the system. In an unprecedented joint operation, both SIS and the CIA had undertaken to help him.

"Thanks for the opportunity of a chat," opened Roosevelt. "I wanted to convey a word of caution about ARNIKA. It comes from the CI guys."

White looked alarmed. "Are they on to him?"

"Not so far," reassured Roosevelt. "But it must only be a matter of time."

White recalled that Penkovsky's first tentative approaches to the

West had proved so inept, passing notes to innocent tourists and startled students, that the CIA had written him off as a crude agent provocateur. It had only been his last-ditch effort to persuade a British businessman to assist him that had borne fruit. It so happened that the individual he had chosen, Greville Wynne, was not only willing to help, but he was already in touch with Dick White's organization. In fact, he had already been assigned a case officer, Dickie Franks, who had been recruiting Western visitors to the Soviet Union as agents for the past eight years, since his return from the SIS station in Tehran.

Instead of attempting to run Penkovsky in Moscow, where hostile surveillance by the KGB was considered too dangerous, a special debriefing operation had been run when he had come to London as part of a trade delegation in April 1961. During his two weeks in the capital, Penkovsky was introduced to his two case officers, Harry Shergold from SIS and George Kisevalter from the CIA. Both were experienced cold warriors. Shergold had cut his teeth in Germany after the war, interviewing refugees to the West, sending spies East, and living from one day to the next in anticipation of an invasion. Kisevalter had the same cautious approach to his work, but his background could not have been more different. He had been born in Kiev and Russian was his first language. He had intended a military career in the U.S. Corps of Engineers, but his linguistic skills had taken him into intelligence, joining the CIA in 1947. Since then, Kisevalter, based in Berlin, had run a series of important cases, but none had matched Penkovsky.

Both White and Roosevelt had been comforted by the extraordinary measures that had been taken to protect Penkovsky from exposure. Neither Shergold nor Kisevalter were permitted to meet SIS's go-between, Greville Wynne, and on the British side only a handful of trusted officers were allowed to learn his true identity. Franks, of course, was privy to the secret, as was Oliver St. John, his immediate superior, an SIS officer with a background in the colonial civil service and an impressive knowledge of the Middle East, where he had once masterminded a spy ring based on a phony news agency in Cairo.

Dick White's team was nothing if not experienced, and the same could be said for his American counterparts. The chief of the CIA's Clandestine Service, Dick Helms, regarded the case as a priority, and his chief of the Soviet Russia Division, David E. Murphy, knew that Penkovsky's information gave the West a whole new perspective to the so-called missile gap.

The origins of this myth lay in the Pentagon's exaggerated assessment of developments in Soviet rocketry and Nikita Khrushchev's outrageously inaccurate claims about Russian capabilities. According to the Kremlin's propaganda, largely swallowed uncritically in the West, still shocked by the Russian lead in the space race as manifested by Sputnik, Soviet scientists had made tremendous progress in the construction of long-range rockets. Indeed, figures of around two hundred weapons a year had been quoted, which was far in excess of the numbers still being tested, with mixed results, in the United States. Hence the "missile gap," a strategic imbalance in intercontinental delivery systems capable of transporting an atomic warhead to its target halfway around the globe. Not surprisingly, an alliance of the U.S. Air Force and influential politicians had alerted the public to the scale of the numerical inequality and had highlighted the dangers. Would the Russians maintain their lead? Might they be tempted to launch a preemptive strike before the United States reached parity? At a time of international tension and mutual distrust among the superpowers, such debates acquired supreme importance.

Yet Penkovsky's evidence, known to only a few in the West, indicated that far from having an advantage, the Russians possessed only a small number of rockets, and none had been deployed operationally. In short, Khrushchev's talk of superiority in the development of long-range missiles was pure fantasy. The reality, according to the spy, was a lack of technological progress that was a grave embarrassment to the Kremlin and a failure that was viewed with increasing alarm by the hard-liners in the Politburo.

Khrushchev's attitude had been one of bluff. He would simply deceive the West and give his scientists enough breathing space so they could perfect their research and catch up with the West. But a minority in the Politburo regarded this approach as dangerously foolhardy. What if the Americans discovered the true position. Would they not try to capitalize on their advantage while there was still an opportunity? Khrushchev's opponents preferred a massive diversion of resources into work on an effective super weapon designed to send a nuclear warhead into space and back onto a target in North America. This ambition had been wrecked in an accident in October 1960 when Marshal Nedelin and three hundred senior technicians and artillery experts had been killed while watching an experiment. This was the kind of inside information that made Penkovsky so valuable to the West.

White shook his head gravely. "It's the sheer volume that's so breathtaking. I don't know how he gets away with it."

"That's just my point," answered the American. "He won't come out because his wife is pregnant and she can't, or won't, travel. He won't leave her."

"So we have to anticipate the worst?"

"Apparently our CI people are getting a little anxious. Remember when he thought he was under surveillance last year?"

White recalled the incident. It had been just after his longest trip abroad, nearly four weeks in Paris at the end of September. Four weeks of debriefings, French tarts, and gluttony. By the end of the visit Penkovsky was ready for a nervous breakdown . . . as were his SIS and CIA handlers. The strain of conducting illicit interrogation sessions by day, and constant whoring by night, had taken everyone involved to the limit of their endurance and had quite exhausted the CIA station chief's list of reliable call girls. Upon his return to Moscow, Penkovsky had reported a suspicious new arrival in the apartment above him. He had been placed under observation, but had this been a routine matter or a full-scale investigation? Penkovsky did not refer to it again.

"I thought all that had blown over," remarked White. "Nothing seemed to come of it. You're not suggesting he's been taken into control? That they've turned him round?"

"Not yet. There's nothing solid; just a worry that has emerged. You know what McGee's office is like. Their job is all plots and conspiracies. It's always the worst case scenario for them."

White acknowledged his companion's assessment of McGee's

staff: hardened cold warriors with an exaggerated idea of the KGB's capacity for deception. The latest gossip was that they had reassessed Michal Goleniewski, the Polish defector who had put so many traitors behind bars. Apparently, some of the older hands had become convinced that their ace source had resumed contact with the KGB in New York.

"I think we have to assume that if he really is determined to stay in place he will be caught, sooner or later. Either a leak in the West, or a slip-up in Moscow." They walked on in silence, turning over the implications. Both men were sufficiently removed from ARNIKA to consider the situation objectively. Case officers, as a breed, invariably got too close to their agents and then lost their objectivity. It was only natural, White knew, to think one's source is going to hold out forever, against the odds. He had learned his lesson well. His best agent, a diplomat in the German embassy in London before the war, had established his reputation as a brilliant recruiter and agent-runner. Fortunately, the Americans had never realized the full truth about Wolfgang zu Putlitz: He had been Anthony Blunt's lover during the war, and was now living in the Soviet Zone of Germany, a committed Communist. White shuddered at the memory, It was all too easy to put excessive faith in one's protégé. It wasn't until zu Putlitz had suddenly decided to move East that anyone had considered he might have been a Soviet spy all along. White swallowed hard, and Roosevelt gave him a sideways glance.

"Don't get me wrong, we have no reason to believe that any of our people in Moscow are in jeopardy. It's just that we ought at least to consider Soviet involvement. Keep an open mind."

"Wise counsel, Archie. It's appreciated. Let's hope that when the moment comes ... if it comes ... he'll warn us."

Penkovsky had been given a series of clandestine signals to indicate the worst had occurred. His usual routine was to photograph documents at home and then leave the exposed films in one of several prearranged hiding places known as "dead drops." Then there was the regular tradecraft to indicate which *dubok* had been used, and when it was ready for collection. Usually the signal was nothing more elaborate than a piece of tape on a particular lamppost on the Kutuzovsky Prospekt. If he had a personal message to convey, he simply typed it out, photographed it with his Minox, and then destroyed the original text. In addition, he had several emergency procedures. A reference to his parents in the message meant he was under hostile control. There was also a telephone number to ring, with different people to ask for. A call for Yuri meant KGB interest; Konstantin was a plea for help, and Andrei signified that a surprise nuclear attack was imminent.

"Let's keep our fingers crossed," concluded White optimistically as they returned to Horse Guards Parade and their waiting cars. He had little idea that his star performer was soon to give the doomsday warning.

Westport, Frankfurt

Thursday, 15 March 1962

Later that same afternoon, Miler emerged from the self-contained apartment that for the last three months had been home to the Golitsyn family. He was in a state of shock, having heard the most extraordinary story of his entire career. But could it all be true? Certainly the Westport staff had considerable reservations about their principal guest. He was stubborn, opinionated, and demanding, and had become increasingly hostile to the debriefing team. Evidently he believed he merited special treatment, and it had been the lack of progress made by the Soviet Bloc Division regulars that had brought Miler across the Atlantic to the quiet suburb of Niedderad.

He had just spent four hours with Golitsyn, attempting to extract from him what everyone else had failed to obtain, an indication of what the CIA might expect if he were taken to the States. The experience had left him mentally exhausted, but he was still keen to draft a cable to McGee while the confrontation was fresh in his mind.

Golitsyn seemed to possess all the right credentials. His curriculum vitae to date had been impressive: a degree from the University of Marxism-Leninism and a diploma in counterintelligence from the KGB's Higher Intelligence School. Service in the American section of the First Chief Directorate, operational counterintelligence duty in Vienna, and graduation from the elite KGB Institute. He had also been selected to assist in the drafting of a plan for the KGB's reorganization on behalf of the CPSU's Central Committee. In short, Golitsyn was a KGB high-flyer, with access to some of Moscow Center's most sensitive secrets. Furthermore, he was an incorrigible name-dropper, casually mentioning his friendship with such legendary First Chief Directorate figures as Colonel Voronin, head of the British subsection. And yet he was unwilling to surrender his meal ticket, the valuable data that was the best currency in the intelligence market, for a guarantee of resettlement and lifelong protection. The Soviet Bloc Division was still wary of their new client, and the mistrust had been reciprocated.

Miler reviewed the notes he had taken of the interview, and then realized how insubstantial the encounter appeared on paper. He had been sent to accomplish a definite objective, but all he had before him were nuances and hints. It was as though Golitsyn had been teasing him ... implying he knew great secrets but retreating when challenged to be more specific. Impulsively, he reached for the scrambled telephone on the desk beside him and placed a call to the chief of the CIA's Counterintelligence Staff. The Operations Center at Langley made the connection and when McGee came on the line he wasted no time exchanging pleasantries with his subordinate.

"What's he got, Scotty?" demanded McGee.

"A lot, is my guess," replied Miler.

"But specifically ... ?"

"Nothing." Miler sighed.

"So the Soviet Bloc Division has been sitting on this guy for weeks and has failed to extract anything of any use? Are we wasting our time on him?" McGee's displeasure came over loud and clear.

"He's volatile; the Bloc Division is scared he might just ship out ... the French, Germans, or Brits would welcome him with open arms and he knows it. He also has a major conspiracy theory, based on a briefing he received last year. No details, just vague hypothesis."

"So what's the delay?" McGee demanded impatiently.

"The Soviet Bloc Division won't vouch for his credentials. He's difficult as hell to deal with."

"What happened when he was fluttered?" McGee was referring to an incident more than six weeks before when Golitsyn refused a polygraph.

"He wouldn't take the test because Piotr is Russian. In fact, he won't talk to anyone if they can speak the language. He's willing to be fluttered in English or German, and that's it."

"What does the Soviet Bloc Division say?"

"It drives them wild. Piotr is their most experienced operator. Sure he's a Russian, at least in origin, but he's the best. You can imagine what he says about this guy."

McGee paused for thought. To interfere with the Soviet Bloc Division, especially on a case they were unwilling to endorse, would be asking for trouble. If Golitsyn went sour on him there would be blood—McGee's blood, most likely. But the chance to initiate three major cases ... what a coup!

"Scotty, what is it going to take?"

Miler waited for a long moment before replying. "I've given this a lot of thought. There's something irrational about the guy. For all the bravado ... I think he's scared."

"That we'll send him home?"

"No ... not that. He's really weird. It doesn't make sense, I know, but I reckon he thinks we're going to kill him."

"Where the hell did he get an idea like that? Are those gorillas from Soviet Bloc Division treating him okay?" McGee's anger made his voice tremble.

"Sure. They're fine." Miler tried to reassure McGee. "It's not all their fault. Listen, I'm not sure about this, but it's the only explanation for the way he's fencing with us. It's just an idea, but supposing he has been led to believe that we kill defectors when we've no more use for them."

"That would certainly explain why we've had so few," acknowledged McGee.

"Exactly. We've only ever received a handful in the West ... and we keep them under wraps for years afterward for their own protection."

"A policy the KGB can present as evidence that we eliminate defectors after they've outlived their usefulness," muttered McGee thoughtfully. "You could be right. No wonder he keeps tantalizing us with useless snippets of information. If you're right, it's just his way of keeping himself and his family alive. The trouble is, if he's willing to believe we behave like that in the West, no amount of persuasion will budge him."

"The only solution is to demonstrate that he's been deliberately misled by KGB propaganda."

"I agree. What have you got in mind?"

"What we need is a KGB defector of similar rank ... someone Golitsyn has heard of, so we can disprove the lies."

McGee chuckled. "A living, breathing, authentic Soviet defector who can tell STONE how splendid life is in the decadent West. I think I have just the man."

Saturday, 17 March

Two days later, Miler was still at Westport, but instead of interrogating Golitsyn alone he came to the same apartment with a tall, athletic-looking man in his late thirties. He had short-cropped black hair and a tan that had been acquired playing tennis in California. His name was Yuri A. Rastvorov and until January 1954 he had been a First Chief Directorate case officer working under diplomatic cover at the Soviet embassy in Tokyo. Since his defection, Rastvorov had been living, under a new name, on the West Coast, enjoying the life of a playboy, hanging around the tennis clubs on the beaches in Malibu. Miler casually introduced Rastvorov and then after a few minutes excused himself, leaving the two men to chat in Russian.

Golitsyn was never to allude to this incident again, but the transformation in his attitude to Miler—and only Miler—had been total. Suddenly the defector began cooperating, and although he was still hesitant on some issues, Miler could tell that simply proving that Rastvorov had not been led to a shallow grave by the CIA had been enough to convince him that Miler at least could be trusted. On his next transatlantic call to McGee, Miler described the change in attitude. Now the defector was talking in terms of "at least three big leads. All First Chief Directorate colleagues running important cases ... in London, Paris, and Washington."

"Any names?" demanded McGee hungrily.

"None yet. Claims he has enough on the Soviet case officers involved to identify the sources. It looks real good, Leo."

"Okay. You'd better bring him over. I'll take responsibility with Soviet Bloc. Bring him over quickly. Show him we mean business. Ashford Farm is clear and we'll put him there."

"What about the wife and child?" asked Miler.

"Them, too. Bring 'em all," McGee said expansively. "Ashford'll be good for them. It'll demonstrate our good faith. If he's as good as he says, Soviet Bloc will have some explaining to do. Imagine ... three hot CI cases."

"And if not?" Miler asked in a worried tone.

"Then we'll think again. But we'll worry about that later. You do what you can on your end. I'll see the deputy director for authorization and send you the cable later today. We're not going to sit on the sidelines any longer."

Miler felt better already. He had a feeling about Golitsyn. It was the line-crosser's confidence that was so impressive. It was as though he knew he would get his own way in the end despite the obstacles placed in his path by bureaucrats. He just exuded inside knowledge. During their conversation an hour or so earlier he happened to mention that General Rodin, another First Chief Directorate heavyweight, was in London under diplomatic cover with the rank of counselor. He was calling himself Nikolai B. Korovin, and had recently taken over the *rezidentura* from Sergei Kondrashev. This was the kind of gem that the Brits would kill for. This was hitting pay dirt.

While Miler set about finding four seats on a military air transport to Andrews Air Force Base, McGee had sought and obtained an urgent interview with the new chief of the Clandestine Service, Dick Helms, who managed the euphemistically named Plans Division from the fourth floor.

"I need to bring a hot one in from West Germany," said McGee bluntly. "I need an immigration sanction today."

"Who is he?"

"STONE, the KGB First Chief Directorate guy from Helsinki. We need to talk."

"Is this the uncooperative Soviet the Bloc Division has been working on at Westport?

McGee nodded. "Bloc screwed up. He doesn't trust them so it's up to us. Scotty Miler has gained his trust and now it's up to us. It's our duty." He let the words sink in.

"What's on offer?"

"Good cases. Current ones ... in Paris, London, and right here, goddammit." That was bound to attract Helms, the CI chief had calculated. "STONE's contemporaries are all case officers. Some of his friends have been assigned overseas to task agents, run high-level penetrations. He can show us where. He also knows about a big conspiracy ... some kind of complicated deception, but on a grand scale."

"And why can't Soviet Bloc handle this? Why bring him here? You know what that means?"

McGee knew the implications all too well. The DCI was empowered by Congress to grant a limited number of citizenships to aliens. This discretion was usually exercised after an individual had shown his worth. Thereafter he was invariably referred to as a "one-ten," after Public Law 110, the 1949 Central Intelligence Agency Act. If Golitsyn was brought into the States, the CIA had no authority to deport him if he subsequently failed to deliver. The embarrassment factor was considerable, especially if J. Edgar Hoover ever learned of the debacle. But there was another matter to be taken into account. If the CIA could expose a Soviet spy on home turf, it would be quite a score against the FBI. Indeed, the prospect of more good cases abroad was very attractive. As a result of Goleniewski's information, the CIA's standing with foreign agencies had never been so good, even if the Bay of Pigs fiasco, which had wrecked his predecessor's career the previous spring, had left the Clandestine Service a little tarnished on the Hill. McGee stepped in to deliver the conclusive argument.

"This man STONE is a potential star. He had terrific access and his behavior is thoroughly professional. We have to reciprocate. He wants to come to the U.S. He doesn't feel safe in West Germany and I don't blame him. Miler has a theory that the KGB tells its men that we kill defectors after we've squeezed them dry. STONE has not exactly confirmed this but the change in his behavior once he was reassured has been eloquent. Once he's here, he'll cough. I guarantee it."

Helms smiled. He had thought of pulling STONE out of Soviet Bloc a week ago, and had learned that the CI Staff was getting impatient. He had even known of Miler's unscheduled trip to Europe. He didn't care. If STONE was all he promised, he would be quite a catch. Every week that Soviet Bloc Division fumbled, STONE's meal ticket would diminish. Who knew its shelf life? The Soviets would have instituted a damage control exercise to mitigate their losses as soon as Golitsyn's defection had been spotted. Agents would have been warned, operations suspended, tradecraft altered, compromised personnel withdrawn. Yet three long months into the case, Bloc was still insisting on running STONE its way. Clearly it hadn't worked; now McGee was taking personal responsibility, putting his trust in a Soviet. It was highly unusual for CI to express a commitment so forcefully—and so early in a case.

"Have you got a safehouse lined up?" Helms asked finally.

"We'll use Ashford Farm, but we'll have to change the staff. STONE's developed a language phobia. No Russian speakers. It's worth accommodating him as a token of our support."

"Very well," Helms said to indicate he had reached a decision. "I'll talk to the DCI later, but you have my sanction." Helms signed the three-part docket McGee had brought with him, retaining one of the carbon copies. "Good luck."

honeytrapped, and continued to supply classified material; the French secret intelligence service, SDECE, was riddled with KGB agents, and a mole had even penetrated de Gaulle's cabinet. Signals had already been dispatched to Ottawa in Canada, where local investigations had been initiated. Only time would tell if Golitsyn's accusations would hold up. However, of the handful of CI officers who had met STONE, none doubted his veracity. He was a walking encyclopedia of the KGB's clandestine activities even if he had not run any sources personally, and McGee's men intended to squeeze him dry.

But for all the serials—each an individual allegation of treachery or a counterespionage clue, the cross-referenced card indices that documented a hint to a traitor's identity somewhere in the world— it was STONE's talk of *dezinformatsiya* that really concerned Miler. STONE knew of a highly secret operation promising diabolical consequences that, a few months ago, had been in the planning stage. The spies and agents of influence would be tracked down eventually. Some might take months or even years to isolate from the serials, but each case would be concluded. Some would be prosecuted, a few might negotiate a deal to retain their freedom. Others would have their activities leaked in their own countries and thereby discredited. But Miler's mind had dwelt on the novel concept of a large-scale, long-term deception for strategic gain. This was no *maskirovska*, the ploy of concealing Soviet military strength, so familiar to every Western intelligence agency. STONE was talking, albeit in vague terms, of a massive undertaking, with potentially apocalyptic consequences.

STONE's tale had a compelling quality to it. A special disinformation section had been created in May 1959, in great secrecy, within the elite of the First Chief Directorate. Its objectives were closely held, and unusual security restrictions had been imposed on the KGB officers transferred to the unit. Its modus operandi had been discussed, in broad terms, at an interdepartmental conference addressed by General Aleksandr Shelepin, the former chairman of the KGB who had taken over from Ivan Serov in December 1958. This was to be deception on an unprecedented scale, using sophisticated techniques that had received authorization from the Politburo's Defense Committee. A complex operation, and one of Machiavellian cunning and ingenuity was under consideration, and the consequences would be global in nature. Apparently, it had been planned in 1960 and had commenced in earnest late in 1961. The trouble was, STONE had little idea of exactly what was afoot. Still, certain deductions could be made from the kind of specialists that had been selected to supervise it. In overall command, said Golitsyn, had been Agayants, once head of the political intelligence faculty at the High Intelligence School and now assigned to France. At the outset he had gathered together some fifty counterintelligence experts, including Colonel Grigorenko, a specialist on émigrés who had previously acted as an adviser to the Hungarian security apparatus, the *Allami Vedelmi Batosag*, and Colonel Kostenko, an aviation authority. It might be inferred from this composition that the operation was perhaps technical in nature, involving aircraft, with a political content and intended to be directed against NATO. The inclusion of Grigorenko, who had worked on emigration operations overseas, also suggested that defectors might have a role to play. His specialty had been infiltrating agents into groups of genuine refugees seeking asylum in the West. The problem was that STONE knew none of the details regarding the latest scheme. He could only say that the resources and manpower earmarked for the project made it one of considerable importance, and one of great political significance. Unfortunately, he had rather expected the CIA to know something of it already. Although Miler had initially been tempted to bluff Golitsyn, he had been forced to admit the truth. The Agency had absolutely no idea whatsoever of any massive scheme that threatened to undermine the Western alliance. The very thought of it made Miler shiver, for it brought to mind Pearl Harbor.

Admiralty, London;
Wednesday, 4 April 1962

It was just past eleven on an unseasonably cold Wednesday morning, after the forty-three-year-old First Lord of the Admiralty had replaced the telephone receiver on its cradle, that his intercom buzzed noisily. He was much younger than most of his subordinates, but he was, despite his relative youth, the Royal Navy's political master. He casually leaned over and depressed the flashing button that indicated his principal private secretary from his private office was on the line.

"Yes?" drawled Peter Carrington, the sixth Baron Carrington. For the past three years he had been the First Lord of the Admiralty. Up until his appointment, by Harold Macmillan immediately after the 1959 general election, he had served in Australia as British High Commissioner. Before that he had held junior ministerial posts in the Ministry of Agriculture and Fisheries, popularly known as Ag and Fish, and the Ministry of Defence.

"Your eleven o'clock appointment, my lord. Sir Clifford Jarrett and Sir Roger Hollis."

"Please show them in." Carrington was intrigued. His private office had made all the arrangements for this meeting, liaising directly with Sir Clifford, the senior permanent civil servant in charge of the Admiralty. While he saw Jarrett almost every day, he had not met Sir Roger, whom he felt his immediate aides had rather expected him to know. But although the name might have been familiar to the secretary for the Admiralty, who was accompanying him, and other Whitehall bureaucrats, who else would be expected to know the identity of the director-general of MI5? The First Lord had enjoyed little firsthand experience of intelligence matters. He had served in the Grenadiers during the war, and his tenure in Canberra had occurred just after the famous Petrov defections. There had been a Security Service representative at the High Commission, a Security Liaison Officer who operated under diplomatic cover, but he had hardly come into contact with him. Actually, the only Hollis he had come across had been Christopher, who had been the M.P. for Devizes until 1955. They had both been to Eton, of course, but Christopher had been much older. A discreet inquiry by Carrington at the club, Pratt's, had established that Roger was Christopher's younger brother, and Britain's security chief since 1956.

Carrington got up from his desk and strode with his natural air of self-confidence, mistakenly interpreted by his political opponents as unjustified arrogance, toward the heavy, ornate door that led to his private office and reached it in time to greet Sir Roger Hollis. His visitor, slightly hunched, was about fifteen years older than the First Lord, being in his late fifties. They shook hands, and Carrington gestured the two men toward the leather armchairs opposite his desk.

"What can I do for you, Sir Roger?" asked Carrington, never one to waste time. "Not more bad news on the security front, I trust?" Carrington had been obliged to take the flak when Soviet spies had been found at work in the Underwater Weapons Research Establishment at Portland just over a year earlier.

"I'm afraid so, my lord. We have just received information, from a source we believe to be reliable, that there is a Russian spy operating in the Admiralty. I have already explained the background to Sir Clifford."

"Good grief," exclaimed the younger man. "Do you know who it is?"

"Not yet. Our investigations have started, but we've not been able to narrow down the suspects."

"How can we assist you?" asked Carrington.

"My men will need assistance from the director of Naval Security, and I would be grateful if you could let him know the gravity of the situation, when you get a discreet moment." Hollis was always meticulous about observing the usual Whitehall conventions. For him to have gone straight to the navy's director of security, without approaching either Carrington or Sir Clifford first, would have been an unforgivable breach of protocol.

"Of course, Sir Roger. You will have his full cooperation. Who else knows about this?"

"I am seeing Sir Norman Brook tomorrow so the prime minister can be informed, but no one else should be told apart from the First Sea Lord and, of course, Sir Clifford."

Jarrett, whose official title was secretary for the Admiralty, nodded imperceptibly. Many in Whitehall regarded him as the epitome of the unseen, all-knowing civil servant. Certainly he knew more about the department's administration than anyone else alive, for he had worked there since his transfer from the Home Office in 1934. Sir Roger had limited the circle of those to know about this latest affair to the very minimum: Carrington as the Admiralty's political chief; the First Sea Lord, who was the service's operational supremo; and the administrative head, Jarrett. No chance of a leak from such a group—or so Hollis hoped.

"I need hardly say that this is a matter that requires total secrecy," added Hollis, anticipating a demand that the director of Naval Intelligence, Admiral Sir Norman Denning, should be indoctrinated into the case. He was ready to resist, for despite the DNI's distinguished record, and his membership on the Joint Intelligence Committee, such a move would widen the number of those in the know and, he reasoned, the spy might even be in the DNI's own division.

"Indeed," replied Carrington, still a little shocked by the disclosure. "Have you any idea how senior the spy is?"

"We only know that a quantity of *Dreadnought* material has reached Moscow, the leakage has been going on for some time, and there are some, er, unsavory aspects to it all. Beyond that, we are pretty much in the dark. It may be a lengthy process to ferret out the culprit, we shall probably have to check every one of the fifteen hundred staff here." With that, Hollis rose to leave; the First Lord, however, wanted to know more.

"Can you be sure the information didn't come from Portland? The DNI tells me that two of the latest Soviet sonars, the FENIKS passive array and the HERKULES active sonar, found on the new *Romeos* are directly attributable to classified data betrayed by Houghton."

"We have reason to believe that some of the *Dreadnought* material was of a class that Houghton could not possibly have supplied," said Hollis evenly, choosing his words with care. "This would appear to be an entirely separate, unconnected business."

Carrington and Jarrett exchanged glances. The research work stolen from the Portland underwater facility had enabled the Soviets to copy the Royal Navy's designs and develop countermeasures. On that occasion the Americans had been less than pleased about the breach of security, but they had at least shown some understanding. *Dreadnought*, on the other hand, would be quite a different matter. The first British nuclear submarine, it had been built in England by Vickers using American technology and with an entirely American atomic plant. It was, in many respects, a U.S. *Skipjack*, and if American expertise had been betrayed by a British spy, the Americans would be rightly furious. Carrington and Jarrett had both understood the implications, although Hollis probably had little appreciation of the possible political consequences across the Atlantic.

"I don't envy you your job," murmured the First Lord. "What with the Portland case last year and that Blake affair, you must have been a busy man."

Hollis nodded. "Last year we locked up more Soviet agents than at any time since the Russian revolution. Three KGB illegals as well as three home-grown traitors. Unfortunately, our efforts are not always appreciated. What we regard as a success—a spy eliminated from the scene and put behind bars—is regarded as a security scandal by the press. But by any standards six Russian agents in jail is not bad." Hollis broke off. He was a self-conscious man, not used to dealing with politicians. He needed all the allies he could find, having endured no less than three major security inquiries in the past few months, but he was anxious not to appear too defensive about his department's performance. The director-general realized that men like the First Lord would be watching his every expression for a sign that matters were out of control. Accordingly, Hollis remained quite impassive, almost aloof. It was an act it had taken years to perfect, and he was eager to avoid being drawn into an exchange that might lead beyond the bounds of propriety.

In truth, Hollis himself knew only the bare bones of what was at hand. He knew, for example, that the CIA had invited the SIS chief of station in Washington, Maurice Oldfield, to attend the debriefing of a Soviet defector. He knew that Oldfield had been sufficiently impressed to request the assistance of a case officer from the counterespionage branch instead of Harry Stone, his counterpart in the Security Liaison Officer's office in the embassy. His director of counterespionage, Martin Furnival Jones, had assigned Arthur Martin to the task, and he had returned the previous week with no less than 153 serials, the authentic clues to espionage. "D" Branch's research subsection had been working overtime ever since Martin's exultant homecoming, and the serials had been divided up among the senior case officers. Hollis also knew that Ronnie Symonds, an ambitious MI5 investigator, had already made a start on screening the sexual proclivities of likely suspects on the Admiralty's payroll. According to STONE, the Admiralty spy was a homosexual, but that was the extent of his knowledge. These cases were best handled by "D" Branch, with the deputy director-general taking a watching brief. Hollis had no desire to be involved in the minutiae. His principal objective was to persuade Whitehall and, as a last resort the politicians, *that MI5 had initiated the investigation.* He was determined that his department had to be seen as dynamic, constantly on the hunt for spies. It would never do for them to learn that all this activity amounted to a defector's meal ticket. More importantly, they should never be allowed to realize that the defector had chosen to go to the Americans.

"Is there really no link between last year's Portland ring and this spy?" asked Carrington. It was a good question, and one that was safe for Hollis to answer. After all, he reasoned, he did not want to appear too uncommunicative. The key to perpetuating the myth of MI5's omniscience was to be ambiguous or imply greater erudition than was strictly justified. On this topic he could be quite candid, with a relatively clear conscience.

"Our information comes from a different source, if that is what you mean. As I have indicated, this investigation is quite separate from the rest, and you may be assured that there were no loose ends overlooked last year."

"So two episodes where our submarine secrets have been compromised, perhaps in parallel, is a coincidence not a conspiracy."

"That is my advice at present," Hollis replied evenly.

"I'm relieved to hear it. Are there any measures you would advise taking to mitigate the loss?"

"I beg you to do nothing that might alert the spy. It's vital he's not tipped off. He could be literally anywhere in the building. I will be in touch again, through Sir Clifford, once I have something more positive to report. In the meantime, it must be business as usual. If either of your private office staff query this meeting, just say I was anxious to develop our liaison with the director of Naval Security. After all, it's quite true."

Carrington and Jarrett nodded their agreement to the subterfuge. "It seems we have quite a way to go yet. Don't hesitate to let me know if you need any help," said Carrington as he launched himself to his feet, an indication that he had heard quite enough for one day.

Moscow; Thursday, 24 May 1962

Captain Alexis Davison, USN, was doing something unusual: He was actually practicing his profession as the embassy's doctor. He usually spent most of his time on the seventh floor of the embassy, on the corridor of secure offices reserved for Paul Garbler's CIA station. For in addition to being the assistant air attaché and a Russian-speaking physician, he was also a co-opted intelligence officer. Garbler's staff of ten, all operating under "light" State Department cover, endured constant KGB surveillance whenever they left the mission, so part-timers like Davison were occasionally pressed into service to perform tasks that other members of the CIA station, such as Hugh Montgomery, could not hope to get away with unobserved.

As a fully qualified doctor, Davison was also called upon to give medical advice or conduct examinations. On this particular day he had been called down to the embassy's small dispensary on the second floor of the north wing by a consular officer, Jack Matlock, of the Immigration and Visa Office. Because of the building's strange configuration, Davison had been obliged to climb up to the ninth floor in order to leave the secure area, sign out with the marine guard on duty, and then take the elevator down to the suite of rooms known, somewhat misleadingly, as the embassy hospital. The hideous building on Tchaikovsky Street, about a mile west of the Kremlin, had once been an apartment block, and the rushed conversion that had been completed in 1952 had been a disaster. One consequence of the alterations had been the extraordinary arrangement that had left the Americans accommodated in a rabbit warren–like collection of tiny rooms, narrow passages, ancient elevators, and flimsy partitions. The National Security Agency eavesdroppers occupied the top floor, leaving the ambassador and the secure communications facilities on the floor below, the ninth. On the seventh and eighth floors were where the sensitive work was carried out by Garbler, Montgomery, and their colleagues.

When Davison arrived on the second floor, Matlock introduced him to a strikingly pretty Russian girl who could not have been more than twenty.

"Alexis, this is Marina Prusakova, for whom we are processing a visa application. She has had her prints taken, and the medical examination is the last formality. She speaks no English. Good luck." Matlock smiled, handed Davison a standard, government-issue buff immigration file, and left.

Davison introduced himself to Marina in his perfect Russian and soon put her at her ease. As he did so he learned more about her background, gently questioning her as he probed her ears, monitored her heart rate, and shone light into her eyes, all the while listening to her monologue.

"I am by training a pharmaceutical assistant, and I have been working in a large hospital in the center of Minsk. I have an American husband and we only arrived in Moscow this very morning. We have checked into the Hotel Ostankino, on the outskirts of town."

"How long have you been trying to get an exit visa?"

"We have been waiting for permission to travel to America for more than a year, and now it seems we will be on our way to the West in a couple of days."

"What does your husband do?"

"Alik works in a television factory. We were married in April last year, and our baby daughter, June, was born three months ago, in February. Doctor, how did you learn such good Russian? You have no trace of a foreign accent."

"My mother is Russian," Davison explained. "She's called Natasha. And my father was a physician, so I had no choice about my future." She laughed.

He soon discovered that Marina was apprehensive about starting a new life in an unknown country, and he offered some help. "My mother must have felt much the same as you do now. I'll give you her number in Atlanta, and if you ever feel the need to talk, just call her. She loves making new friends. Where are you going to live?"

Marina seemed unsure. "Alik's mother and his brother are in Fort Worth, Texas, and he hopes to find work there. His family will help us find somewhere to live."

"What sort of work?" Davison asked as he completed Marina's medical chart.

"Alik once served in the U.S. Marines, and specialized in radar, so we hoped he will get a job in the electronics field ... perhaps in another television factory."

Davison was anxious to hurry through the examination because he had an important appointment to keep before lunch. He had been asked by Hugh Montgomery to check lamppost number thirty-five on the Kutuzovsky Prospekt for the telltale signal from the station chief's star agent. It would be some months before Davison even heard Penkovsky's name, for the security surrounding his identity had been rigid, and there had been no need for him to be fully indoctrinated into the case. His part in the operation was strictly limited to surveying the signal sites and maintaining a telephone watch on particular nights. Davison regarded the assignment as a tremendous responsibility. He knew that Montgomery, who had only recently been posted to Moscow from Athens, was an experienced case officer, but he did not know his way around the streets as well as Davison. Nor could he move about with the same freedom. Montgomery had almost certainly been spotted by the KGB as a career CIA officer, and Garbler, too, but who would suspect the embassy doctor on his first overseas assignment? This, of course, was the Agency's strategy. Mixing recognizable intelligence officers with complete unknowns so as to keep the opposition's surveillance teams on their toes.

As Marina Prusakova's blood pressure was entered on her medical report Matlock returned, accompanied by a slim young man in his early twenties with receding brown hair. His Russian was poor, and his appearance seemed to unsettle his wife slightly. Davison added his signature to the medical report and handed it back to Matlock.

"If you come back this afternoon with a photograph of your

daughter," Matlock told them, "we can add her to your passport, and you will be all set. We've made reservations for you on the *Maasdam* from Rotterdam on the fourth of June, so you have a day or two, just enough time to get visas from the other embassies. Your train will pass through Poland, East Germany, and West Germany on the way to Holland, so Marina will need transit visas for each. But don't worry, they won't hold you up. Enjoy your voyage home, Mr. Oswald."

Langley, Virginia;
Thursday, 21 June 1962

McGee was in attendance to address the Watch Committee. It was a rare event, and he was determine to savor every moment of it. The deputy director of Central Intelligence, Lieutenant General Marshall S. Carter, made a brief introduction. He had only been in his post for a month, having received Senate approval early in April, and he was still finding his feet. His background was entirely military, and his appointment by President Kennedy had been a surprise move. Accordingly, those gathered in the soundproofed room were wary of his presence, unsure of his role. Carter limited himself to explaining McGee's position as chief of the Counterintelligence Staff, and gave him the floor.

"As I understand it," opened McGee, with typical irreverence, "you fellows gather to ensure our great nation is not taken unawares. Finger on the pulse, so to speak. So I'm hoping you can put a problem that has been identified by my staff into its proper context. It is my belief that we are being conned, but I don't know how, why, or by whom ... yet.

"You all know Soviet Bloc Division's dismal record ..." he put a hand up to acknowledge the universal groan that came from the assembled CIA officers, "but I am not here to rake over the past. Only to articulate a few facts. They are as follows ..." he then turned to his briefing notes.

"One. The First Chief Directorate is in bad shape, thanks to Goleniewski. We have wound up a large number of its operations and it must hurt like hell.

"Two. Up until 1960 we have been able to run only one successful penetration into the Soviet intelligence apparatus. You're all

51

familiar with the case of Major Piotr Popov; his loss in 1959 was a tragedy. This is not the time to continue the postmortem of that particular business, but it's clear that at some point before his arrest he came under KGB control. My point is simply this: Our best source in Moscow was run by us for precisely six years, between his first approach to us in 1953 and his detection in 1959. For part of that time he was probably doubled against us, but that is another issue. What I want to emphasize is our relative lack of success in this unique field."

"Relative to what?" asked a hostile Jack Maury, head of the Soviet Bloc Division. He was understandably sensitive to any criticism of his division. He was also acutely aware that STONE had been removed from his control and taken over by McGee's so-called counterintelligence experts.

"Relative to fact three," replied McGee, undaunted. "Namely the extraordinary windfall of Soviet sources we have been fortunate to receive in recent months. It began with ARNIKA last year. That case is still running, so suffice to say that this is GRU in origin. Then we had an approach from SCOTCH, a KGB officer at the United Nations. Now we have another KGB singleton, FOXTROT, who has made contact and offered to collaborate. What distinguishes each of these individuals is their professionalism, and their apparent willingness to remain in place. They don't seem to want to come over. Statistically, we are now in touch with no less than three Soviets simultaneously—more than we have ever achieved in the Agency's fifteen-year history."

"And what about your defector, STONE?" someone asked.

"I was coming to him. He's of interest for two reasons. First, his disclosure of a secret concept known as *desinformatsaya*, which roughly translates into a grand strategic deception. Second, his certain knowledge that the First Chief Directorate has launched a sophisticated operation of some kind."

"Leo, are you trying to tell us that all these Soviets are plants?"

"No. I am merely reporting a curious phenomenon. We have too little to go on yet to draw that conclusion; the evidence is not all in. But it's odd that for more than a decade we only got to deal with one walk-in at a time. Now, suddenly, they're forming a line."

"What else can you tell us about the three you're suspicious of?"

"Not much, at the moment. ARNIKA is familiar to all of you, and seems to be an authentic source, although his overtures were originally rejected because he was regarded as a likely agent provocateur. However, the experts tell us that his data checks out. So be it. He's GRU and we have no complaints. I know very little about SCOTCH because he's being run by the Bureau, and I will not take up your time with our liaison difficulties over there. He's a well-placed First Chief Directorate officer under U.N. cover, and the Bureau is pleased as punch."

"And the latest?" Maury asked warily.

"A second Chief Directorate type who made his pitch last week in Switzerland. Soviet Bloc is running him, but on his terms. No contact in Moscow, only third-country meets. Evidently FOXTROT is quite senior, well connected, and travels abroad without difficulty."

"And where does STONE fit in?" asked Maury.

"He doesn't. He certainly doesn't conform to the pattern set by the others. You'll recall that he just turned up on Frank's doorstep. No pitch, no offer to work in place to earn his meal ticket. In fact, quite the reverse. He burned his boats by bringing his family, too."

"Is there any common denominator that links them, perhaps in their testimony?"

"Not yet. ARNIKA is supplying us with technical data on Soviet rocketry as well as regular GRU material. SCOTCH claims to be in the collection business in the U.S., and FOXTROT says he can tell us about security procedures in Moscow. Apart from being professionals, they have virtually nothing in common."

General Carter now took over the meeting. "I suggest everyone pitches in and gives an overview of local matters of concern. We'll start with Soviet Bloc."

The Soviet Bloc Division representative was cautious. He could tell McGee was in a fighting mood. "We're playing our sources by the book," Maury said defensively. "In our perception, this recent windfall is nothing more sinister than the culmination of years of steady groundwork. The climate is changing and not everyone trusts Khrushchev. Nor is Semichastny a popular boss. He replaced Shelepin as chairman of the KGB last November and he's something of an unknown quantity. Indeed," he paused to steal a glance at McGee, "it may well be that STONE's defection was prompted by Semichastny's appointment. He may not be the ideological convert he presents himself to be, but rather the victim of internal dissention in which he backed the wrong horse. It's a matter of record that he fell out with his *rezident* in Helsinki ... but only time will tell. As a division we have not had an opportunity to deal with the CI analysis you have just heard ... but we will respond when we have studied it in detail."

Carter turned to the European Division and nodded. The tall, prematurely gray analyst gave a brief résumé of the tense situation in Berlin. It was almost direct from Bill Graver, the CIA's chief of base in the divided city, who had sent a long cable the previous evening outlining what he perceived to be Soviet strategy in central Europe and the threat posed to Berlin's Western sectors. He was followed by Far East, which anticipated some Indonesian expansion and further political activity in Saigon, and the Africa Division. Then Carter turned to the Near East Division.

"OK, Walter. Any ideas?"

"Soviet pressure on the Turks," replied Walter Penrose. "We've got God knows how many intercept facilities along the Black Sea, quite apart from the Jupiter sites. This makes Ankara a target for destabilization, but there doesn't appear to be anything special on at the moment. In fact, the regime is so robust that when it was suggested at a NATO meeting in Oslo last month that the new Polaris subs might make the Jupiters obsolete, Selim Sarper, the Turkish foreign minister, was unamused. They like the Jupiters, even if the Russians don't."

"Latin America?"

"We have twelve hundred Bay of Pigs hostages in Havana. They've been sentenced to thirty years' imprisonment and Castro wants $53 million for their release. He has us over a barrel. There's been a Soviet buildup on the island, but I would have to get the Cuban Intelligence Center to give an update. Once Castro has consolidated he may start again in Venezuela or Argentina. His chief lieutenant, Che Guevara, is from the Argentine and he's a committed Marxist. Cuba is on the way to becoming a Soviet satellite, but there's little scope for what Leo has in mind."

"Communications?"

The scientist from the Office of Communications peered over his old-fashioned half-moon tortoiseshell glasses. "Every overflight now has to have approval from the Committee on Overhead Reconnaissance, so our U-2 missions have been curtailed severely." Other members of the Watch Committee averted their eyes. The CIA's contract pilot, Francis Gary Powers, who had been shot down in May 1960, had been returned to the Agency just four months earlier in a spy swap completed in Berlin. The resulting debriefing, conducted at Ashford Farm, had been a major embarrassment because it had indicated that the pilot had consistently lied about exactly how his plane had been downed. If he had remained awake and had been flying at an altitude of over eighty thousand feet, as required by his flight plan, he would have been invulnerable to attack from MiG-21s or SAM missiles.

"Nevertheless," he continued, "we have no reason to suspect any major switch in Soviet strategy. Their camouflage is minimal and we can monitor any movement of strategic significance. At present we are concentrating on military order-of-battle with an eye on Berlin, but there's no buildup there ... yet."

"Very well," concluded Carter. "Would the CI chief care to sum up?"

McGee rose to his feet. "Somewhere, something is under way. We have great confidence in STONE. He has provided leads to First Chief Directorate penetrations in every NATO country. This guy is a kosher source, and he's convinced that men of a certain caliber have been gathered together inside the KGB for a particular enterprise. We would be wise to heed his warning. We know from bitter experience with Popov that the Soviets are perfectly willing to run high-risk double-agent operations. His case was a watershed. It was not a few partisans in the Ukraine or émigré guerrillas in Albania. This was a complex example of trading some authentic data for a broader advantage. If we are on the right track, it may herald an offensive of some kind. The only question remaining concerns its nature. That is up to you gentlemen to figure out before it's too late."

Gibraltar; Tuesday, 26 June 1962

Tom Waters stepped out of the Transport Command Viscount at Gibraltar and followed the other three men in civilian clothes into the military section of the terminal building. His performance at the JIC in front of Loehnis had apparently been sufficiently impressive to have had the director's personal approval for his temporary reassignment from Cyprus to Palmer Street, GCHQ's discreet office in Victoria, conveniently close to the Secret Intelligence Service's headquarters just a few hundred yards away in Broadway. Waters's new task was to follow up his initial report and collate the relevant intelligence concerning the phenomena of the missing Russian ships.

Although the director's memorandum had implied praise for his traffic analysis, Waters was well aware that Loehnis wanted action. He required a detailed account of what was happening to the Soviet merchant fleet, and why. Furthermore, he wanted it quickly. Waters had assumed that it had been Loehnis's own naval background that had inspired his interest. A cynic would have said that if Soviet aircraft had been vanishing in the Middle East he probably would not have taken the slightest notice. But Loehnis hated mysteries, and he wanted to know what was going on.

It was evident from his interview with Roosevelt at the CIA station in Grosvenor Square, and his briefing by the Naval Intelligence Division next to Admiralty Arch, that nobody else seemed to share his director's curiosity. Roosevelt had run checks on the *Omsk* and the *Poltava*, but there was nothing suspicious about either of them. They had been built for the Baltic lumber trade but in recent months had been operating out of the Mediterranean.

The CIA clearly had better things to concern itself with than elusive freighters. As for Naval Intelligence, their prime concern was craft that traveled beneath the waves. No attempt had been made to collate the movements of particular vessels, and therefore Waters had undertaken his own study. In addition to the ships he had already identified as having dropped off the map over the past two months, four more bulk carriers had exited the Aegean at night and then maintained radio silence. The *Bratsk*, *Divnogorsk*, and the *Metallurg Anosov* had all displayed these odd characteristics, and now Waters had arrived at the mouth of the Mediterranean to test his theory with the *Volgoles*, which had left the Black Sea two days earlier.

Once through the customs barrier Waters was met by a youthful officer in the Royal Navy uniform of a lieutenant. He reached out and took his overnight bag. "Cable and Wireless?" he asked disingenuously.

"Good afternoon," smiled Waters.

"A pleasant flight, I trust," said Simon Hardwick, introducing himself as he took Waters's overnight case. "I gather it's the Rock Hotel, and then I'm to indoctrinate you into what we do with the taxpayers' money down here? Climb aboard. Do you need to check in with your outfit here?"

"No. This is strictly a sideshow. They probably don't even know I'm here."

"It'll stay that way. Your radio people hardly mix with us. Come to think of it, they don't really mix with anyone. Too secret I suppose."

"Thanks," replied Waters, maneuvering himself into a dark blue Land Rover, with "RN" painted in white on the hood. Moments later they were roaring across the airfield toward the town. Five minutes later they had negotiated the light, mid-afternoon traffic and climbed to the Rock Hotel, overlooking the bay to the west and, in the hazy distance, Algeciras. Having checked into his room, Waters rejoined Hardwick for a ride to the Naval Operations Centre Annexe.

"I hope you're not claustrophobic," remarked the lieutenant as the Land Rover roared past the Rosia Cold Stores and then ground to a halt at a barrier at the foot of a steep incline. Both men showed their identification to the armed Royal Marine on guard, and then continued up the track. "There's more inside Gib than outside, if you know what I mean," said Hardwick. "The whole of the Rock is literally riddled with tunnels, almost all of them big enough to drive down." He took a sharp turn to the right, signposted Harley Street Bypass, and changed down in gear to tackle a traffic hump in the road by Gort's Hospital.

"Is this all limestone?" asked Waters.

"Yes. Ideal for tunneling. Much of this was excavated during the war, but they're still working on the Great North Road." He gestured over his shoulder. "That's supposed to link the military complex with the civilian chambers. Mostly reservoirs, pumping stations, and power generators at that end. This is the business end. Hundreds of galleries, all on different levels. Three hospitals, numerous oil storage tanks, and heaven knows how many old gun batteries and magazines. That's where we're headed."

"It's like a small town in here," said Waters, as they accelerated away past the Royal Electrical and Mechanical Engineers workshops.

"It *is* a small town. As well as the natural caves, which are vast, there's a whole system of connecting shelters. And every entrance is protected by a blast wall, so it's about the safest place in Europe. Good place to be when the bomb drops."

"Is it all still used?"

"Only part of it now. But it's kept ventilated. That gives the constant temperature of sixty-two degrees, day or night, summer or winter. It's a terrific environment to work in . . . if you like being underground."

"And CAESAR likes being underground?"

"CAESAR likes being secure, and there's nowhere as safe as this." They were approaching the Buffaderd Battery, and slowed for another military barrier. Their passes were checked again, and they drove on, turning up a narrower tunnel signposted to the Beefsteak Magazine.

"This is CAESAR's home. Come in and I'll introduce you to the duty officer." He opened a steel door and walked down a long, dimly lit passage with peeling paint, then through a second door into a large cavern. Inside were dozens of ancient Nissen huts, neatly placed together in rows, like soldiers on parade. They continued across the concrete floor toward a large double door marked RNOC (A). Once inside, Waters could see that he was in a first-floor gallery, like having a box at the theater, with a large auditorium below. But the only performers were machines: dozens of what looked like teletype printers, interspersed with the occasional visual-display unit. The room had the air of a hospital operating room, with a continuous low buzz of air-conditioning. Manning the equipment were no more than eight or ten operators, some in naval uniform, some in jeans. On three sides of the building were huge floor-to-ceiling screens, each subdivided into sectors, with the vague outline of a map just discernible.

"Welcome to CAESAR," said Hardwick. "I'll give you a brief guided tour, and then we can wait for your little operation. Do you know much about what we do here?"

"Listen to submarines?"

"More or less. We track everything, although our objective is Warsaw Pact traffic. I suppose it's not so different from what you chaps at Cheltenham do." He pointed to the batteries of electrical paraphernalia. "Those terminals monitor the underwater hydrophone arrays, but it's not quite as simple as that. The difficulty is working with water as a medium. Acoustic energy can travel long distances in water, and does it much faster than in air. About four times as fast, as a matter of fact, but there are a lot of variables. Temperature, salinity, and pressure all affect the speed. So does the chemical composition on the water. You wouldn't believe how filthy the Mediterranean is becoming, and just here the sea flows in both directions at different depths. Anyhow, we have to deal with this dynamic environment, as well as the currents, countercurrents, and the topography of the ocean floor, all of which have an impact on the sounds we pick up. Then there's the fish and microorganisms. They all make a hell of a din. Our task is to listen to the clatter and extract the man-made, artificial sound of cavitation from the background."

"Cavitation?" asked Waters in a puzzled tone.

"The disturbance caused by the propeller blades churning the water. The vortex created by the tips contain air bubbles that collapse with a characteristic hissing sound. We also enjoy hearing pumps, steam turbines, gear trains, lavatories, and any other kind of machinery. Then we have the hydrodynamic noise of the water rushing over the hull. Even at quite low speeds, the free-flood holes and protrusions generate quite a lot of sound."

"How big are the arrays?"

Hardwick hesitated. "It goes against the grain to show you all this, but my orders are that you have a Cosmic clearance. I'm to tell you everything. Very well," he shrugged, "they're bloody enormous, the size of a double-decker bus, and chains of them stretch right out into the Atlantic. This is just one choke point of several, all linked together." Hardwick pointed to a glass booth in one corner. "That's the communications center, which can switch our surveillance monitors over to Brawdy in Wales and Tudor Hill in Bermuda. All at a flick of a switch. From here we supervise three other choke points, in the Bosphorous, in the Straits of Kithera and Karpathos at the mouth of the Aegean, and then the Sicilian Channel. These are the really narrow gaps of shallow water the Soviets have to run through before they can reach the Atlantic from the Black Sea. We listen to 'em all the way. Then we follow them out into the ocean. We can track them if they go north past Portugal, across the ocean to the Azores, or south down to Ascension."

"So this is one gigantic listening device," said Waters, unimpressed at the magnitude of it all.

"That's not the whole story. Sound is just one dimension. If a boat raises a periscope or radio mast we will catch it on radar, and if it's near the surface we can sometimes find a telltale hump from the water displacement. When a submarine moves, it inevitably causes electrochemical changes in the immediate seawater. The hull generates various electrical potentials, and a current flows from the hull using the water as a conductor. This changes the electromagnetic field and we can spot that with sensitive detectors. In addition, a huge ferrous bulk affects the earth's natural magnetic field, and that also registers on our apparatus. Thus, our static arrays include several different kinds of passive devices to spot a sub. We are also experimenting with thermal tracing, to find the exhaust emission in the sub's wake, and the bioluminescence that is created by the turbulence of the props. All the data is fed into a computer, which discriminates between the various options, and then we try and plot a position."

"Can you tell a Soviet from one of ours?"

"Quite easily. The Soviets are still using what is essentially the U-boat technology that they acquired from the Germans at the end of the war. The majority of their subs are Zulu-, Whiskey-, and Foxtrot-class diesel electrics, which were designed more than fifteen years ago, long before sonar had become so sophisticated. Most modern craft have a single propeller, which creates a noise that is modulated at the natural frequency of the blades to produce an idiosyncratic beat. But the Soviets use two or three propellers instead of one. This is very helpful because instead of producing a single rhythm, they develop an intermodulating beat that is easy to recognize. They are also incredibly noisy, and their hulls are loaded with bollards, domes, and other fixtures that interfere with the slipstream. It's hardly believable, but the Soviets still use long wire-towed antennae, and these tend to vibrate at their natural frequency. Some of the more ancient Whiskeys even have nonretractable snorkels. They make a heck of a din."

Waters was surprised. "Surely they must realize how vulnerable they are?"

"One day it will dawn on them to invest in anechoic tiles and screen their interiors to suppress their noisy boats, but not for a long while yet, I hope. This is at the cutting edge of technology. It takes a lot of research to develop the countermeasures needed to defeat CAESAR. For a start, they'll have to rejig all their machine tools to mill engine parts with a precision they can only dream of now. They'll need a couple of decades to catch up with this box of tricks. Perhaps longer."

"Unless they can steal it."

Hardwick nodded. "I've heard that some of this may have been compromised by the spy ring at the Portland Underwater Weapons Research Establishment that was caught last year. God knows what they gave away. I won't bore you with the technical stuff, but in deep water there are some quite easy tactics that reduce the chances of detection right at the limit of our range. There's no sign at the moment that the Soviet commanders have been enlightened, but it may happen any time. It's all a matter of hiding between the layers of water of different densities. Although their technology is hopelessly outdated, there are a few tricks they could use to their advantage."

"Don't tell me," pleaded Waters. "Need to know, and all that. I'm after different game this evening."

"This is your ship, the *Volgoles*?"

"According to my calculations, it should be transiting your choke point tonight."

"Wouldn't it be simpler to track her with some maritime reconnaissance aircraft?"

"Probably, but no one in London is willing to authorize the sorties. And our allies are far from convinced about the point of all this. In any case, I'm keen to avoid tipping off the Soviets to what I'm up to."

"And what exactly is that?"

"To establish why Soviet freighters are manifesting some very strange behavior. Like radio silence, transiting Western strong points at night, and registering phony destinations."

"Have you checked the radar logs?" Hardwick asked thoughtfully.

"It's scarcely believable, but there aren't any. I can't match the names of particular vessels to radar plots through the Straits. It seems that as long as a ship follows the rules of the road, it's free to pass in and out of the Mediterranean without anyone taking any notice. What's so odd is that several Soviet ships seem to have slipped quietly into the Atlantic without anyone noticing."

"I can assure you, we would notice them if they were warships."

"But they're not. That's my point. They are the lowest of all priorities, which is why I'm experiencing a little difficulty in having this matter taken seriously."

"And tonight you want to hear the *Volgoles* pass through our screen?"

"No," replied Waters. "What I expect to hear is something really quite different."

Over a light supper in the duty officer's cramped cubicle, Hardwick described how individual Soviet submarines could be identified by CAESAR. "We have on file recordings of virtually every Soviet submarine that has passed through one of our choke points. Each has had the ambient noise filtered out and is distinct. It's a little like a fingerprint ... every one is slightly different, and easily recognizable. Thus we can monitor the movements of a particular craft, but we can't really predict them. Is that what you want to do?"

"Unless I am very much mistaken," Waters said quietly, "the *Volgoles* is going to slip through the Straits this evening. I want to see what happens."

"But our objective is to listen to the subs, not the surface vessels. We don't record the ships."

"That is exactly my point. According to the study I've been conducting, several Soviet freighters have sailed into the Atlantic unnoticed, attracting very little attention. There could be an entirely innocent explanation for this phenomenon, but I can't find it. What I need to establish is whether this is some unusual activity, related to the radio silence imposed on some selected merchantmen, and perhaps part of a larger scenario."

"Of course," replied Hardwick, "there is always Soviet naval activity around here. At the moment we have an intelligence-gathering vessel keeping station in international waters."

"Is that usual?" asked Waters in surprise.

"It would be unusual if it wasn't there. It's the *Linza*, and it's almost always cruising off the Rock. We call it a gatekeeper."

Waters was intrigued. "Does it listen in to your wireless traffic?"

"We assume it does. There are three other Okean-class side trawlers in the Red Fleet, and they all pretend to be engaged in hydrographic research, or some such nonsense. But they don't fool anyone. They've retained their characteristic trawler masts, a tripod well forward and a pole aft, but a huge wire antenna in between is festooned with receiver coaxials. They've got every imaginable directional aerial, including some unusual loops for high-frequency direction-finding. All the original compartments, built by the East Germans, have been converted to accommodate a complement of about sixty and a mass of electrical equipment. In any event, we've never spotted any of the crew fishing. It may be that this particular ship is involved in helping submarines get through the choke point.

Waters looked puzzled. "By running alongside to mask the sound of the submarine?"

"No, the *Linza*'s not big enough for that. It's only just over seven hundred tons; and its top speed is only about twelve knots, so it wouldn't be fast enough either. The best way of beating the surveillance, apart from using a large ship as a mask, is by exploiting the thermocline."

"The what?"

"The layers in the sea. Salinity and temperature affect the way sound travels under water, and there's a permanent layer that can be used to shield the sound of a submarine if the commander knows exactly where it is. His problem is that it can be found at different depths at different latitudes, and it varies with the seasons. Around here there is a diurnal that we call 'the afternoon effect,' which is a consequence of solar heating of the surface. If a submarine can find the exact thermocline, and then operate just above it, much of the sound it generates will be reflected up to the surface and dissipated instead of being bounced back down to the sensors. This is an extraordinarily skilled undertaking and depends upon hourly samples being taken of the water at predetermined depths throughout the day to monitor the location of the thermocline. That's what the *Linza* does. We suspect that this data is somehow communicated to an approaching submarine so it can take advantage of the layer in the choke point. This information can be vital because the layers can cause a submarine to porpoise. This happens when a submarine hits an isothermic layer unexpectedly, and either gains or loses depth without warning. It's pretty unnerving for the crew."

"Can you check on the *Linza*'s position now?"

"Not instantly. The radar plot is patched through to CAESAR so it's easy to punch it up on the screen." He turned to a monitor beside the duty officer's desk and selected a few buttons. Gradually a green hue appeared on the screen, and the sweep of the antenna beam became more obvious. "There's a lot of interference and clutter from the African coast, but this is fairly typical. It takes a few calls to pinpoint a particular blip as an identifiable vessel."

"Is each blip a ship?"

"Most of them. You may get the occasional false echo, but the image won't last."

"But there are dozens of ships out there."

"Well, that's what you would expect in one of the world's busiest seaways."

"Can you tell one ship from another?"

"Not really. A small yacht may show up really well on the screen if it's carrying a reflector at its masthead. There's not much chance of judging relative size with this equipment, which is scheduled to be replaced soon anyway. Similarly, a fishing boat with a low profile may hardly register at all, unless it has a reflector. That's the basis of the cigarette smuggling that goes on between here and Ceuta or Tangier."

As Waters watched the dull glow of the monitor, he noticed two pulses merge. He pointed it out to Hardwick. "This pair has just joined up."

"That often happens. Depending upon their position relative to our radar, if two ships come close enough, their reflections will fuse together. I gather that occurs even on the very latest technology."

"So if I wanted to get a ship through the Straits undetected, I could simply run beside a larger vessel at night."

"It would be an extremely dangerous exercise, and no responsible master would attempt it."

"But it would be possible, in theory."

"Rather impractical, actually. Their relative positions would have to be altered to keep the second ship in the radar shadow of the first. This would require continuous but gradual changes in speed and course, and quite exceptional navigation. Although attractive theoretically, I doubt it would really work. It would also be quite a hazard for other shipping."

"Very well," replied Waters. "But can we monitor the progress of the *Volgoles* relative to the *Linza*?"

"We should be able to set that up," confirmed Hardwick.

"And can we combine CAESAR as well?"

"We can certainly try." He then made a series of telephone calls through the Naval Operations Centre. After a few minutes of peering at the radar screen, and marking up some of the blips with a grease pencil, Hardwick turned back to Waters. "How sure are you that the *Volgoles* is coming through tonight?"

"I can't be certain, but unless the ship has been delayed or put into a port, it should have got this far by now. All the others I've studied over the past two months have averaged three days across the Mediterranean. On the assumption that it will only proceed through the Straits in the dark, I anticipate the *Volgoles* anytime after nightfall."

"According to Ops, we have an unidentified contact from the northeast quadrant, steaming at a steady eighteen knots, and making a course for the Straits. It could be the *Volgoles*."

"It hasn't been positively identified?"

Hardwick shook his head. "Nor will it be unless its master chooses to, and there's no reason why he should. He is perfectly entitled to navigate these waters without making any kind of contact and, as I said before, provided he keeps to the rules of the road we won't interfere."

"Any sign of submarine activity?"

"We have to consult CAESAR for that. Come next door." Both men returned to the larger plotting room and approached a seaman at a console.

"Any Soviet deployment tonight?" Hardwick asked.

"Two so far, sir," he replied. "A Whiskey-class diesel, designated Kilo Tango, which transited through our area two days ago, and a November-class nuclear, designated Bravo Lima out by the Canaries."

"Can you be more specific?" asked Hardwick.

"Yessir," replied the operator, punching keys on his control panel. "The Whiskey is the *Pskovskiy Komsomolets*, commissioned in 1951, and the November is the *Seljabinskiy Komsomolets*, launched in 1958."

"Is that a normal deployment?" asked Waters.

"About right, I should say," said Hardwick. "The Whiskey doesn't pose much of a threat. It's a medium-range, shallow-water submarine based in the Black Sea or Baltic that's been mass produced at about four Soviet shipyards. Seven years ago they churned out about ninety of them. In effect, they're German World War Two, Type-21 U-boats. Nothing to worry about. They're in and out of here all the time."

"And the November?"

"Well, that's quite different. The original November was the *Leninskiy Komsomolets*, which made history in April 1958 by being the first Russian nuclear-powered sub. Actually, it was not exactly a breakthrough; it was really an old German-designed Foxtrot fitted with two pressurized water reactors and steam turbines. There are only two shipyards in the Soviet Union capable of building atomic submarines—Severodvinsk in the White Sea and Komsomolosk on the River Amur's estuary, in the Pacific—so we could monitor its progress quite well. Its props have a distinctive four blades and," he leaned over the seaman's shoulder to decipher the figures on the display screen, "we have clocked this one at thirty knots submerged. Most impressive."

"What's it armed with?"

"Torpedoes. Maybe nuclear tipped, we can't tell. It's classified as a hunter-killer, on station to detect our subs, but it's hopelessly noisy."

"Just how much information do you have on each submarine?"

"A lot. There are now 285 Soviet subs operational, that's about double the Red surface fleet, but of that number only eighteen can be described as modern boats, and we know of just four nuclear-propelled. That's two other Novembers, apart from this one, and a new missile sub we have designated Hotel. All the others are diesel electrics. If we take this November as an example, I can tell you that it is equipped with a SNOOP TRAY radar, which you're probably familiar with, and a medium-frequency sonar pinched from Portland. Crew of eighty, and the skipper is Captain Vladimir Nikolayevich Chernavin."

"You even know his name?" Waters asked in amazement.

"We have to, in case we need to communicate over the underwater telephone. He might be called upon to surrender. It's very demoralizing for his crew."

"Are you sure he's still the skipper?"

"Oh, yes. Unlike NATO fleets, the Soviets don't rotate their commanders. Young Vladimir Nikolayevich will stay on the *Seljabin-skiy* until he's promoted, and then intelligence will read about it in one of the Red Navy's magazines. Incidentally, his sub is named after a Young Communist organization. Very sound, ideologically speaking."

Waters was amused. "Which side of the Straits is our diesel?"

"At present it's about thirty miles east, making around ten knots, with no quiet-running routines," said the rating.

Waters looked at Hardwick quizzically. "Much of the Mediterranean is too shallow for the long-range Soviet subs to operate effectively, although their attack craft will come in from time to time. You can be sure that the November will stay out in the Atlantic. Naturally, they all hate the choke points, and it would be a little odd if Kilo Tango comes back this way after just two days."

"You're sure it's the same sub?"

"No question. We measure these characters on their first voyage, and then update our recordings every time we get the chance. He can't change his characteristics while operational. That takes a major refit."

"So why would he be heading back?"

"Change in orders, new patrol, perhaps an emergency on board. Your guess is as good as mine. It's just that the skipper would not do this voluntarily, because he knows that it amounts to endangering his boat."

Waters held up three fingers. "So we have one submarine out in the open sea, another heading toward us, and a likely candidate for the *Volgoles* moving in the same direction?"

"Correct," replied Hardwick.

"Then indulge me. Will the courses of the merchantman and the diesel converge?"

Hardwick moved to a chart table and made a few calculations. He then took a ruler and marked two courses on the overlay. He glanced at his watch, did a little more arithmetic, and then announced his conclusions.

"Conditional upon both vessels keeping their present courses and maintaining their speed, they will probably rendezvous at about midnight, or a little earlier."

Waters smiled uneasily. "Let's wait and see."

Opa-locka, Florida;
Wednesday, 11 July 1962

Manuel Ruano was one of the lucky ones. Unlike Pepe, his brother, he had been given another chance to live a reasonable life. But now he had to make up his mind, and quickly. He had been called in by a colleague of the man he knew as Frank Bender, but he was an old hand at this sort of thing, even if he was only twenty-four years old. When he had received the telephone message, he had hesitated to make contact again. Was it worth it? Should he just walk away from it all? Surely he had given enough already. He had given his left arm, from just below the elbow. He had every right to ignore Bender. But as he strolled toward the unused air base, Ruano knew that he wanted to be involved again. There was still work to be done.

Manuel and Pepe Ruano had been involved from the beginning. They had even known Carlos Santana, the first of the volunteers to die accidentally in Guatemala, whose serial number had given the name to Brigade 2506. They had gone to TRAX, a coffee plantation thirty miles inland from the Pacific coast, where they had been trained by veterans of the Hukbalahap rebellion in the Philippines. They had also attended a grueling jungle warfare course at Fort Gullick, in Panama. Nobody could say they were ill-prepared.

Shortly before the invasion, code named ZAPATA, the entire brigade had been flown from the plantation's airstrip to TRAMPO-LINE, the tiny fishing village of Puerto Cabezas in Nicaragua, ready for embarkation on the evening of 14 April. Ruano remembered the excitement of the Cubans: Fifteen hundred heavily armed exiles, all determined to rid Cuba of Fidel Castro's

70

oppressive regime. They had spent two nights at sea in chartered rustbuckets, and then had landed on the Zapata peninsula, at the Bahía de Cochinos.

What had happened over the following hours had been a disaster, but Ruano was not keen to recall any of that. Nor did he want to remember his capture, outside Buenaventura, after a mortar had exploded nearby and peppered his left arm and side with shrapnel splinters. Instead of being taken to a medical station, he had been tossed into a meat truck and transported to Principe Castle, in Havana, along with 134 of his comrades. The journey had taken eight hours, and when they emerged from the container, nine had been crushed or suffocated. It was only then that Ruano's wounds had been treated, and it had been too late to save his arm.

The amputation had been carried out in the primitive hospital wing of the fortress, and Ruano had spent the following year in a cell packed with others who had been seriously injured. Eventually, exactly a year after the ships had set out from TRAMPOLINE, sixty of the injured were flown to Miami airport. Ruano had been among them, but not Pepe. He had been one of the 114 exiles who had perished on the blood-soaked beaches of the Bahía de Cochinos.

The original Bay of Pigs operation had been run by Bender at arm's length, from Quarter's Eye, an anonymous government office in Washington facing Ohio Drive and the Potomac River. Opa-locka had provided logistic support, but the main operations center was in Coral Gables. The "front office," calling itself Zenith Technical Enterprises, Inc., was in a densely wooded compound on the south campus of the University of Miami and was staffed by a team of three hundred Americans, all agents or contract employees of the CIA. Code named JM/WAVE, the project had cost a small fortune and had been planned in minute detail. Now that the recriminations were over and some of the planners sacked, it had fallen to William King Harvey to pick up the pieces left by Bender. Harvey's Task Force W intended to call in each of the repatriated survivors for a debriefing. New networks had to be built on the island, new personnel indoctrinated into the realities of life in Cuba. Following the failure of the invasion, the Agency had acquired a new set of priorities. One was to extract the remaining prisoners incarcerated in camps and prisons scattered across Cuba and the Isle of Pines. According to the latest estimates, more than a thousand were awaiting trial for participating in the invasion. So far, only five had been executed, apparently for crimes alleged to have been committed under Batista's rule. The CIA was anxious to conclude the negotiations that had been conducted for the past six months, haggling over the price to be paid for their release.

Although Castro still had control over the prisoners, the economy was in ruins. The United States had announced a trade embargo in February and ration books had been introduced a month later. Coupons were needed to purchase food, clothes, shoes, and even the most basic of household items. The CIA was keen to reestablish a presence in Cuba, and Bill Harvey had been given the assignment. Harvey was everything Bender had not been. He was a rough, tough, hard-drinking, gun-toting, cigar-chewing professional, and he had turned to Ruano for help. Not much had changed. Bender had relied on Ruano while planning ZAPATA, and he was one of the few men the CIA officer trusted implicitly. They met again at the Stuft Shirt Lounge at the Holiday Inn on Brickell Avenue, a popular rendezvous conveniently close to the Opa-locka base.

"I have to tell you candidly," said Harvey, "we are deep in the brown stuff. We need to know what is going on. What is the condition of the men in the Principe fortress? Why has Raúl Castro gone to Moscow? What is happening at Lourdes, where dozens of antennae have been erected by Russian technicians? Have the Soviets really been interrogating the ZAPATA prisoners? What is the Soviet connection? Have they really pumped $100 million in aid into the economy?"

"Have you no sources left in Cuba?" Ruano asked in a tone of disbelief.

Harvey shook his head. "We have agents, of course ... but they're of doubtful reliability, especially after last year's disaster. It's hard to know how many assets have been turned by the DGI. Communications are more difficult than ever. It's said that the KGB has introduced some sophisticated equipment to track down the illicit transmitters; so the few we possess have kept silent. As for couriers, even the local diplomats are too frightened to risk a visit to the Villa Marista."

Just the name of the feared DGI interrogation center was enough to chill Ruano. Once a Marist seminary, the building in the Vibora district had developed an appalling reputation under "Chino" Mayans, Castro's security chief.

"Manuel, you have suffered for the cause. Nobody has done more, sacrificed more." Harvey glanced awkwardly at the Cuban's arm. "But there is much more to be done. We need someone like yourself, with the courage of a lion, to go back and make contact with our sources."

"You're as ruthless an old bastard as Colonel Frank was," replied Ruano with a smile. "You know I can't refuse you. There's not much they can do to me that they haven't done already. You want me to go back? I'll go back. But you have to promise me that next time we get the military support we were promised."

"You have my word," said Harvey. "ZAPATA was a catastrophe, but it was not the end of the war. We will carry on, and next time we'll succeed. At least Washington now understands the problems. Next time it will happen properly, but we need to lay the groundwork now."

The conversation then passed to more mundane matters, such as Ruano's family, with Harvey making all the correct, tactful inquiries to build his agent's confidence. Then they settled on the arrangements for his return to Cuba—by a fast boat from the Everglades—and a method of communicating—via a dead-letter drop in Havana.

Ruano was an experienced agent and would have no trouble getting ashore and moving around the country. Far from being a single island, Cuba is an archipelago of sixteen hundred islets and cays, and only a limited stretch of coastline could be guarded. Consequently, scarcely a night went by without a high-powered speedboat making the crossing from Key West. Getting in and out of Cuba was not a problem. The real skill lay in retaining one's liberty once there.

Harvey knew the hazards. Old Frank Bender had done much to

undermine confidence. Bender's real name had been Gerry Droller, and he had been born in Germany before the war. After service in the OSS he had run the CIA's Swiss desk; eventually he was transferred to the Latin America Division. Bender's appointment had been crazy. But Harvey understood about running agents in denied areas, having run the CIA's base in Berlin for three years, and he recognized Ruano as a source in a million. Here was a deeply committed agent, one who had lost his brother and his left arm to Castro's regime, yet the fire in his eyes was undimmed. Few had better credentials in the émigré community, and although he was obviously now known to the Cuban State Security apparatus, he was a sufficiently skillful operator to avoid getting into trouble.

Once Ruano had completed the contract formalities and been placed back on the payroll, Harvey packed him off to Useppa Island, a former resort off Fort Myers on the Gulf coast where the Agency had established a Cuban Intelligence Center to coordinate all future operations against the regime. Most of the new officers posted to Useppa had only a fraction of Harvey's understanding of what was afoot in Cuba. Certainly they knew about the ZAPATA fiasco. Who didn't? But none of them knew the background like Harvey. That had been part of the problem with Bender. Harvey had done his research, gone back in the files to the days when the U.S. government had secretly backed the young Fidel Castro's 26th July Movement against the totalitarian Batista. In 1958, Robert Wiecha, operating from the consulate at Santiago de Cuba, had delivered $50,000 in cash to the Movement, and Park Wollam, another undercover CIA officer, had helped set up Radio Rebelde. And since then, so much had happened. Fidel had betrayed the revolution and taken power for himself. Staff at the U.S. embassy had been reduced to eleven, and then in January last year diplomatic relations had been severed. Worse still, the Russians had begun to appear. The Red Army had sent over Lieutenant-Colonel Anastas Grigorich to retrain the army, but in a more sinister development, two KGB colonels, Valentin Trujanov and Mikhail Furmanov, had been spotted at El Condado, near Trinidad, where an estimated four hundred Soviet counterinsurgency experts had been accommodated in a purpose-built camp. It had been troops instructed by these firm disciplinarians that had defeated the men of Brigade 2506 as they waded ashore.

Harvey knew the history of Soviet intelligence interest in Cuba. It dated back to April 1943 when Batista had opened diplomatic links with Moscow, and a veteran of the Spanish civil war, Grigori Bashirov, had subsequently established himself in a plush apartment on Second Street in Miramar. The CIA had been unconcerned, mainly because Captain Jose Costano, the deputy director of Batista's notorious secret police, the BRAC, had been a long-term asset and a fervent anti-Communist. He could be relied upon to keep the local branch of the Comintern in check. But matters got really serious when Colonel Ulianov arrived in February 1960, hot on the heels of the official visit made by Soviet Foreign Minister Anastas Mikoyan. Costano had been executed, and under Ulianov's guidance Aldo Vera had taken control of Castro's security apparatus. Suddenly a Caribbean island less than a hundred miles from the Florida coast had become a threat.

Harvey had come under pressure. State had produced alarming figures to demonstrate that Soviet technical and military aid had been pouring into the island. A huge Soviet complex at Lourdes, twenty-four miles due south of Havana, near San Antonio, had sprouted huge radio masts. The evidence of an escalating Soviet interest had dated back to October 1960 when Paul Bethel, the U.S. press officer, had been stopped at a roadblock on his way to visit the Soroa caves in Pinar del Rio. A group of Cuban militia and unmistakably Caucasian civilians, speaking poor Spanish, had turned him back a mile away from the entrance to the famed caverns. That particular mystery had never been solved, but the suspicion remained that some kind of underground bunker was under construction. For what purpose? Intelligence officers hate unsolved puzzles, and Bethel's report had stayed on the Cuban desk as an open file ever since, a mystery to be unraveled.

Since the Bay of Pigs, the CIA's Cuban Intelligence Center had acquired all the attraction of Calcutta's black hole. Career-wise, it had been regarded as a dead end, and the Latin America Division was strewn with ZAPATA victims. Langley had reacted with predictable vengeance against those held responsible for the failure, even though many of those closest to the front line believed the blame should have been shouldered elsewhere. But that's politics. Everyone had shrugged and accepted the inevitable. The White House and Capitol Hill had called for blood and the sacrificial lambs had been offered. The legendary Allen Dulles, DCI since 1953, had paid the price, along with several of his senior aides.

But now Task Force W needed answers to questions that no one at Langley found it palatable to ask. Why had Raúl Castro suddenly flown to see Khrushchev? What was the explanation for General Konstantin Slazenko's recent arrival in Havana, accompanied by Major-General Fedor Bendonesko? Little was known about the former, but Bendonesko's background had included commanding the Red Army's mechanized troops. If the Russians intended to guarantee Castro's regime from another landing, Washington had to be warned. Harvey wanted good men on the ground and a secure communications system. Manuel Ruano would provide the first, Leo McGee the second.

Harvey and McGee went back a long time. So long, in fact, that Leo tended to call him Special Agent Bill, for Harvey had once been in the FBI. A minor infraction of Hoover's rules had forced a move to the CIA. Of course, McGee had also worked closely with Bender, who had been in Austria at the end of the war. Leo had been in Rome, befriending the Haganah. The Jews had operated an underground railroad, what they called the *brycha*, for survivors of the Holocaust, escorting the illegal emigrants to Adriatic ports for the onward voyage to Palestine. Leo had gained their trust and worked with Bender to ensure minimum interference from the British while the refugees were moving through the Allied zones in Austria. It had been a traumatic experience for everyone involved, but it had led to a deep friendship between the two Americans, fellow conspirators in a campaign to circumvent the British government's restrictions on emigrants destined for the Holy Land. Since serving together in Europe, the two had gone their separate ways, Bender to Latin America, McGee to Counterintelligence. Bender's fortunes had floundered at the Bay of Pigs, while McGee's talent in the arcane arts had been in increasing demand with the appearance of Colonel Penkovsky. Now Harvey was running Task Force W, and McGee had access to that most valuable of currencies, favors owed.

Over the years, McGee had developed a status within the Agency that was second to none. Whenever a defector's meal ticket offered the vital link for a counterintelligence investigation, the kind of clue that made the difference between a traitor going to prison and the unproven suspicion of a trusted civil servant, McGee had inevitably been the man to deliver the news. Under different circumstances, Bill Harvey might have taken the same role, for he, too, had always been first and foremost a counterintelligence expert. But then, instead of competing with McGee, he had accepted the prestigious Berlin job. While Harvey had been in Europe, McGee had thrived and, most recently, had been the host of STONE's party. The British had visited and come away with veritable gems of information. Security Service case officers had been taken off their assignments and transferred to the pursuit of Golitsyn's unique serials. At this very moment the British Admiralty was being turned upside down in an attempt to identify a homosexual spy who allegedly had been hemorrhaging secrets to the KGB for years. Similarly, the French had been invited to come and feast at STONE's table.

At first it had been SDECE's local station chief, Henri Rolland, who, masquerading under first secretary cover at the French embassy in Washington, had come to hear STONE pontificate on the subject of Soviet penetration of the Paris establishment, in much the same way that Maurice Oldfield had listened for the British. Both men had been dumbfounded. In Oldfield's case, he had cabled for help from London. Rolland had requested an entire interrogation team, and he had got the best. Daniel Doustin, head of the DST, had brought his two most trusted lieutenants and the SDECE's director of counterespionage, Colonel Rene Delseny. STONE's testimony had been devastating. According to the KGB defector, a network known as COLUMBINE had spread its tentacles into every corner of de Gaulle's administration, and had even recruited a high-ranking source in the Elysée Palace.

When Harvey asked McGee for help in Cuba, the counterintelligence specialist did not hesitate. He knew two people straightaway who could act as a conduit for messages left in Cuban dead drops. The Italian defense attaché in Havana was a Jew and an old friend who had helped the *brycha* negotiate the frontier between Trieste and Yugoslavia. He had been granted plenty of help in the past, and McGee could call in a couple of favors. And then there was Rolland, who also happened to be accredited in Cuba. He made routine trips down to the Caribbean, usually for recreational purposes, but no doubt he could also be prevailed upon to cooperate. After all, SDECE had just been alerted to the existence of a major Soviet spy ring in Paris, and one good turn deserved another. Alas, thought McGee, as he considered Harvey's request, if only the British had been in a position to help. Unfortunately, most of SIS's local assets had been eliminated in July 1960 when the British oil interests had been seized. The oil companies had refused Castro's order to process Soviet crude, and wholesale nationalization had followed, which in turn led to the withdrawal of the English personnel ... and the SIS representatives.

Port Everglades, Florida;
Friday, 17 August 1962

As he watched the lights of Port Everglades fade in the distance and the first glimmers of dawn rise on the horizon to the east, Tom Waters gripped the cold steel railing on the flying bridge of a down-at-the-heel converted coaster, the U.S.S. *Oxford*, and contemplated the events that had brought him to Florida so swiftly from the Rock.

Less than a month ago, Waters and Simon Hardwick had been watching, or rather listening to, Soviet submarines at play off Gibraltar. Together they had witnessed a remarkable phenomenon, a Whiskey-class diesel making twelve knots and maximum sound while passing the SOSUS sensors strung across the ocean floor. Underwater, the naval officer had explained, sound travels at just under 1,650 yards a second. That meant that the target, when it was about twenty miles off the Straits, took about twenty-two seconds to be detected by the hydrophones; it took another three seconds for the signal to be relayed back to CAESAR, subjected to spectrum analysis, and processed. However, by the time the plot would come up on the display, the submarine would have moved 157.3 yards ... in any direction. CAESAR's sophisticated acoustic equipment took a continuous plot from the sound source and automatically compensated for the time lag. In a full-scale operation, extra data from sonar buoys, towed arrays, and "dunking" helicopters would enhance the quality of the plot in computer real time and pinpoint the target to within just a few yards of its exact position and depth. But on this occasion the two men had been content to compare the radar plot showing the progress of the *Volgoles*, still maintaining radio silence, as it glided silently through the narrows, with the noisy submarine close by attracting all the attention. It was exactly the reverse of the countermeasures usually deployed by Soviet merchantmen, which were intended to screen an underwater transit from the listening devices anchored to the sea bottom. And all the while, the *Linza* had kept station in the Atlantic, no doubt monitoring every frequency to check whether NATO aircraft were scrambled to identify the surface ship.

When Waters and Hardwick had overlaid the CAESAR track onto the course of the *Volgoles*, all remaining doubt had evaporated. Both vessels had converged and then maintained an identical speed and course. The exercise had been remarkable because, as the naval officer had admitted, the two plots would not normally have been compared unless a Soviet submarine had been lost and was suspected of making a clandestine approach to the choke point.

Having witnessed what he had come to see, Waters returned the following afternoon to Brize Norton and then prepared a report for his director, Sir Clive Loehnis, which was followed by a verbal report. It had been immediately after the JIC meeting on the following Thursday that Waters had been summoned to Palmer Street from Benhall, on the outskirts of Cheltenham, to hear his new assignment. Instead of returning to Cyprus, Waters would be posted to the National Security Agency at Fort George G. Meade for briefing, followed by a ten-week "platform tour." Waters had been more than apprehensive when he heard the nature of the platform ... an obsolete old Liberty ship that enjoyed all the seagoing characteristics of a perpetual-motion machine without stabilizers.

Waters had raised objections, including his tendency to seasickness, but when he had heard the reasons, he reluctantly agreed to cooperate. Loehnis had laid out the scenario, which gave the mysterious voyage of the *Volgoles* a rather more sinister interpretation, and one that threatened to destabilze the world's strategic balance. Loehnis had sketched out the background.

"The fact that the *Volgoles* transited Gibraltar in the way in it did confirms that the Soviets are anxious for us not to pay too much attention to their merchant fleet. The Americans have now completed an analysis of their shipping movements across the Atlantic, with special attention on Cuba, and there is a very clear escalation in traffic. For the first six months of this year, there was an average of roughly one passenger ship and fifteen dry cargo vessels calling at Cuban ports. So far this month, four liners have docked, along with twenty-eight other freighters. U.S. Naval Intelligence reports that two more ships are in the Atlantic, apparently heading for the Caribbean, and one of them is the *Volgoles*."

"How does a buildup of Soviet commercial maritime trade with Cuba affect the U.S.'s global strategy?" asked Waters innocently.

"Cuba is the Americans' Achilles' heel. They are extremely sensitive about Cuba, partly because it's so close to the U.S. mainland, but chiefly because it straddles the oil route. Most people don't realize that sixty-five percent of the oil imported to the United States comes through terminals on the Gulf of Mexico, which means that the tankers have to go through the stretch of sea between Florida and Cuba. It's only ninety miles wide. Furthermore, ships using the Panama Canal have a choice of only two channels: the Yucatan route, which is narrow and dominated by Cuba's eastern tip, and the Paso de los Vientos, between Cuba and Haiti. All this shipping is terribly vulnerable, which is why the Americans get into a state of anxiety so quickly if there's trouble. A single Soviet submarine operating from Cuba could easily seal off the oil supply to the Gulf. It's, therefore, hardly surprising that they cling to their naval base at Guantanamo and try to get rid of Castro."

"So this is all about oil and the possibility of Soviet submarines operating on Uncle Sam's doorstep?"

Loehnis regarded Waters with a very grave expression. "It's much more than that. When it comes to aircraft based in Cuba, the U.S. is wide open. When the NORAD early-warning treaty was formed five years ago, North America established what it believed to be complete protection from surprise enemy attack. Unfortunately, no one had bothered to build any protected radar sites in the south. It's a combination of Maginot Line mentality and Pearl Harbor experience."

Waters played the devil's advocate. "Even on the assumption

that all the Soviet merchantmen that have disappeared were heading for Cuban ports, is there any evidence to suggest the Soviets
are planning something?"

Loehnis picked up a report from Hardwick and looked at it
briefly. "There's plenty of circumstantial evidence that points to
increased Russian interest in Cuba. The old Soviet ambassador, a
GRU veteran named Sergei Kudryavtsev, was recently replaced by
the local KGB *rezident*, Aleksandr Shitov. For the past few years
he has been masquerading as Havana's TASS correspondent, calling himself Aleksandr Alekseev. That's a sinister development. Shitov simply returned from Moscow and sacked Kudryavtsev. The
implication is that the KGB is taking greater control over local
intelligence operations on the island."

"Is this linked to the ships?" Waters was more than a trifle
confused.

"It may be. The CIA tells us that ten days ago a group of Euo-
peans, believed to be Czechs, used the Cuban militia to evacuate
all the homes in the waterfront area of Mariel, one of the ports
about thirty miles from Havana that has been receiving ships from
the Black Sea. Finally, Russian personnel have taken over the management of the El Moro Cement Works at Mariel, and the Titan
Concrete Company at Santiago de Cuba."

"Which means ..."

"The consensus is that the Russians are building a secret submarine base, or refueling facility, somewhere on the Cuban coast.
Mariel was evacuated to prevent prying eyes from seeing the heavy
equipment being unloaded."

"Anything else?" Waters was determined to get every piece of
the puzzle he would be helping to solve.

"Just two items. Our Kremlin watchers have reported the dismissal of a senior Soviet officer. It may not be relevant, but General
Golikov, the director of the Main Political Administration of the
Armed Forces, has suddenly gone into retirement. He's in disgrace,
but there is no obvious reason for his replacement. One possibility
is that he may have quarreled with Khrushchev over the development of a submarine base in Cuba. Nevertheless, the way in which
he has acquired nonperson status indicates that some major policy
disagreement has occurred."

"And this is why you want me floating in a tin box off the Cuban coast?" Waters was not happy about it, but he knew how to accept the inevitable gracefully.

Loehnis shook his head slowly. "Not entirely. Of course, you have more experience than most in listening to Soviet merchant fleet traffic, far more than anyone the NSA can deploy in the Caribbean, but we want you to focus on Lourdes, the big Russian communications center just outside Havana. It won't take you long to determine its function. Is it a relay transmitter for low-frequency signals destined for the submarines, or a terminal for a new base? Who knows, it might be nothing more than an intercept site. The problem is, we need to know. And you may be sure that the Russians will be up to their usual tricks, taking countermeasures. We need someone who knows all their mischief. It's the key to Soviet intentions. The NSA has agreed to provide round-the-clock cover by assigning two naval platforms, operating in tandem, and your presence is vital. There's no one more experienced in dealing with this traffic, and now you even know a little about submarines."

Waters felt somewhat overwhelmed by this unsought responsibility. "Less than twenty-four hours spent in Gibraltar hardly qualifies me as an expert on Soviet submarines. Anyway, there isn't any Soviet submarine signal traffic. They maintain permanent radio silence."

His director seized the opportunity to refute Waters's objections. "Exactly. So therefore you know as much as anyone else. However, now that you've been indoctrinated in CAESAR and all those classified antisubmarine warfare techniques, you can make some use of your newfound knowledge. The navy hates letting people in on its secrets and this will save time. Just get yourself to Baltimore as quickly as you can."

A day of briefing at Fort Meade had been sufficient to convince Waters that he should have put up more resistance to his director. The omens were far from good. Even the NSA staff made little attempt to gloss over the discomforts that one had to endure on their naval intercept vessels. And the *Oxford* was worse than most.

Waters's instructions were short and to the point. He should fly to Fort Lauderdale, Florida, and take a cab for the fifteen-minute ride to the John U. Lloyd State Park on Ocean Drive. At the end of the road, next to Nova University's oceanographic laboratory and the U.S. Coast Guard Station on Lake Mabel, was the NSA's secret naval facility, Port Everglades.

Even before Waters had checked in at Port Everglades he had serious misgivings about the wisdom of taking what amounted to an assignment afloat. The U.S.S. *Oxford*, he had been told, was a converted Liberty ship, built at the end of the war. What had been omitted from the briefing was the fact that the working conditions inside the main accommodation, the area that had once been the cargo hold, were appalling, and that the ship, now designated as an AGTR for Auxiliary General Technical Research, had originally been designed as a short-life steamer. Just over 440 feet long, and top heavy with radio antennae draped on tall masts and running the full length of the superstructure, the *Oxford* and her sister ship, the *Sergeant Joseph E. Muller*, had spent the past twelve months cruising the seas off the east coast of South America, sucking up signals from the ether like a seaborne vacuum cleaner and recording them on tape for analysis and decryption.

Unlike other U.S. navy ships, the NSA's fleet of intercept vessels was crewed in the main by civilians. Thus, when Waters arrived on the dock at Port Everglades he was welcomed aboard by the skipper, a burly Bostonian dressed in T-shirt and blue jeans. Having introduced himself, Commander Reilly had explained the separation of duties on his ship.

"Theoretically I have 285 officers and men under my command, but the reality is that a full two-thirds of that number are people like yourself, civilian technicians. My crew have very little idea about what goes on in the commo spaces, and we don't want to know. Access to the security sections is strictly limited, and the person who really runs this ship is Hank Rusbridger. I'm merely a glorified cabdriver," he paused and laughed. "Come to think of it, there's no glory in any of this either. We can't say where we're going or where we've been, and I sometimes get the impression that not even the brass at Norfolk really knows what we do. Follow me, and I'll find Rusbridger for you. He'll assign you your quarters, quite spartan I'm afraid. This tub was not built for paying passengers. And don't forget, no liquor please. We run a dry ship."

Waters suppressed a comment about the improbability of anyone ever wanting to pay for a voyage on the *Oxford*, which, he noted, was simply identified as AGTR–1 in white on the matt gray hull. He followed Reilly up the gangplank, his duffel bag over his shoulder, and crossed the quarterdeck, past the petty officer of the watch who examined his NSA pass, and ducked into the executive officer's stateroom.

"The taxpayers spent $20 million on this ship," remarked Reilly, "but none of it went to the living compartments. Up until last year this wreck was in mothballs, part of the national reserve fleet in Puget Sound, and then someone thought it could do something useful. Here's the man who knows just how useful our mission is," he said, introducing Rusbridger, a short, sandy-haired man in his late thirties, with an easy grin.

"Take no notice of the skipper," said Rusbridger. "He thinks the commo spaces are full of untold luxury and dancing girls. I'll show you to your quarters." The two men nodded to Reilly and made their way to the tiny cabin Waters was to share with another numbers cruncher.

Now, as Waters gazed across the rolling waves and the *Oxford* gathered speed and turned south, he wondered what the prospects were of finding the truth behind the Soviet buildup in Cuba.

Washington, D.C.;
Friday, 17 August 1962

Five hours after the *Oxford* slipped its moorings and sailed out into the predawn Florida gloom, McGee and Harvey sauntered into L'Escargot, a small, inexpensive French restaurant on Connecticut Avenue in northwest Washington and a well-known haunt of U.S. intelligence officers. Recognizing his guest, Henri Rolland, who had arrived a little earlier and had already ordered a blanc cassis, McGee slid onto the banquette opposite him and introduced Harvey as a colleague. The contrast between the two intelligence professionals could not have been greater. Whereas Harvey was short and rotund, his stomach bulging through his garish plaid cotton jacket, Rolland was the epitome of the suave European nobleman. Nor could their backgrounds have been more dissimilar. Harvey had been a G-man, a cop first and foremost, anxious to catch spies and lock them up. Rolland's life had been spent largely undercover, first in the French resistance and then working during the war in London for de Gaulle's embryonic intelligence service. Since April 1951, he had been masquerading as a diplomat, responsible for SDECE's liaison with Washington, a job he found exceptionally congenial.

After a few preliminaries and the ordering of their lunch from Georges, the ever-discreet maître d'hôtel, the three men got down to business.

"Henri, I need an update on how your people are dealing with STONE's data."

Rolland smiled, knowing full well that the CIA's Counterintelligence chief had not invited him to lunch just to check on what use his NATO allies were making of the defector's meal ticket. Nor

creased, but the Brits say that some of the Russian dry cargo freighters have taken unusual steps to conceal their destinations. Apparently they are practicing emission control. That's no radar, no ship-to-shore, no VHF channels. And almost all have come from familiar arms exporting ports like Odessa, Novorisk, and Stettin. This ties in with DIA estimates, which note new Cuban patrol craft, ground attack aircraft, and armor."

"But isn't that what you would expect after the Bay of Pigs? A greater defensive capability?" Rolland tried to put things into perspective; the Americans had become super-sensitive about Cuba.

Harvey swallowed his martini and said bluntly, "The Russians are not natural philanthropists. They're not renowned for the deployment of personnel and material for no obvious reason, apart from responding to a hypothetical threat. We all know that the political climate would have to change dramatically before the White House sanctioned a new effort to destabilize Castro. In short, there is no logical reason for the Kremlin to make such a massive investment. We're not talking about a few obsolete artillery pieces to deter another invasion. We suspect it's more like 350 tanks, 700 antiaircraft guns, and 40 offshore fast boats. There's no way Castro can pay for all that. According to the refugees we've interviewed, literally thousands of Russians have arrived over the past few weeks. Why? The only reasonable conclusion is the development of a big submarine refueling depot."

"So in time of war the Soviets could either threaten or even enforce a maritime blockade," added McGee.

"So you envision the Soviets exacting a specific price for protection against another Bay of Pigs?"

McGee nodded his head vigorously in agreement. "As I see it, Khrushchev told Castro that he would guarantee his regime on condition that he granted the Red Navy an equivalent of Guantanamo Bay. How could Castro refuse? He hates our retention of an American base on Cuban soil and this would be a way of getting even. He might even see it as a chip to bargain with."

"Furthermore," added Harvey, "this scenario would explain a few other developments of significance: The new Soviet ambassador in Havana is a career KGB officer. Several senior military commanders have also turned up unexpectedly in Cuba. Then there is Raúl Castro's unannounced trip to Moscow and the sudden dismissal of at least two important military advisers."

Rolland was naturally suspicious about the motives of his two hosts. "If you are right in your surmise, why do you need my help? Why hasn't this become one of your intelligence priorities?"

Once again McGee and Harvey exchanged embarrassed looks. McGee took the initiative. "It's fair to say that Bill's predecessor, Frank Bender, did a pretty good job of undermining the Agency's credibility hereabouts with the Bay of Pigs. The fact is that we are alone in this. Nobody wants to know about Cuba and the Agency. The DIA, for example, simply doesn't believe us. The people there have pinned their faith on ARNIKA and very little of his data is even remotely relevant to Cuba."

"What about the buildup in arms. Surely that is a responsibility for the DIA?"

"It is," agreed Harvey, "but the analysts have concluded that until there is solid evidence to the contrary, they will continue to interpret the intensified Soviet activity as being mostly economic assistance."

"What about your own analysts?"

"We don't have them. Two were brought in a couple of years ago, but they fell out with Dulles. When the DCI departed in November, we were left without any intelligence analysts on the Cuban front. I'm ashamed to admit it, but it's true."

Suddenly Rolland realized that he was being drawn into an interagency battle. He now had the advantage, and he was keen to exploit it while the Americans were in such a forthcoming mood. He broached the most sensitive subject of all, the National Security Agency. "I would have thought that, given due regard for their technical expertise, the NSA could have decided matters one way or the other quite conclusively. After all, it is in Cuba already."

"The NSA has endorsed the DIA's findings," said McGee flatly. "It's true it intercepts from inside the Guantanamo perimeter, but it would seem that the Russians are being careful about what they broadcast."

Looking warily at his luncheon companions, Rolland said, "So the NSA is against you as well?"

"More or less," agreed McGee. "The Brits have made noises about the maritime traffic going to Cuba, so Fort Meade has made a token gesture to placate them. One of their fellows from GCHQ has been sent on a Caribbean cruise. They don't take this seriously."

Nor, it appeared, did Rolland. "How practical would a Soviet submarine base be in Cuba?"

"Plenty effective," Harvey snapped. "Thanks to some recent leaks they know all about the measures we have taken to monitor the movement of their long-range submarines. Quite apart from the choke points, the navy operates COLOSSUS, a system of underwater hydrophones from Argentia in Newfoundland down to Andros in the Bahamas. It creates, in effect, a barrier which ensures that we can track the movement of every Soviet submarine. There are only two possible countermeasures: to knock out COLOSSUS's coastal terminals, or station submarines permanently inside the barrier."

"Surely in time of war the first option would be quite legitimate?" objected Rolland.

Harvey started to reply but hesitated for a few moments while a neighboring couple left their table. Once they had passed, he continued. "Sure, and we have already noticed heightened Soviet activity around Cape Hatteras, North Carolina, and Bermuda, two of the key terminals. Both have been subjected to unwelcome attention from Soviet trawlers alleging engine trouble, but probably undertaking reconnaissance missions. There's no doubt they know exactly what we have done, and they are planning appropriate countermeasures. The only reason the Soviets have requested landing rights in Bermuda for their fishing fleet is because one of the main listening posts is located at Tudor Hill on that island. They probably have contingency arrangements to sabotage the site at the outbreak of hostilities. However, if their submarines could operate freely in the Caribbean, having passed over the COLOSSUS line, we would have to completely rethink our antisubmarine strategy."

"I am not so sure I understand," responded Rolland. "I am no sailor, but surely one Soviet naval base more or less would not make much difference?"

Harvey waved his fork impatiently. "It would make all the difference, especially if the facility was in the Western Hemisphere, or on our home turf. The Russians are terribly restricted by their geography and weather. They only possess six submarine bases in the whole world: Vladivostock, Sovietskaya Gavan, and Petropavlovsk, in the east; Murmansk and Severodvinsk in the north; and Leningrad in the Baltic. All are covered by permanent surveillance of one kind or another, and none have direct, unimpeded access to the ocean. In effect, NATO can bottle them all up easily, and in any event, the ports are literally thousands of miles from the submarines' target areas. That means minimal time spent on active patrol, a huge wastage sailing to and from their operational areas, and a constant danger of detection while en route. A fully-equipped base right inside the U.S.'s front line would tip the balance in their favor. It might even give them a first-strike capability from sea-launched ballistic missiles."

Uneasy at the way the conversation was headed, Rolland countered, "Surely they have a first-strike capability anyway?"

McGee replied firmly. "We don't think so. Our latest estimates suggest that the Soviets have only built four intercontinental ballistic missiles."

"This is only the CIA's contention," said Rolland as McGee recollected that SDECE had received virtually all of Penkovsky's intelligence but had remained unconvinced.

"Yes, but it's been confirmed by our satellite reconnaissance, which you may not have seen yet. The very latest Discoverer photographs show that there are just four Russian ICBMs, a single SS-6 Sapwood plus reload on each of the two launchpads at Plesetsk."

"So the deployment of the Red Navy's submarine fleet is absolutely critical," agreed Harvey.

"The Soviets have thirty Zulu-, Golf-, and Hotel-class missile subs, each armed with thirty SS-4, medium-range Sandals. These are two-megaton warheads with a range of about a thousand nautical miles."

"You're saying that at present the United States is invulnerable to Soviet attack, despite everything Khrushchev has stated publicly, unless their submarines can get in close?"

"Exactly. It really looks as though the Kremlin has been bluffing about Soviet missile strength. If the analysts are right, and our pictures seem to confirm it all, the Russians are still experimenting with V-2 technology. The Sapwoods are very unreliable and are easy to spot from the air because of their size and their four distinctive strap-on boosters. The Soviets are nowhere near perfecting the next generation of long-distance delivery vehicles, with true intercontinental range ..."

"... which means they need submarines to bring the missiles within range of their targets," added Rolland.

"Yeah. And they have to be transported to the launch area undetected. The only way this can be achieved is by operating the subs inside COLOSSUS, and having them serviced and refueled there, too. It would take us years to construct a new COLOSSUS line, and in the meantime Khrushchev would have the advantage, leaving NATO vulnerable to nuclear blackmail."

"And that means the loss of Berlin," muttered Rolland, "just when the temperature there was falling."

McGee judged it was the right moment to nudge Rolland. "It might interest you to know that we think there are a couple of snippets from ARNIKA that might be relevant, whatever the DIA thinks."

Rolland leaned forward conspiratorially to catch every word. General Jacquier had mentioned to him some weeks ago that he was not convinced that the British and the Americans were sharing everything from this valued source with their NATO allies.

"He has given us some interesting news that may be relevant to all this. Two Soviet generals have recently been reassigned overseas. They are Lieutenant General Sergei Ushakov of the Antiaircraft Missile Command, and General Slazenko, an infantry specialist. Nobody seems to know where they've been sent. They could be irrelevant, or they may be involved in all this. We really need to find out."

"Where might they have gone?"

"There are only three alternatives. We know that two Soviet

Foxtrot-class submarines have been operating secretly for the Indonesians, so Jakarta is a possibility. Then we have reports that the Red Air Force is supplying bomber aircrews in Yemen, so that enters the equation. Both these recent developments have grave political implications and are a radical departure from how the Soviets usually behave. Finally, of course, there is Cuba."

Rolland was convinced. "I'll do it."

U.S.S. *Oxford*; Monday, 20 August 1962

For the past week Waters had endured the best, and the worst, the Caribbean could offer in midsummer, at the height of the hurricane season. The first two days, sailing south, had been pleasant enough, but then they had caught the edge of a tropical depression, and the following thirty-six hours had been very uncomfortable. Nor was it much consolation to Waters to learn that most of the communications technicians, known simply as CTs, had been equally seasick. At the end of the first few hours, Waters reckoned he had studied every inch of his shared cabin. It was an eight-by-ten L-shaped box painted navy gray, with a wardrobe on one bulkhead and lockers fitted to the other. The only furniture was a small leatherette desk chair, apart from a very comfortable double bunk, a head, shower, and small washbasin. It was the very minimum needed to sustain life for two adults, and in bad sea conditions, with the twin five hundred horsepower General Motors diesels fighting a thirty-five-degree roll, the overall experience had inspired only depression. However, once the weather had settled, Waters quickly got into the routine of doing two shifts in the Special Operations Department, which had formerly been the *Oxford*'s cargo hold and was now universally called the SOD hut.

Apart from the *Oxford*'s two sister ships, there were no other ships like this afloat. The idea of developing what amounted to a clandestine fleet of floating intercept platforms had been borrowed from the Russians, who had adapted some trawlers built in East Germany in the late 1950s. But while the unarmed Soviet vessels were swathed with just as much sophisticated electronic receiving equipment topside, and their giveaway multiple helical antennae, they went through the pretense of being civilian, even though they never did any fishing. The U.S. AGTRs, in contrast, were conspicuously naval in appearance, and their cover of hydrographic research was, as Waters discovered, supported by two members of the wardroom whom he had met on the first day of the voyage. Twice on each shift the *Oxford* came to a stop for the oceanographers to conduct a Nansen cast and a bathythermograph test, which involved taking a seawater sample from several different depths to record salinity and temperature gradients. A six-hundred-fathom line was winched out manually from the fantail, with the sample bottles attached to the end. The objective was to construct a comprehensive record of the thermocline's variations in the Caribbean, essential data for conducting antisubmarine warfare. It also justified the international day signals for hydrographic work being hoisted on the yardarm: red ball, white diamond, red ball. Waters wondered if it fooled anyone. The *Oxford*'s sister ships were the *Private Jose P. Valdez*, and the *Sergeant Joseph E. Muller*, both of which had spent most of their extended life off the African coast. According to *Jane's Fighting Ships*, all were engaged in hydrographic and electromagnetic radiation research, better known in the trade as "collection" or, more crudely, espionage.

During his first morning aboard the *Oxford*, Waters had been granted the rare privilege of an escorted tour of the commo spaces by Rusbridger.

"You're the first foreign national we have ever had aboard," commented the lieutenant as they walked down the companionway toward the SOD hut. The entrance to the classified area was a large steel door, protected with three locks, one on the handle itself, opened by a key, a combination dial in the center, and then a press-button arrangement in which four digits had to be selected in the correct sequence before the locking bolt could be released.

"Is this security really necessary?" asked Waters.

"Only a small proportion of the ship's company have a clearance for special compartmented intelligence, so only the CTs and visiting NSA personnel can have access to the hut or the crypto room. They're called the spooks by the rest of the crew. Even the ship's regular radiomen have never been farther than this. Everything beyond this door is classified above top secret. Most of it is code-worded, too. We have stuff in here that the Soviets haven't even dreamed of."

Once inside the temperature dropped dramatically as the air-conditioning system kept the shift on duty alert and prevented the hardware from overheating. Waters was presented with a quite unnautical scene: an office area packed with computer consoles, electronic receivers of every kind, and several banks of crypto-graphic machinery, all in an atmosphere of laboratorylike sterility. Rusbridger continued the tour.

"The *Oxford*'s mission is to be the eyes and ears of the navy. I expect with your background some of this gadgetry is familiar to you," Rusbridger said.

"Not at all," answered Waters truthfully, who felt as though he had entered an Aladdin's cave of sophisticated apparatus, only some of which he had seen before. "Most of the stuff I'm used to is fit for the Science Museum. This is much more up-to-date."

"Our primary role is that of intercepting all electronic emissions from, on this voyage, Cuba. Usually we cruise slowly up and down the coast, just outside the territorial limit, listening to anything and everything. Our frequency range covers the whole spectrum, so we will be recording conversations over military walkie-talkies well inland as well as radar signals. Everything is recorded and logged, and then subjected to onboard analysis. The commo spaces are divided up into particular disciplines, including direction finding and traffic analysis. Our chief occupation is taking fixes of radar transmissions in the hope of finding a new station. We record the same signal from several different locations and then trace the position of the shore station. Nine times out of ten it's a station we already know about."

Rusbridger moved on to another steel door. "In the next sec-tion are our own transmitters. We have a choice of systems for communicating Stateside or relaying data. They say that with the prefix PINNACLE CRITIC, a message from us will reach the presi-dent in six minutes. We've never had to try it out. In addition to the regular continuous wave morse circuits in the radioshack at the back of the wheelhouse, there's a secure teleprinter down here."

"Are they linked?" asked Waters.

"No. It's not ideal, but we use the CW circuit to call up, and then the appropriate Naval Security Group ground station selects a frequency on which to set the encrypted teleprinter. In addition, we have access to the High Command net, but that's not secure. Finally, we have our special box of tricks, which is our microwave connection. In theory, this maintains an open secure channel on a microwave beam bounced off the surface of the moon."

Waters was dutifully impressed. "Which makes it impossible to intercept?"

Rusbridger grinned. "Well, that's what we like to think. In theory, the only way of breaking into the ten-thousand-watt signal is to place an antenna between us and the moon, or the moon and the NSG station. It's a line-of-sight channel that is set up with a television camera fitted with a powered zoom lens. Frankly, interception is pretty improbable. But best of all, we can use the channel while maintaining radio and radar silence. When we enforce complete emission control we actually disable all the ship's transmitters by removing the keying components and locking them away. However, this little gimmick can't betray our position, or so they tell us."

Waters picked up on his host's uncertainty. "You said 'in theory'?"

Rusbridger sighed and said, "Well, this gear is still in the experimental stages. It's dependent upon the transponder and dish receiver on the forward mast being exactly in alignment with a particular point on the moon. The transponder is highly directional, but it's the sixteen-foot dish that always seems to be out of synch. The engineers have dreamed up an immensely complicated hydraulic system to keep both steady whatever the direction or roll of the ship. Unfortunately, it's so clever we can't get it to work— either that or it's completely useless. I haven't made up my mind about it yet."

"Presumably you can direct the beam virtually anywhere in the same hemisphere?"

"That's right, provided it's all working. I sometimes think we have more men up the masts mending dipoles or lashing antennae than down here in the research spaces. Do you know, we have forty-five different antennae up there? It would be a miracle if all the systems worked simultaneously."

In the farthest recesses of the commo space was another steel door with a peephole at eye level. "This is the cipher vault, and not even you can go in there. There are only half a dozen of us cleared to do so, and we have to be accompanied at all times by a designated CMS custodian ... the Communications Material Systems. It's where we keep the KW-7, KG-14, and KL-47 cipher machines, together with the key lists sufficient for the duration of our voyage. Anyone breaking in here will set off thermite charges that will melt the contents in a few seconds. Over here," continued Rusbridger, guiding his visitor away from the cipher room, "is our passive sonar center. We have a 'big ear' on board that allows us to listen to submarines. Listen, I emphasize, but do not touch. We can also deploy a towed array, but not in daylight."

Waters pointed to one of the large high-voltage cable terminals close to a bank of instruments and tape decks. "How is all this hardware powered?"

"We use a lot of juice, especially on the air-conditioning. The main engine room has two hundred-kilowatt generators for the ship, but the auxiliary engine room has two sixty-kilowatt genera-tors for the research space with an emergency twenty-five-kilowatt generator as a backup. This runs all the electronic surveillance operations twenty-four hours a day while on patrol. Every radio frequency ever known to have been used by Eastern bloc navies or maritime fleets are monitored around the clock. And in here"—he pointed to a cubicle devoted to steel filing cabinets, all fitted with combination locks—"are the classified publications. They list every Communist ship we are ever likely to encounter. Full regis-tration details, silhouettes, and photographs. Whenever we come across a new ship, it's added to the manuals. So we perform a visual observation and identification function as well as an elec-tronic intelligence-gathering one. Below we have a fully equipped photographic lab."

"Very impressive," agreed Waters. "But when do we really get down to the business we're here for?"

Rusbridger glanced at his watch. "We should be over the target in the next hour or so."

What Rusbridger and Waters were referring to was the *Oxford*'s real mission on this voyage. Although the ship would continue to act normally, intercepting and recording coastal radar emissions, its primary mission was to monitor Cuba's overseas voice circuits. Most of the CTs had already tuned their apparatus to the transmission frequencies used by the huge Soviet signals center at Lourdes for their long-distance communications, and other ingenious advanced technology monitored the Soviet's receiving equipment. Even if the Lourdes complex was simply engaged in intercept work and was not sending, the *Oxford*'s sensitive antennae could detect the very faint emitted radiation that betrayed the exact frequencies being kept under surveillance by the Russians. But the ace up the sleeve was an unusual device now lashed to the deck awaiting deployment, code-named RIMMER.

The origin of RIMMER, as Waters had been told during his briefing at Fort Meade, had been the knowledge that Cuba's entire telephone and cable system had been constructed by an American company, ITT, which happened to enjoy a close relationship with the CIA and the NSA. With the assistance of the very engineers who had designed ITT's system and laid the cables, the NSA developed a highly innovative induction antenna that, when placed alongside the main cable on the ocean bed, picked up every signal. And because the Soviets were well aware that their radio traffic was the subject of routine hostile interception, they tended to rely on the land lines for what they evidently believed to be secure communications.

RIMMER's only drawback was the necessity to locate the exact position of the underwater cable and to deploy the apparatus in the correct manner so as to achieve optimum reception. Even the *Oxford*'s intricate inertial navigation system, which used overhead satellites to determine her position with pinpoint accuracy, down to only a few feet, had failed to achieve the standard of precision required for such a delicate operation. However, two experiments had already proved that once a submarine had laid a pattern of remote-controlled sonar beacons, the state-of-the-art paraphernalia on board could bring the *Oxford* to precisely the required position, and thereby could compromise the integrity of a transatlantic cable hidden deep underwater. As Rusbridger had explained, it was a little like adjusting an aircraft on the glide path when making a final approach for landing. As the *Oxford* neared, the acoustic beacons were triggered into action, broadcasting a very weak signal that was received and interpreted by a computer guiding the ship's progress. Once directly above the cable, RIMMER was deployed over the side and winched down to straddle the line that carried virtually all of Havana's telephone and telex traffic.

On this occasion, as Waters noticed, the procedure worked faultlessly, although Commander Reilly had insisted they wait until dark before the covers were removed from the long tubular container that held RIMMER's delicate sensors and it was lifted over the fantail. Positioning RIMMER in the best place took two tries because of the gentle swell, but on the third attempt the SOD hut reported perfect reception. The banks of tape recorders were switched on, and the three translators on board were summoned to start sifting through the voice channels.

It had been Water's fluency in Russian that had proved the clincher for this assignment. Loehnis had reinforced his argument by pointing out that the U.S. Navy boasted very few professional linguists. Of the three on the *Oxford*, two were Spanish-speakers and the third had not yet qualified in Russian. Most of the low-sensitivity transcription work was farmed out by the CIA and NSA to émigrés who were under contract, but there were only a handful of people with the right language skills and the necessary security clearance. And since the NSA did not regard this project as a priority, it had not been prepared to transfer key personnel to the venture. Waters, however, had been granted the clearance and, thanks to his attendance at the interpreters course at RAF Crail in Fife during his National Service, and the advanced program run by the Foreign Office at Bodmin, had acquired a handy knowledge not only of Russian but of much of the current military terminology.

Waters joined his new colleagues in a small cubicle in the SOD hut and clamped a pair of bakelite headphones over his ears, and then began selecting voice channels on the switching console at his side. As soon as he started, he was amazed by the clarity with which he could hear the conversations being conducted over the cable so far below. There was a constant crackle of background noise, mainly static interference, but he was quite used to working with far more difficult material. None of this, he reminded himself, was anything like the traffic he had to pluck out of the ether on his single sideband watches.

Waters continued at his desk late into the night, eavesdropping on the international circuits, moving quickly from one to the next, noting names whenever they occurred, listing locations mentioned. Due to the eight-hour time difference between Cuba and Moscow, the Russians in Havana evidently had to conduct their business in the early hours, so it was not until dawn that Waters had returned to his quarters, exhausted yet exhilarated by his experience. As he switched off the bulkhead lamp over his bed, he smiled about one particular conversation he had listened to, and one that he intended to report back to Cheltenham. Apparently, in the interests of maintaining security, one unit of Soviet soldiers, under the personal command of a certain General Dankevich, had not been told of their destination when they had been given their embarkation orders at Odessa, so they had no idea where they were headed. As a result, they had packed winter clothes and brought their skis.

Havana; Wednesday, 22 August 1962

It had been a breathlessly hot day, and the evening had been no better. The food in the shabby cafe on San Lazaro where he had dined alone had been awful, and the air-conditioning in the Havana Libre, formerly the Hilton, had broken down again. Outside there was a stench of diesel fumes, but few private cars on the roads. This week the fuel ration had been allocated to public transport vehicles only.

Rolland had flown into Rancho Boyeros Airport from Mexico City four days ago, and he wished he could have caught a plane out that same evening. Unfortunately, he had not been able to empty the dead-letter drop on 23rd Street, opposite what was left of the monument to the *Maine*, until this morning. Harvey's instructions had been typically elaborate. The drop would not be ready until a flowerpot had appeared on the second-floor balcony of an apartment on Belascoain Street, above a tailor's shop that, ironically, happened to be frequented by some of the leading revolutionaries. The pot had only been put in position the previous evening. By the time Rolland spotted the signal it was quite late, and he had to wait until morning to avoid walking the streets late at night.

The ambassador, Robert du Gardier, had been very suspicious of Rolland's unannounced arrival, but had been sufficiently discreet to make no obvious comment on it. Both men assumed that the DGI had bugged every room in the chancery building, but talking in riddles came naturally to men from the Quai d'Orsay. Just to give Jose Abrantes's notorious security men something to think about, Rolland had also made a couple of courtesy calls—first to

103

the Italian ambassador, Raffaele Ferretti, who had been besieged with refugees seeking asylum, and then on the splendid old veteran Swiss diplomat, Carl Burckhardt, who had been brought back from retirement to look after the American interests section. With each he had engaged in banal conversation about the fate of the political prisoners detained in the Cabana Fortress after the Bay of Pigs fiasco, but Burckhardt had disclosed an interesting item of gossip. Apparently, his driver had met an air force officer in the bar of the Commodore Hotel who claimed to be Castro's personal pilot. Somewhat the worse for wear, this man had boasted that the Americans were soon to be in for an unpleasant shock. Rolland stored the warning away in his memory.

Having set a few hares running for the secret police to chase, Rolland had indulged in some basic tradecraft to keep any remaining enthusiasts occupied. He had engaged three complete strangers in quite innocuous conversation, knowing that each person would be placed under surveillance and followed until he had been identified. The skill was to do this so naturally that the opposition would not realize what had really happened. The unwitting decoys would keep the security men occupied, quite harmlessly, for hours. The next objective had been to establish whether he was still under hostile observation. All the movie stunts of "shaking tails" or "dry-cleaning" were entirely impractical countermeasures because they served merely to betray one's status as a professional intelligence officer. That was half the battle lost, so Rolland, like other skilled practitioners of his arcane art, made his moves with commensurate subtlety.

Even when he was satisfied that he had probably shed whatever surveillance team might have accompanied him from the Havana Libre, Rolland had a few tricks up his sleeve. The first had been to make contact with Juanita Castro by telephone. Naturally the line was monitored, but the conversation would have established him to those listening as someone with access to the regime's inner circle. This would be of little value if he was dragged off to the Villa Marista, but at least it would caution anyone unwise enough to consider compromising him in some elaborate setup. He also walked round to 11th Street, where Celia Sanchez lived, and dropped a short letter at her apartment, letting her know that he was back in Havana for a few days. Seeing Celia would be mixing business with pleasure, for they had been lovers before the revolution.

Celia was almost as much of an enigma as Castro himself. She came from a similar, wealthy landowning background in the east of the island, and had certainly never been a Marxist. She had also read law at the University of Havana, although their paths had not crossed there because of their age difference. Castro had graduated from Belen, the exclusive Jesuit college, in 1945, aged nineteen. Celia had been four years younger, and as a radical student had been inspired by Castro's disastrous attack on the Moncada and Bayamo barracks in Oriente in July 1953. Batista had spared Castro's life, following the intervention of the rector of Santiago University and the archbishop of Santiago de Cuba, and allowed him to stand trial for insurrection. Castro had defended himself in court, and taken the opportunity to portray himself as a reincarnation of José Martí, Cuba's national hero. He had advocated justice and freedom from persecution and denounced Batista and his army's repression. As a law student, Celia had attended the trial and been spellbound by Castro's oratory and his stated commitment to democracy and educational, agrarian, and housing reforms. Few present, apart from the judge, had been unaffected by the charismatic young defendant. For Celia, it had been a seminal experience, and during the two years Castro spent in prison Celia had become a political agitator and an early recruit to the 26th of July Movement, the anti-Batista organization named after the date of the Moncada assault. Castro had been sentenced to fifteen years imprisonment, and Celia had had little prospect of seeing him again, but after twenty-two months Batista had pardoned him in an amnesty. Once released, Castro divorced his wife and moved to Mexico where he planned another ill-fated revolt, a general strike timed to coincide with an invasion. Bad weather had delayed Castro's amateur armada, and Batista's troops had counterattacked. Faced with overwhelming odds, the rebels had fled to the heavily wooded mountains of the Sierra Maestra, where they continued to operate as guerrillas, and where Celia had joined them.

Tall, slim, and astonishingly good-looking, Celia had been a sensation on her arrival in the rebel camp, and she quickly became Castro's confidante. Rumors abounded that she was also his mistress, but no one ever said so in their presence. She gave him wise counsel, and it was in part due to her advice that Castro adopted a moderate manifesto and thereby succeeded in uniting many of Batista's fragmented opponents. When, in January 1959, Castro had eventually seized power, Celia had been in his entourage. And when, in April, Rolland was sent to Cuba to assess the new regime, they had been introduced at a government reception. Each had been attracted to the other, and their discreet affair had been snatched in hotel rooms and borrowed beach houses. The combination of the dashing French diplomat and the beautiful sophisticate turned revolutionary had been a volatile mixture, but one that had lasted. On the occasions they met, they rarely discussed politics, preferring instead to indulge in torrid, unrestrained lovemaking of the kind shared only by two people who knew that neither could make any lasting commitment to the other. For Rolland, his relationship with Celia, if discovered, would have meant the end of his career; for her, the penalty might have been more severe, for she had become Castro's nominal secretary and a figure of some influence in Havana.

Celia was part of the reason Rolland had opted to stay in Washington in spite of the attractive posts he had been offered from time to time in Paris, and certainly the main motive for his periodic visits to Cuba. Each time he followed the same routine: He would leave a brief, uncompromising message at her apartment and then wait for her to arrange a clandestine rendezvous. She adored the thrill of her illicit romance, safe in the knowledge that Rolland would never betray her. This was no intellectual liaison but a vastly satisfying experience shared by two compatible lovers, one a young woman who had spent three years in the *cordillera* enduring the most primitive of conditions, the other a suave sophisticate willing to devote himself to ensuring she obtained complete sexual satisfaction. The paradox had given both free rein to their substantial appetites and allowed them to gratify their fantasies.

Rolland had always been careful not to jeopardize the intrigue by taking every precaution to avoid discovery. He rarely revealed to his SDECE superiors his unique source of information, and he was reasonably sure the CIA had never been tipped off. Furthermore, his feigned disinterest in local political developments had given Celia the confidence she needed to sustain the relationship, even though it became more dangerous as each month went by. However, Rolland had decided, on this trip, to break the unwritten rules. There had been a couple of encounters that had given him cause for anxiety.

On the way to the Vedado district the previous day, which was where Celia Sanchez's apartment was located, Rolland had taken the usual precautions and in doing so found himself in San Pedro Street. Usually a bustling avenue choked with traffic and residents, the Frenchman had been struck by what he now saw. The road had been completely filled, not by moving vehicles, but by literally dozens of Soviet-made trucks that had been parked, three abreast, end-to-end, the whole length of the street. It had been an extraordinary sight, but he had been careful not to linger or be seen counting them. Before moving on, however, he had been struck by an oddity: The drivers were not Cubans. They were all fit young men, all white, with severe military haircuts. What had made them particularly conspicuous was the fact that they were all wearing much the same kind of sports shirts. Indeed, as Rolland looked closer, he realized that of the thirty or so drivers he could see milling around, they all seemed to share identical taste, for there were only two styles and colors of shirt on display. Rolland had hurried on.

The change of atmosphere in the capital had also struck the French visitor as peculiar. He had been to Havana several times after the Bay of Pigs, and the wave of arrests that had followed the disaster had affected everyone on the island. No firm figures of those taken into custody had been released, but some well-informed observers reckoned it must have been near 35,000. The Palacio de Deportes, the stadium with a capacity of 10,000, had been requisitioned to accommodate those interned and been quickly filled. The headquarters of Castro's feared security apparatus, a huge green office block on Fifth Avenue between 12th and

14th streets, had overflowed with people grabbed off the sidewalk by snatch squads. So many suspects had been arrested that Ramiro Valdez, the hated commissar, had taken over several neighboring buildings. But despite the repression, rumors were rife, and Rolland heard them in the cafes: The ports had never been so busy, yet there was nothing to eat in the shops. Russians, not Czechs, had taken over much of the waterfront in Mariel. And perhaps most sinister of all, the docks were idle throughout the day ... the ships were, without exception, unloaded at night by foreign labor.

When Rolland listened to the gossip, it made the hairs on the back of his neck stand up. It was the same kind of sensation he had experienced during the German occupation at home in Romorantin, south of the Loire and not far from Orléans. The demarcation line between Nazi-occupied France and Vichy had been drawn just a few miles away, along the River Cher, and as a young man he had crossed it with impunity, carrying messages for the local resistance group and occasionally guiding a Jew on the run. Those had been exciting times for a young man of just nineteen. Now Rolland felt the nagging anxiety he had known while waiting half the night in the thick undergrowth along the banks of the Cher, watching for the German patrol before slipping into the icy water to swim the four hundred feet to the so-called free zone. And there had been the traitors to contend with as well as the German troops. He had once joked, on his return to Paris after the liberation, that his greatest surprise had been to discover that 13 million Frenchmen had been members of the resistance. It had not seemed like that at the time!

The clincher, for Rolland, had been the message he extracted from inside the matchbox left by Harvey's agent. It was brief and did not answer the questionnaire that had been despatched a month earlier. The message consisted of just two items: the name Vasili Mendeviev, as the Soviet who had recently taken over the running of the Titan Cement Works at Santiago de Cuba; and the description of a long missile, the length of a telegraph pole, spotted late at night on a Soviet transporter moving west from Mariel toward Guanajay. As instructed, Rolland destroyed the note after memorizing the contents. It was just as he had extinguished the flames in his washbasin that Celia had telephoned and welcomed him to Havana. It had been the mention of the name Jose Luis that had identified the beach house where they should meet later that evening. Anyone intercepting the call would never have guessed that two lovers had arranged an assignation.

When they met, it was as though they had hardly been away from each other. Celia looked as ravishing as ever, her supple brown body poorly concealed by a brightly colored *pareo* bathing wrap. She was tall and elegant, with the kind of posture some women paid a fortune to acquire at finishing schools while others inherited naturally. They stood for a moment on the veranda of the small bungalow-style house, gazing at each other.

"Mon Dieu," said Rolland, "you look better than ever. I've missed you."

"You liar," laughed Celia, tossing back her long dark hair. "I know you spend all your time chasing pretty American white women in Washington. What a life you lead. Come indoors. It's too hot out here."

Rolland took her arm, walked inside, and then kissed her hard on the lips. "They don't make women in America like you," he murmured, as he kissed her cheek, and then her ear. He knew she could never resist that, and it was true what he had said. Celia's family was of mixed blood, and although she had clear gray-blue eyes, her skin's natural tan suggested that one of her grandparents had been a mulatto. She shivered and tightened her grip on him.

"How long are you staying?"

"I have to leave tomorrow morning. I've a flight to Mexico, but I'll be back again soon enough."

"I think you're what they call a jet-setter," smiled Celia, teasing him, "with a different girl at every airport."

His hand moved down and slipped under her bra to the beautifully rounded shape of her breast, and he cupped it gently, his fingers moving over her hardening nipple. He heard her sharp intake of breath and drew away briefly. "Nothing changes, eh?"

He kissed her hard again, pushing himself closer to her. "We have a lot of time to make up for," he said, leading her to the bedroom. Moments later they were on the bed, her wrap discarded on the floor. She had a bikini on underneath, but he unclasped the bra top and allowed her full, firm breasts to be revealed. Then, slowly, he caressed them, his fingers drawing tantalizing circles around the stiffening dark tips of each. Then he drew her to him and he hugged her hard before moving his lips down her neck to rest on her nipples, which, in turn, he manipulated softly with his tongue. She reached out and pulled his cotton jacket off. She sat up on the pillow, her bronzed body arched back while she tried to undress him, but Rolland was preoccupied, his fingers exploring her velvet softness.

Soon both were writhing and panting on the disheveled sheets, hardly waiting to have rid themselves of their clothes. Once naked, they made love quickly and earnestly, and then did so again, with just as much passion but at a more lingering pace.

Two hours later the electric fan in the high ceiling was still idling, pushing a barely perceptible breeze over their exhausted, intertwined bodies. Celia got up and, without bothering to put on her wrap, moved to the kitchen. Moments later she was back, a long frozen daiquiri in each hand. "This will revive you, decadent white man."

Rolland looked up gratefully, and admired her unashamed nakedness. It was now getting dark outside, but there was enough light through the shuttered windows to see the soft lines of her magnificent body and the curves of her delicious breasts. He watched in wonderment as she settled on the side of the bed, leaned over to balance the glasses on the small table, and then kissed him deeply. He had been caught unawares by the swiftness of her response, but the subtlety of her touch stirred him, physically drained though he was, and they began to make love again.

Finally, after they had both climaxed for what had seemed the umpteenth time, Rolland rolled onto his back, cradling Celia's head on his shoulder, gently stroking the softness of her hair. "*Cherie,* I have to get back tonight. I don't want to cause you problems."

"Don't worry. We're quite safe tonight. Fidel has gone away for a few days. He's not due back until tomorrow or the day after."

"Where's he gone?" Usually Rolland would never have asked such a risky question, but under the circumstances it seemed quite natural.

"He's taken up caving. It's his latest craze. Last year it was scuba diving, now it's exploring potholes. He's very enthusiastic."

"Does he go alone?"

"Oh, no. He is taken by a guide from Poland, called Marciej Kuczynski."

"A Pole? Is that safe? You know that in America they have Polish jokes like the English mock the Irish. Does he know what he is doing?"

"I suppose so. According to Fidel, he has mapped all the caverns under the Gobernadora Hill near Guanajay. That's the first time it has ever been properly surveyed."

Rolland made a mental note to remember that detail. "How did this Kuczynski get here?"

"He came back with Raúl from Moscow last month. He and Fidel have been inseparable ever since. I had no idea there were so many caves on the island."

"They say that all the caves in Russia are man-made," replied Rolland softly. He had once attended a NATO briefing in Paris on Soviet civil defense measures. According to the intelligence officer who had lectured them, the entire Soviet hierarchy had built itself an underground nuclear bolthole, the so-called Soviet National Command Authority, at Sharapovo. It had been rumored that when the Kremlin realized how far the bunker was from Moscow, a special seventeen-mile tunnel had been dug to the Vnukovo airfield so the elite could fly straight to their protected headquarters and avoid the peasants choking the roads on the surface. But this was not a tactful subject for Celia. Their relationship was based on sexual compatibility, not a shared political ideology, and now was not the moment to jeopardize anything. Luckily, Celia laughed at his whispered remark, but made no comment. Rolland knew it was time for him to get back to his hotel, and time he alerted the CIA to Castro's interest in the caves of Pinar del Rio province. It had sounded odd to him, but perhaps the CIA knew more about this mysterious Polish expert.

McCoy Air Force Base, Orlando, Florida; Wednesday, 29 August 1962

It was five hours before dawn, and Jim Schneider had just finished a breakfast of steak and eggs in an annex off the Physiological Unit of McCoy Field. He was thirty-two years old and had been undergoing this ritual for the past two years, ever since his "transfer" from the air force reserve. He had come from a reserve unit deactivated after the Korean War, and had volunteered for "interesting, single-engine, single-seat work." After two interviews he had undergone an intensive physical at the Lovelace Clinic in Albuquerque, New Mexico, and had then started training at the Watertown Strip on Groom Dry Lake in the Nevada Desert. What had followed was far from routine, and the curriculum had included such esoteric subjects as chemical warfare, escape and evasion, survival, and mission planning as well as the more familiar topics of tactical doctrine and reconnaissance procedures. His civilian posting to the First Weather Reconnaissance Squadron (Provisional) had been entirely cosmetic. In reality, he was on the CIA's payroll as a pilot for what had once been the world's most secret plane, the Utility Two.

The U-2 was no ordinary plane. It did not even look normal, more like a huge unwieldy glider with a wingspan more than double the length of the fuselage, a full 103 feet from tip to tip. Constructed of plywood and plastic on a metal frame, the fragile wings weighed less than a third of conventionally built spans its size. The other characteristic that distinguished it from other aircraft was its lack of a proper undercarriage. Instead of the usual tricycle arrangement with the gear under both wings, the U-2 operated on a bicycle principle, with two retractable wheels under the body and a short, detachable outrigger strut, like a pogo stick, at the wingtip, which was jettisoned just before takeoff. For landing, the plane balanced on the two wheels and then, when it came to a stop, tilted over onto the reinforced wingtips, which were slightly turned down to prevent damage.

The single-seat plane's strange configuration gave it an extraordinary weight advantage that allowed it to soar to incredible heights. Powered by the same J57 Pratt & Whitney jet engine found on the F-100 Super Sabre fighter, it could attain 80,000 feet, an altitude at which no other aircraft could be sustained, and well over the long-standing world record set by an RAF Canberra of nearly 64,000 feet. Elaborate arrangements had been made to allow the U-2 to cruise at this remarkable level for long periods. A special fuel mixture had been created by Shell to resist evaporation and burn in the oxygen-poor atmosphere that had just 3 percent of the density at sea level. The engine had been adapted to develop a mighty 17,000 pounds of thrust and could maintain a speed of 450 mph in the thin air despite a reduction in thrust to 500 pounds. As befitted such a remarkable plane, each one was handbuilt under conditions of great secrecy by Lockheed at their "skunk works" at Burbank, California, and then painted a sinister matt black so it would be difficult to spot against the darkness of the sky.

After breakfast, Schneider walked over to the Physiological Unit's prep room and began the long process of climbing into his flight suit. First, he undressed and reversed his long underwear so the seams were on the outside. Under the air pressure he would endure in flight, the slightest ridge in his underclothes could leave unbearable welts on his skin; experience had taught him that this was the best remedy. Then, with the help of an attendant, he put on one of his two made-to-measure rubber flight suits and held out his arm so the unit's doctor could take his blood pressure. Once he received a nod of reassurance that everything was in order, Schneider slipped on his gloves and snapped the circular metal fittings closed. He took great care in these preparations; his life would depend upon the integrity of the suit. He would be flying at 70,000 feet, an altitude at which his blood would boil if his suit failed. This was not some idle rumor. During his training, Schneider had been put into the pressure tank, and he had watched a glass of water beside him boil as the pressure had been reduced. The warning begins at about 25,000 feet, when the gases in the gastrointestinal tract start to expand. Oxygen, carbon dioxide, nitrogen, and hydrogen-sulphide occur naturally in the digestive system; any expansion of the digestive organs would push them up into the diaphragm and interfere with the pilot's breathing.

Every U-2 pilot's fear is hyperventilation. The mildest physical exertion can double the need for air, and it was not unknown for aircrews to lose consciousness. And because of the plane's intrinsic instability, even a brief blackout can spell disaster. At maximum ceiling, the U-2 had to be flown with great care, the pilot constantly checking the controls to keep it in the narrow range between stall and mach buffet. Two "barber pole" needles on the airspeed indicator gradually converge at altitude, and the pilot's objective is to keep the airspeed needle in the narrow gap between 404 and 412 knots. This needs a featherlight touch, for the alternative was known to the crews as coffin corner. At the mach limit, the airflow over the U-2's wings is supersonic and generates shock waves that buffet the airframe, and a quick temperature change or turbulence can produce a lethal buffet. Thus, a momentary loss of concentration can cause midair breakup or a flame out. A gentle glide down to 40,000 feet would allow the engines to reignite and recover the stall, but there was no antidote for disintegration. Nor was bailing out an option over 25,000 feet if the pilot wanted to use his chute and survive the experience: Weight considerations had prevented an ejector seat being fitted; instead, a pilot had to open the canopy and clamber out as best he could.

Schneider chilled slightly at the thought of turbulence aloft, and then stretched his arms so the attendant could put on his emergency survival vest. He wriggled his feet into his flight boots, laced them up, and then sealed them. The final stage was the addition of the visored helmet, which resembled a goldfish bowl. The attendant lifted it over his head, lowered it into the metal retaining slots, and snapped the security triggers shut. He was now hermetically sealed into the suit, his air supply provided on demand by a tiny regulator that allowed a slight positive pressure within the oral-nasal cavity. This was dependent upon the silicon rubber oxygen hoses linked to a small portable controller that was designed to maintain absolute suit pressure in the event of sudden decompression. A special check valve attached to the suit prevented any reverse flow, and he was able to communicate through an integral microphone and speaker circuit built into the helmet, which obviated the need for bulky headphones. For the next two hours, while he studied his flight plan, he would breathe pure oxygen to remove the nitrogen from his bloodstream and thus prevent the bends in the event of an emergency depressurization of the cockpit. The oxygen went into Schneider's lungs under pressure, requiring him to make a conscious effort to exhale, a reversal of how the body usually breathes. It was a very tiring process but none of the pilots complained. Schneider had done it so often that he could concentrate on the color-coded map on his lap without difficulty.

Schneider's prebreakfast briefing had detailed his flight plan. It called for a takeoff to the east and a steady climb to the southeast before turning toward the Caribbean. The objective was an overflight over the western end of Cuba just after dawn, approaching the island from Grand Cayman airspace. The British, of course, would not have raised any objections to the route, even if they had been consulted. U-2s had been operating in secret from Lakenheath in Norfolk, England, crewed by British pilots, for some years. Most of the flights had been lateral aerial reconnaissance missions, flying along Soviet territorial limits, using mirrors and an oblique long-range camera to photograph objects up to ninety-three miles away. Up until Gary Powers's fateful U-2 flight on 1 May 1960, the plane had been considered invulnerable to attack. The main Soviet antiaircraft weapon, the elderly SA-1 Guild missile, had proved utterly worthless, exploding harmlessly in the distance. Nor had the MiG-19 or MiG-21 fighters been any more successful. At the U-2's operating levels, the Soviet interceptors simply went ballistic and failed to respond to their controls, whereas the U-2 maneuvered easily and, uniquely, could turn and move out of the way of any threat. Neither of the Soviets' most advanced fighters could come within twenty thousand feet of the U-2, and their puny cannons had a range of less than a mile. Then the Soviets developed the SA-2 missile, which tipped the balance in their favor, but only marginally. Designated Guideline by NATO, this was a two-stage antiaircraft rocket with a 286-pound warhead that was detonated by a proximity fuse. With a ceiling of eighty thousand feet, the missile exploded as close as it could to its target, leaving its lethal fragments to envelop several hundred feet of airspace.

The CIA had discovered an intrinsic flaw in the Guideline's design: To attain its high altitude, it was powered by an extremely potent booster that generated a tremendous speed. However, its high speed rendered its aerodynamic control surfaces ineffective in the thin air, so ground-control radar was relatively useless, a weakness that gave the weapon only a 2 percent kill ratio. The CIA had also perfected an ingenious electronic countermeasure, code named GRANGER, which prevented hostile, radar-guided weapons from locking onto the U-2. Unfortunately, when Gary Powers had encountered *fourteen* SA-2s over Sverdlovsk, one had exploded sufficiently close to damage his right stabilizer, which then broke off, causing the plane to flip over, followed by an inverted spin and the destruction of the wings. Powers had managed to escape and parachute to safety, the victim of a lucky shot by the Soviet SAM battery.

That is not to say that there were no other hazards to flying the U-2. Quite apart from the temperamental nature of the aircraft, grueling physical demands are made on the pilot. The force of gravity is multiplied in flight, sometimes by a factor of six, which momentarily gave Schneider a weight of around 1,020 pounds. Then there's the oculogyrical illusion, a phenomenon caused by overstimulation of the ear's semicircular canals. The result is a confusion of the signals passing between the eyes and brain which mean that a target in plain sight might appear motionless, or even appear to move in the opposite direction. In addition, the pilot sometimes has to cope with a somatographic illusion, brought on by sudden acceleration or deceleration that leaves him with the impression that the aircraft has adopted a nose-high altitude. Only a check of the instruments can overcome the dangerously misleading sensation. Compared to the flight experience, which would leave Schneider several pounds lighter through perspiration and so exhausted that he would be unable to fly for at least two days, the menace of hostile aircraft was minimal.

What Schneider did not know as he strapped himself into the aircraft's cramped cockpit, on top of his parachute, was the lengthy wrangle that had taken place in Washington to authorize his mission. The DCI, John McCone, had put in a request to the Committee on Overhead Reconnaissance, chaired by the president's National Security adviser, McGeorge Bundy, for U-2 coverage of Cuba in response to Harvey's report on 15 August, two weeks earlier, but although COMOR had given its consent, the weather had been too overcast. After two days of frustration, McCone had asked the air force to fly a low-level photographic mission, but this had been refused by Kennedy's defense secretary, Robert McNamara, as too risky and potentially provocative. McCone had been obliged to wait until Wednesday, 22 August, to see the President, who had congratulated him on his forthcoming wedding. McCone, a widower, was to marry a Seattle heiress, and was due to leave Washington the following day for the wedding ceremony. When told of McCone's anxiety about Cuba, Kennedy authorized a U-2 sortie, but until today the weather had been unfavorable.

Once strapped into his seat, Schneider closed the canopy and sealed off the whining noise of the turbine generator. He plugged into the onboard communications system, checked his oxygen supply, and began his routine preflight checks, starting with the uncomfortable maneuver of reaching behind his head to test the circuit breakers. Once completed, he went through the familiar list: pilot heat off; INS modeswitch ... on; suit cool ... lever up; flaps ... up; throttle friction ... set; spoiler ... arm; ADF, TACAN, ILS ... on; IFF ... mode and code set as briefed; defog handle ... in; pitch trim ... set point five degrees nose up; continuous ignition ... on; flight instruments ... check; tee block ... one notch open.

Schneider signaled to one of the ground crew to ensure that the movable tail section was set correctly, and then indicated that the pogo sticks should be unlatched for taxiing off the stand. Then, with a slight nudge of the throttle, the aircraft rolled forward and Schneider transmitted a short signal to the tower.

"Tango Two Charlie, ready."

"Tango Two Charlie, you are clear to go," was the brief response. Radio traffic on U-2 flights were kept to a bare minimum, everyone being fully aware that intercept operators at Lourdes or on some Soviet trawler were scanning the frequencies for telltale exchanges.

Schneider moved the aircraft to the end of the runway and then reached out for the fist-sized throttle lever on his left. The plane moved gently forward, gaining speed with every second, and discarding the outriggers on the wingtips. Then, quite suddenly, it lifted into the air in a dramatically steep climb at a sixty-degree angle, having used less than a thousand feet of the tarmac. Two minutes later, he paassed fifteen thousand feet. With the airspeed indicator at 160 knots, Schneider, looking down with an exhilarating sense of levitation, could see the remainder of the runway still directly below him.

At 23,000 feet, Schneider checked the altimeter and eased back on the stick for a conservative climb. Then he went through the flight checks: aileron control ... elevator response ... rudder. All responded positively, so he sent two quick clicks over the radio to signal to the base that all was well. Complete radio silence would be maintained until the conclusion of the mission unless something went wrong. He then checked the power percentage, the exhaust gas temperature, and turned to the small green card attached to his leg. The graph on the reverse recorded the cabin pressure, and he marked in confirmation that he had checked the suit vent and the pressure and quality of the oxygen. Finally, he set the fuel counter on the sump tank cursor at sixty-five gallons and engaged the autopilot. This allowed him to relax and look out for the first waypoint. Over land this meant moving the view sight by the toggle on the lower-right instrument panel so he could watch the territory below through a reverse periscope; over the Atlantic, he would settle for the inertial navigation system, which gave him his exact position to an accuracy of within just a few feet and would guide him to Puerto Rico and his next waypoint.

At 71,100 feet, Schneider reached his predetermined cruising altitude; he glanced at the outside temperature gauge. It registered minus fifty degrees. His attention was drawn for a moment to a slight flicker on the intruder alarm indicator, but it was nothing. During the first hour of the flight, Schneider had little to do except listen and verify, climb and adjust. At this height the huge fan engine was eerily quiet, for there was nothing for it to reverberate against. There wasn't really very much to it, he thought to himself. It was getting the aircraft back on the ground that often caused the problem.

Just as dawn was breaking over the Leeward Islands on the horizon, Schneider reached waypoint three on his flight plan and disengaged the automatic pilot to begin a long gentle turn north. Too sharp a turn, at this altitude, can create the kind of turbulence that U-2 pilots fear, with one wing stalling in the thin atmosphere while the other experienced mach buffet. Gradually, Schneider saw the outline of the Isle of Pines emerge over his right wingtip, and then Cuba itself appeared on the horizon. Fifty miles from the target he switched on the view screen and cameras, and as the coast approached at a speed of 410 knots, he scanned the skies below for the contrails of hostile aircraft. MiG-15s, -17s, and -19s had been seen in Cuba, but Schneider's only concern was the MiG-21 Fishbed, which had not been seen operationally, although several dozen were supposed to have been spotted at Santa Clara. The Cuban MiG-17PFU and MiG-19PM interceptors each carried four AA-1 Alkali missiles, which follow a radar beam that locks onto a target. Fortunately, the missiles were fairly primitive and had to be fired from a plane flying on the same level if they were to follow the radar beam. Since none of the MiGs could hope to reach Schneider's altitude and stay level, there was little chance of an Alkali posing a threat to his U-2. In any case, the GRANGER system would neatly unlock the Alkali's radar signal by transmitting a false echo.

Underneath Schneider's U-2 were seven large perspex ports, all linked to a Hycon 73B camera specially developed for the CIA by Dr. Edwin Land, who had invented the Polaroid camera. The apertures were protected from temperature changes and the high-altitude humidity caused by the extreme fluctuations in temperature. Land's "B camera" combined a long focal length with a precision-engineered Hycon lens that, using the latest Kodak fine-grain film, allowed details of just two inches to be caught from seventy thousand feet. The state-of-the-art lens had been produced by a Harvard astronomer and optical expert, Dr. James Baker, and the camera itself boasted a mechanism to automatically compensate for aircraft movement and altitude changes. Its exposure was also controlled to cope with bright light that was reflected off clouds. Once Schneider had activated the camera his task was to fly along the route outlined in blue on his flight plan, crossing the west side of the island and then moving down its twelve-hundred-mile length. The camera automatically recorded the scenery below on a continuous nine-by-eighteen-inch filmstrip for nearly three hours. Over the airfields at Guanajay and Santa Clara, and San Julian, Argentina, Schneider checked his view screen for hostile fighter activity, but saw none.

Once back over the sea, heading toward Haiti, Schneider turned north over the Turks and Caicos Islands and set a course for McCoy. The last obstacle to be overcome was the landing. The U-2 cannot be throttled back like normal aircraft—this invariably causes a flameout—so the engine bleed valves and spoilers are opened and the landing gear and flaps lowered during the long descent. This has the effect of maintaining speed but reducing height. At lower altitudes, the U-2 is more difficult to control; instead of the delicate touch needed higher up, the pilot has to wrestle with the stick to get a response. As Schneider lined up for his final approach he initiated the most critical procedure of all, pumping fuel from one wing to the other to get an equal balance. The touchdown speed was always slightly different, and was calculated by the plane's gross landing weight. The smallest error could result in the U-2 bouncing back into the air in a stall and crashing. Two of his colleagues, both highly rated CIA pilots, had been killed while coming in to land. Fortunately, there were none of the crosswinds that can make the final moments of flight so dangerous, and when the plane was just a foot above the runway he stalled the engine and allowed the aircraft to bump onto its bicycle undercarriage. The plane quickly lost speed and, just before coming to a complete halt, tipped over onto its left wing.

While Schneider was unstrapping himself from his seat and the ground crew was unfastening the canopy, two technicians were already opening the camera compartment and extracting the film cassettes for transfer to an air force jet with a clearance for immediate takeoff to Andrews Air Force Base. From there it was whisked by car to the old Naval Gun Factory on the Anacostia River in downtown Washington, D.C. By the time Art Lundahl had returned from lunch to the newly created and still secret National Photographic Interpretation Center, the filmstrip was already being processed.

Washington, D.C.;
Wednesday, 29 August 1962

At the corner of M and First streets in Washington stands Federal Building 213, a dilapidated warehouse with no windows. From the street, it is obvious that the windows have been bricked up, and only the high chain-link fencing, topped by barbed wire, and the outsize air-conditioning plant make the property stand out in this run-down neighborhood. It certainly seemed an unlikely location for one of the U.S. government's most secret organizations, and Arthur Lundahl was its equally unlikely director.

Lundahl was a native of Chicago who had originally set out to become a geologist, but the war and the navy had interrupted his studies. He had worked in the Office of Naval Intelligence, and later was appointed chief engineer at the U.S. Navy's Photo Interpretation Center in Anacostia, Maryland. In 1958 the CIA recruited him to run its new Photographic Intelligence Center, which was to expand and become the NPIC in 1961.

Lundahl had been involved in the U-2 project from the beginning and had played a key role in the development of the high-resolution camera. Each aircraft carried 11,954 feet of special Mylar-based Kodak film that was exposed by the Hycon in a panoramic strip. When necessary, it was enhanced by the infrared Wild-Heerburg camera, with its twelve-inch lens, located in the U-2's nose. On this occasion, the product from Schneider's U-2, code named IDEALIST, gave an unprecedented resolution of sixty line pairs per millimeter. At the end of the war, Lundahl was still working on fifteen lines per millimeter. What made the IDEALIST material so remarkable was the way in which the huge airborne camera, which weighed 450 pounds, used all seven of the U-2's ports to make a near duplicate exposure. When examined together, with the aid of a stereoscopic viewer, the overlap gave the prints a three-dimensional quality right across the breadth of the island.

The first prints of the negatives from Schneider's films were examined by two photo-interpreters, one of several hundred based at the NPIC, who were used to looking at Cuba, albeit from a greater height. In recent months both the SAMOS and the second-generation Discoverer satellite reconnaissance systems had become operational, which had provided the imagery experts with short strips of film to examine. But because the satellites had been placed into polar orbit, they did not do full justice to the long, spindly island, which stretches east to west. On the other hand, the Discoverer series, code named CORONA, had provided the best quality, based on a film that had been recovered after it had been exposed and ejected in a capsule from the orbiting satellite. Unfortunately, technical problems had dogged the program from the outset, and only a handful of the satellites launched had completed their mission successfully.

Launched in conditions of great secrecy from Vandenberg Air Force Base, Point Arguello, on California's Pacific coast, 150 miles north of Los Angeles, the Discoverer series had depended on a Thor IRBM booster with a Lockheed Agena-B upper stage. After two years of testing, the recovery procedures had been perfected, and Lundahl's team had been concentrating on spotting ICBMs at suspected Soviet ranges. And instead of losing two to three hours while the capsule was located and regained, an Air Rescue Squadron had devised a method of scooping it up while still falling, suspended on its parachute, in the recovery zone.

Two Discoverer launches, code named ETA and THETA, had been made in July, and both capsules had been recovered after flights lasting four and a half days. Then, on 2 August, a Thor Agena-D had sent A KAPPA into an 82.2-degree orbit to photograph the northern test site at Plesetsk, where the first four SS-6 Sapwoods had been spotted the previous year. This had been followed on 5 August by a high-resolution satellite that circled the globe on a similar flight path for just one day. The imperative for the increased reconnaissance activity was the disclosure that the Soviets had resumed their nuclear tests and had just exploded a thirty-megaton weapon on the Arctic island of Novaya Zemlya. In addition, two spacecraft, Vostock 3 and 4, had been launched together, the first time two manned craft had orbited simultaneously. Accordingly, yet another Discoverer, designated A SIGMA, had been propelled into space that very morning, its film capsule scheduled to return to earth in four days time. Aware that the Pentagon was becoming increasingly anxious about the clear lead the Soviets had established in the space race, and not a little concerned about the Kremlin's unannounced resumption of nuclear testing, Lundahl knew that his analysts would soon be working late into the night to complete their reports on the latest satellite photos. The additional U-2 burden was therefore unwelcome, but not unexpected.

The black-and-white IDEALIST prints Art Lundahl had before him were of the highest caliber, and the conditions under which the photos had been taken were clearly excellent. As the exposures had been timed for shortly after dawn, tall objects were highlighted by a twenty-degree shadow. Equipped with his stereoscopic viewer, Lundahl peered at the prints and for the next three hours concentrated on the magnified images. He spent much of the time scrutinizing the Cienfuegos naval base, on the Caribbean coast, for signs of any new wharves that might accommodate Soviet submarines, but there were none to be seen. He then turned to the Guanajay area, as McGee had suggested in his typically mysterious way over the telephone the previous afternoon. Just how McGee had learned that an IDEALIST mission over Cuba was imminent was beyond him. Such information was not only classified but strictly compartmented. It was only after a brief conference with two women colleagues, who had been studying the negatives, which gave an even higher resolution, that Lundahl took action. First, he ordered up several enlargements from the laboratory, and then he conducted a search of the computerized files for some comparison prints. After a quick check in classified manuals that catalogued all the Eastern bloc artillery pieces, Lundahl placed a call on his secure line to Ray Cline, the CIA's director of intelligence at Langley.

"Ray, are you sitting down?" asked Lundahl.

"Go ahead, Art. Tell me the worst. Have you found a submarine facility?"

"No, but I've got an SA-2 Guideline battery at Artemisa, and at seven other locations in west Cuba. These are new SAM sites, photographed on an IDEALIST mission this morning."

"Art," said Cline grimly, "I've got to ask: Is there any chance they're anything else?"

"No way. We've been looking at Guidelines for a long time, ever since they went on display in Red Square four years ago, and they're very distinctive. Ninety-five feet long—really two rockets in one. Four big fins at the end of the booster, four smaller ones halfway up at the separation. There's no mistake. I'll send the enlargements right over."

"Thanks, Art. I'll alert the White House and the DCI."

It was only after he had replaced the receiver on its cradle that Cline remembered that the DCI was out of town. At that moment he would probably be tucked up in his honeymoon bed at Cap Ferrat in the south of France.

Cline was extremely concerned about the discovery of Guidelines in Cuba. While they posed no direct threat to the United States in that they had nowhere near the range needed to infringe American airspace, they would be bound to inhibit future IDEALIST missions. The COMOR group would be reluctant to risk another Powers incident at this critical time if there was a chance that another U-2 might be shot down. The revelation made him uneasy. He reached for the telephone and put in a call to the deputy director, Marshall Carter.

"General, we have SAM batteries set up on the western end of Cuba. We ought to convene a Task Force W first thing tomorrow morning. I propose to notify the DPP, send a cable to the DCI in France, and invite Art Lundahl to make the presentation."

"I concur," replied Carter, "but tell me this: SAMs are defensive weapons. What on earth are the Cubans defending?"

"It could be a submarine base, or it could be the hardware the Soviets have shipped over."

"But there's no way the Cubans could handle this. The Soviets must be running the show. That's the way they operate."

"Very likely," said Cline.

"In which case we must have the CI Staff in on this as well. McGee has been working on some elaborate Kremlin strategy and the Watch Committee is monitoring developments. This sounds unpleasantly like a major Soviet move, so you had better call Jack Maury as well."

Langley, Virginia;
Thursday, 30 August 1962

Once General Carter had taken his place, Lundahl walked across the room, pulled a drape off the tripod, and revealed a large black-and-white print.

"Gentlemen," he began, "I will not waste your time. During an overflight of Cuba yesterday morning by an Agency U-2 this photograph was taken." He paused briefly to retrieve a wooden pointer and gestured to the tripod. "There is no doubt that this is a Soviet-made SA-2 Guideline surface-to-air missile battery. It is identical to the hundreds we have photographed in the Soviet Union and kept on file. It is a modern, effective weapon that is particularly good at bringing down high-altitude aircraft. Its weakness is that its radar system is a little primitive and will not lock onto low-flying aircraft. Until we obtain further imagery we will be unable to give you exact figures, but yesterday we counted a total of eight separate SAM sites, all on the western end of the island."

"Since the SAM is a purely defensive system, with no offensive capability, is there a direct threat to U.S. national security?" asked Carter.

"In the folders before you are all of Guideline's vital statistics. I think you will all agree that it does not pose a direct threat, but its deployment in Cuba will undoubtedly have political implications."

"Surely the only relevant question," MeGee interjected, "given the nature of this missile, is: What is it guarding? The Soviets would not donate this kind of hardware gratis. It is there for a purpose."

"Would you care to elaborate?" asked Carter.

"By all means," replied McGee. "Over the past few months there has been a steady buildup in materiel reaching Cuba. The statistics, as collated by my office, are unambiguous." He glanced down to his notes to refresh his memory. "Up until July the Soviets were averaging about fifteen dry cargo ships a month calling in Cuba. In July that doubled, and so far this month we have counted thirty-seven freighters and six passenger ships. Furthermore, these arrivals have taken place in conditions of unprecedented security. The ships have maintained radio silence and they would appear to have deliberately avoided detection by sailing through the Straits of Gibraltar at night. Once in Cuba, the ships have been unloaded at night, by Soviet personnel. This is particularly significant. Whatever those ships were carrying . . . the Russians didn't trust the Cubans to unload it.

"Now let's turn to the hardware in Cuba. According to the DIA's estimates, about forty Komar-class gunboats have been delivered, as well as a quantity of MiG-15 Fagot, MiG-17 Fresco, and the top of the range MiG-21 fighters."

"Am I correct in saying that these aircraft are strictly fighters and have no ground-attack role?"

"Not entirely. Although the MiG-21 Fishbed is primarily designed to operate in a dogfight, armed with two Atoll heat-seeking missiles, it can be converted to carry a nuclear payload. This version requires a longer takeoff. It is worth noting that one of Bill Harvey's agents has reported that the José Martí runway is currently being extended to sixty-five hundred feet. Make of that what you will.

"The DIA still has no clear estimate of how many Soviet troops have been sent to Cuba, or what units are involved, but we have some circumstantial evidence, from a technical source, to suggest that among the Soviet brass recently arrived in Havana is Lieutenant-General Pavel B. Dankevich of the Strategic Rocket Forces. We do not believe he is on vacation.

"Finally," continued McGee, "we have some very sensitive political intelligence. Castro's brother Raúl, who is the minister of defense, led a delegation to Moscow early last month, for what reason we do not know. We also know that Fidel has recently developed an interest in speleology."

"Spel . . . what?" asked the deputy DCI.

"The study of caves."

"And your conclusion?"

"In the absence of any submarine installation, it is my view that whatever is happening in Cuba is the major event predicted by our defector STONE. Personally, I think the Soviet plan is to deploy atomic weapons there—if they haven't already done so."

"Can you support that?" asked Carter severely.

McGee came back firmly; he felt absolute assurance. "Only through logic. We have been working for weeks on the basis that the Soviets intended to build a submarine facility in Cuba. Well, we've checked, and there simply isn't one there. But look at the advantage to deploying a few strategic missiles. It's a wonder they haven't done so before. Even the DIA now admits that ARNIKA's assessment of Soviet rocket strength is correct. They probably have less than a dozen ICBMs with sufficient range to threaten North America, and even they are unreliable. So instead of pursuing the ICBM program, which must be a long-term undertaking, why not move your shorter-range MRBMs or IRBMs closer to the target and gain an immediate strategic advantage? And where better than Cuba? Castro is so insecure he would sell his grandmother for additional protection. He wants, and has got, a completely re-equipped army . . . literally hundreds of new tanks and artillery pieces. Why should the Soviets be so generous?"

"But surely history is against you," remarked the Soviet Bloc Division chief; it was the first he spoke. "The Soviets have never stationed ballistic weapons on the territory of their Warsaw Pact allies. And if they don't trust the Romanians, Bulgarians, Hungarians, Czechs, and Poles, why should they be so keen to accommodate Castro, who declared his conversion to Marxism only eighteen months ago? He's the new boy on the block; Khrushchev would be crazy to entrust nuclear weapons to him."

McGee pressed his case boldly. "But supposing there was an overriding incentive for Khrushchev? He knows the missile gap is a fallacy, and it will take him years to catch up and match our strategic arsenal. At present he is almost completely powerless. His ICBMs are liquid-fueled and take hours to prepare for launch.

That means they have no value as second-strike weapons, and he is vulnerable to nuclear blackmail. However, if he sited MRBMs or IRBMs, of which he has plenty, in Cuba, he suddenly achieves a very credible second-strike capability, to say nothing of his new-found capacity to initiate a surprise attack."

"So the SAMs are a prelude to the deployment of these shorter-range surface-to-surface nuclear missiles?" asked the DDCI.

"In my estimation there is no other logical explanation. It certainly fits all the facts as we know them. If it isn't missiles, then the MiG-21s will be equipped with atomic bombs. Hence the lengthening of the José Martí airfield. Either way, it's a nuclear delivery system, and that was probably the substance of Raúl Castro's trip to the Kremlin."

"Where do the caves come in?" asked Maury, skeptically.

"Cuba is honeycombed with caves, some of them really vast in scale. Where better to store mobile missile launchers? Far away from our cameras. Not even infrared could pinpoint them underground."

"I agree," said Carter. "You may be interested to know that before the DCI went overseas he handed the president a memorandum outlining exactly this scenario. He is convinced Khrushchev will deploy MRBMs in Cuba and is willing to take the political gamble so as to gain Berlin, or at least bargain away our warheads in Italy and Turkey. The next step is to convene the Intelligence Board and get more data. We need another U-2 flight straightaway."

"But what of the risk," objected an unknown voice. "If the Guidelines are operational it would only be a question of time before a plane is brought down."

"That's a matter for the politicians, but I will strongly advise the administration that we must obtain more data."

The meeting was closed, and Lundahl watched over McGee's shoulder as the younger man peered at the photograph through a magnifying glass. "You're really sure that's a SAM?" he asked.

"It sure is. But I'd like to know how you knew to tell me where to look for it."

"A trade secret, I'm afraid."

U.S.S. *Oxford*;
Saturday, 8 September 1962

As he languished in the Caribbean, Tom Waters knew that he was in the epicenter of momentous events. So, for that matter, did the whole crew. The regular radio broadcasts switched over the ship's speakers four days earlier had disclosed the news from the White House that the Soviets had placed SAM missiles in Cuba, and President Kennedy had publicly warned the Russians that he would not tolerate the deployment of any offensive weapons on the island. What the public had not known was that the Soviet ambassador, Anatoli Dobrynin, had held a private meeting with Robert Kennedy, the attorney general, at which time he conveyed a personal message from Khrushchev, assuring the American government that no ground-to-ground or offensive weapons would be introduced in Cuba.

Having eavesdropped on so many Russian conversations on the line between Havana and Moscow, Waters had gained the distinct impression that he was no longer in the somewhat esoteric business of monitoring the movements of Soviet cargo ships. Certainly the *Volgoles* had come and gone, and Waters had been concentrating in recent hours on the *Omsk*, which was in the process of docking at Mariel, but suddenly the stakes had been raised. The President had revealed that an aerial reconnaissance flight the previous Wednesday had shown surface-to-air missile sites in Cuba, and by taking the matter to the public he had reduced the diplomatic options available to him. He had taken the opportunity to reassure his American audience that no offensive weapons had been deployed in Cuba, but Waters was not alone in wondering about the President's strategy. Either he had been remarkably shrewd, acknowledging the Soviet buildup so it could not be used against him in the forthcoming congressional elections, which was Rusbridger's interpretation, or else he had been extraordinarily naive, accepting worthless Soviet promises at face value. Whatever the case, no mention had been made of the *Oxford*'s clandestine role, monitoring the Soviet voice channels, and recognizing the indiscreet military slang used by the antiaircraft battery crews as they attempted to link up with the air defense radio network. As Waters knew, the Soviet Union operated a fully-integrated air defense force, known as the Voiska Protivovozdushnoi Oborony, which coordinated all the various separate defense functions of running the radar stations, manning the SAM batteries, operating the fighter airfields, and vectoring the interceptors onto their targets. This unified structure, quite unknown in the relatively fragmented divisions of responsibilities in the NATO chain of command, had evidently been superimposed over the relatively primitive Cuban system, and the initial chaos had produced some interesting signals intelligence and had betrayed the location of the main Soviet communications center. According to the triangulation made by the *Oxford*'s technicians, it was just outside Camagüey. All this intelligence product had been beamed back to Fort Meade, bearing a new security designation PSALM. The prefix ensured the material would receive priority treatment at all stages, and the introduction of a special code name, within the existing code word compartmentation arrangement, spoke volumes to Waters, and everyone else on board, regarding the heightened sensitivity of their mission.

But what about the President's reference to aerial reconnaissance? Had he been wise to disclose the source of his information, or had he been advised to mention an overflight so as to conceal the true source, perhaps an agent on the ground, or even his own contribution? While Waters pondered these unknowns, those in Washington authorized to handle PSALM data were under increasing pressure from the White House to provide up-to-date intelligence. They had already been handicapped by inclement weather in the Caribbean, which had forced the cancellation of Thursday's U-2 flight over Cuba. For all its technical ingenuity, the plane's cameras were impotent when clouds obscured the target.

The Psalmists also had to wrestle with the consequences of an unrelated incident that had occurred the previous week on the other side of the world. On Thursday, 30 August, a U-2 based at Atsugi, Japan, on an air-sampling mission over the Sea of Okhotsk, had strayed accidentally over Sakhalin Island. The Soviets were particularly sensitive about Sakhalin because of the many military installations they had there: the radar complex at Yuzhno-Sakhal-insk; the air bases at Smirnykh and Dolinsk-Sokol, and the Red Banner naval yards at Korsakov and Aleksandrovsk. Three fighters had been scrambled to intercept the intruder, but the U-2 had little difficulty evading them. The real problem had arisen over the lack of authority for the overflight. Unlike the photo-reconnaissance sorties over Soviet territory, which had to be sanctioned individually by the Committee for Overhead Reconnaissance, these routine high-altitude air sampling flights, known by the acronym HASP, did not usually infringe Russian airspace. The program's purpose was to scoop up the air at predetermined heights and force it through special filters to detect telltale traces of radioactive residue from nuclear weapons tests.

Paradoxically, the greatest threat to the Cuban IDEALIST project was about to occur in the Far East. On the following morning, while Waters was still asleep in his bunk, a U-2 based at Taoyüan, a few miles southwest of the Taiwanese capital of Taipei, took off and headed for the Chinese nuclear test center at Lop Nor in the province of Sinkiang. The pilot, one of six Formosans who had trained with Jim Schneider at Laughlin Air Force Base two years earlier, was on a routine reconnaissance mission, following one of two familiar routes across the People's Republic to monitor Communist progress with their first atomic weapon or their development of medium-range missiles, which meant a detour to the rocket ranges at Chuang-Cheng-Tzu in Gansu. On this occasion, the pilot, Colonel Chen Wai-sheng, flying one of a pair of aircraft supplied by the CIA to Chiang Kai-shek's Nationalist government two years earlier, had activated the airborne cameras in the U-2's belly and turned, near the city of Yümen, for the final seventeen-hundred-mile leg of the flight home. However, just south of Nan-chang, the aircraft had been blown out of the sky by a Chinese version of the Soviet SA-2.

Peking had waited five days before delivering a strongly worded protest to the State Department, alleging that the CIA had masterminded Taiwan's U-2 flight program, which was met with a curt denial. However, even if the incident had been played down by the diplomats, a total ban had been imposed on any further CIA overflights. The State Department had decreed that further missions were to be flown by regular air force aircrew, and emphatically not CIA personnel, in case yet another one of the vulnerable planes were to be lost. The ban had meant that new USAF aircrews had to be transferred to Laughlin and McDill Air Force bases for conversion training on the U-2s, which effectively ruled out any IDEALIST material for ten days while the pilots were getting used to their new aircraft.

Although Waters knew nothing about the difficulties being experienced by the Psalmists in Washington, he was well aware of the U-2. So, indeed, were most of the British personnel with access to RAF Akrotiri in the Sovereign Base Area at the southeastern extremity of Cyprus. The strange, spindly planes had swooped down on the island after flights from Lakenheath in Norfolk and Giebelstadt in West Germany. The odd, unmarked aircraft had taxied straight into hangars at the far end of the airfield and the American ground crews had been segregated from the other airmen. These unusual precautions had heightened interest in the mysterious planes, but there had been no leakages. Word had spread that the high flyers were engaged in weather research for the U.S. space program, but the cover story had failed to impress the GCHQ staff from Mount Olympus, who had often driven down to use the base's Naval Army Air Force Institute facilities. They had heard the tales and seen the U-2s come into land. They had also noticed the airtime slots reserved for long enrypted transmissions to Port Lyautey, NSA's regional headquarters in Morocco, at the conclusion of each flight. For as well as flying aerial reconnaissance and HASP missions, the U-2 had proved itself to be a marvelous airborne SIGINT collection platform.

Instead of dwelling on such esoteric matters, Waters was preoccupied with rather more mundane things: the domestic trivia of the telephone link between Havana and Moscow, and the movement of the Soviet merchantmen. During the past few days he had studied the *Latvia*, the *Muritsky*, and the *Aneckcahapobch*, but his attention had been drawn particularly to the *Omsk*. Registered in Vladivostok, the freighter had recently been launched in Osa, Japan. It boasted eight cargo compartments, according to the *Oxford*'s classified manuals, and a reinforced bow. It was this unusual feature that made Waters wonder as the vessel silently maneuvered into the harbor at Mariel. Why would the Russians go to all the trouble and expense of building a ship to sail in icy seas only to use it in the Mediterranean, Atlantic, and Caribbean? Was this yet another example of legendary Socialist bloc inefficiency, or was there another reason? He had also noted bulky domed objects under tarpaulins on deck and the fact that the *Omsk* was riding high in the sea, her Plimsoll line clearly visible high above the waves, even from the distance that Waters had watched her. Something very odd was going on in Cuba, Rusbridger agreed. But exactly what, who could say?

Dolphin Square, London;
Wednesday, 12 September 1962

For the past two hours, Ronnie Symonds had been concentrating on every sound from the apartment below, on the eighth floor. Sitting hunched over the electronic equipment installed a month ago by MI5's technical support section, he listened as its sole occupant made himself breakfast and prepared to go to work. Symonds had been eavesdropping like this virtually every morning for the past month, but today was different.

He had a special reason for being tense. He could not forget that, back in April, when STONE's tip had alerted the Security Service to the existence of a Soviet spy in the Admiralty, he had disagreed with his colleagues' assessment of the case. Patrick Stewart, who had been in a wheelchair ever since he had lost the use of his legs in the war, had undertaken the original analysis of STONE's meal ticket, tracing the circulation of documents that Golitsyn had seen in Moscow and compiling a list of suspected spies. At the top of his list had been a thirty-seven-year-old civilian employee in the Admiralty, a clerk in the Naval Staff's secretariat named John Vassall. But when Symonds had conducted a preliminary investigation of Stewart's list, he had moved Vassall's name nearer to the end. Initial inquiries had shown Vassall to be a devout Roman Catholic, and he had spent two years in Moscow as an assistant to the naval attaché at the British embassy, without any adverse reports. For the past six years his work at the Admiralty had earned nothing but praise.

Now, six months after Symonds had started to ferret out the Soviet source, he knew the case was reaching its conclusion. And yet there was only the most minimal circumstantial evidence pointing to Vassall. Certainly, he had enjoyed access to the classified documents STONE recalled having seen; and true, MI5's surveillance on him had revealed him to be an active homosexual. But as Symonds reluctantly admitted to himself as he pressed the headphones to his ears, there was nothing else to link Vassall to the Russians.

MI5 had tried everything to trap Vassall. He had been kept under constant observation by MI5's skilled watchers, and the apartment directly above his had been borrowed from its owners so microphones could be placed in his ceilings to pick up his every move. Even his suspected KGB contact, a first secretary at the Soviet embassy named Nikolai P. Karpekov, had been placed under surveillance. The fact that he had unexpectedly returned to Moscow the previous Thursday had disturbed Symonds's entire team. According to STONE, Karpekov was a top First Chief Directorate case officer. Why did he suddenly leave London just as attention was focused on Vassall?

Symonds was only too well aware of how much depended upon finding the KGB mole. "D" Branch, MI5's counterespionage division, had gone to unprecedented lengths to identify the leak. An observation post had been established on an upper floor of New Zealand House in the Haymarket, which had an unrivaled and almost unrestricted view of all approaches to the Admiralty. Radioactive dust had even been sprinkled on the papers of those under suspicion in order to see whether they were being removed illicitly from the building. Geiger counters had been placed by each exit but none had registered the presence of the treated documents. When the sensitivity of the apparatus had been increased, it had been triggered by the luminous dials of wristwatches. The experiment had eventually been abandoned when it was realized that the Admiralty had too many doors to cover and the management had begun to murmur about possible health hazards.

Had the spy suspended operations? Had he been warned by Karpekov before he had fled? Symonds had no idea, so he had opted for the last resort, a clandestine search of Vassall's apartment. To the readers of spy fiction, which Symonds was not, such matters are commonplace, but in the real world, populated by intelligence bureaucrats anxious to protect their pensions, a break-in could not be treated lightly. Of course, Vassall's desk in his office had already been rifled, three times in fact, but Colonel Macafee had provided the necessary authority on each occasion. Private property was quite a different matter. Once the locksmith from "A" Branch had opened the door the searchers would be extremely vulnerable, either from nosy neighbors, the security conscious porters in the apartment block, or Vassall's housekeeper, Mrs. Murray. Even the police, close by in Rochester Row, were an anxiety as MI5 had no special immunity from arrest. So the request from Symonds's immediate superior, the D1 Arthur Martin, had been routed through to the branch director, Martin Furnival Jones. A solicitor who had practiced law before the war, Jones had a healthy respect for the criminal statutes, and had passed the recommendation on to the director-general himself for approval. Being such a cautious individual, no doubt Sir Roger Hollis had cleared it himself with the deputy under-secretary at the Home Office, Philip Allen.

A lot hung on this operation, thought Symonds. Quite apart from the reputation of the Security Service within Whitehall, there was also the question of STONE's integrity. He had persuaded the CIA that a mole had burrowed deep into the Admiralty and had betrayed hundreds of secrets. What would happen if MI5 failed to identify the spy. Would it be assumed that none had existed and STONE's information unreliable, or would people begin to wonder about MI5 itself?

While Symonds turned over the alternatives in his mind he heard the man below switch off his radio. Moments later the front door slammed shut, so he pulled off the headset and signaled to Leslie Jagger, who was finishing a cup of tea.

"He's off to work. Tell the watchers."

Down below, on Grosvenor Road, two innocuous-looking cars, each containing three men, had taken up position: one by the garage opposite the ornate main entrance to Dolphin Square, the other by the bus stop. The watchers knew, having kept Vassall under surveillance for the past three weeks, that he would catch the number 24 bus to Whitehall and alight outside Horse Guards

Parade for a short walk to his office in the Admiralty. As Vassall emerged from the elevator in the lobby of Hood House, another watcher, a middle-aged woman, joined the end of the bus line. Moments later, Vassall was standing behind her. One of the team would already be on the bus, scouring the rush-hour passengers for any known Soviets in case a "brush-past" contact was attempted.

Once the lead surveillance car reported that Vassall had caught his bus, Symonds nodded to Jagger and they made their way down the stairs to Vassall's apartment. The front door was fastened with a straightforward Yale-type lock, and Jagger had it open in just a few seconds. His prowess at picking locks was legendary, as was his own colorful career. During the war, when he had been a sergeant-major in the Rifle Brigade and a prisoner of the Italians, he had escaped from four different PoW camps—only to be recaught. Since then he had concentrated on refining his art and developed lock-picking techniques for each new type of mechanism as it came on the market. However, he usually advocated obtaining a duplicate key for most illicit, or "black," entries. "Even the most skilled operator will leave tiny scratch marks when tackling a lock, and these marks will be spotted by an experienced intelligence officer," he used to tell his pupils in the training course he gave in the basement of MI5's headquarters.

Once inside Vassall's apartment, Jagger's assistant was stationed by the door with a small radio receiver linking him to the lookouts posted close to the two entrances of the building. Then Symonds and Jagger drew the curtains on the windows overlooking the gardens of Dolphin Square and began a thorough search of the one-bedroom apartment. The first discovery was in the bottom drawer of a desk, an Exacta Varex IIA camera. Handling it gently, and making a note of its position in the drawer so it could be replaced without alerting its owner, Symonds scrutinized the aperture and focus settings, F3.5. The Makro Kilfitt Krar 40mm lens was adjusted for taking close-ups.

"It's empty," he remarked. "That means there's probably a spare film here ... somewhere."

Symonds's certainty that the apartment contained 35mm film was founded on two details in Vassall's personal file. One had been his training as a photographer in the RAF during his National Service. With that professional background, would he have chosen an East German model if he was choosing a camera himself? The other curiosity was the missing film. Vassall had bought a couple of 35mm cassettes two weeks ago, at Boots in Victoria Street. Where were they now? It was half an hour before a triumphant Jagger called Symonds out of the bathroom where he had been dismantling the lavatory cistern.

"Bingo," he said simply, pointing to the corner bookshelf in the sitting room. The lowest shelf had been removed, revealing a small cavity underneath. Inside were fourteen exposed Kodak 400 ASA Tri-X film cassettes and a Minox camera.

"Right, gentlemen," smiled Symonds. "Let's pack up and get out. Everything back to normal please." He then moved over to the telephone instrument, which had been fitted with a small device that converted it into a permanently live microphone. "You can tell the D1 we have reached our objective," he said clearly, without even lifting the receiver, addressing the intercept operator on the top floor of MI5's headquarters.

Later in the afternoon of the same day, as Vassall left the Admiralty after work by the northwest door in The Mall, he was approached by a burly man in a raincoat and bowler hat.

"William John Christopher Vassall?" he asked.

The younger man went pale and nodded.

"I am Superintendent George Smith of the Metropolitan Police," he produced a small warrant card, "and I must ask you to accompany me to Cannon Row police station."

"Wh-why," stammered Vassall. "What's wrong?"

"Please come with me," replied Smith firmly. Gripping Vassall by the elbow and taking his attaché case, Smith guided him toward an unmarked Humber parked at the curb. Both men climbed in the back and, without turning, a woman in the front said something unintelligible into the radio. Moments later the car sped off, turning at the Admiralty blockhouse toward Horse Guards Parade and the Foreign Office. While crossing Parliament Square, Smith continued with the formalities.

"I am now going to caution you. You're not obliged to say anything unless you wish to do so, but anything you say will be taken down and may be given in evidence."

"I don't understand why you're doing this," replied Vassall, his voice faint. "I've done nothing wrong."

"In which case," said Smith archly, "you won't object if we search your apartment, will you? Keys please."

Vassall groaned and fumbled in his trouser pocket for his key. He knew the end had come.

London/Washington, D.C.;
Monday, 17 September 1962

Under normal circumstances, Vassall's arrest and his swift confession would have been the cause of great jubilation in Langley and London. According to his first formal statement, made in the tiny police station in Cannon Row, directly under the shadow of New Scotland Yard's ornate towers, he had been persuaded to become a spy by his friend "Grigori," who had supposedly been in trouble with his bosses in the Soviet Ministry of Foreign Affairs. It was, as his Special Branch interrogators recognized, a classic tale of a homosexual honeytrap, and the man Vassall had known as Grigori had actually been General Rodin, using the name Nikolai Korovin while under diplomatic cover in London. The subtle exercise in blackmail had stretched back over seven years and had started with an indiscretion by Vassall in Moscow. Since then, he had been supplying Rodin and his successor, Nikolai Karpekov, with photographs of documents he had borrowed overnight from the Admiralty. Apparently they had suspended operations temporarily during the Portland case, but had resumed once the fuss had died down. Then, a week ago, Karpekov had failed to show up at a rendezvous, and the films had gradually accumulated in their hiding place. When developed, they comprised no less than seventeen complete secret documents.

It had been a pathetic story, but it had represented a significant breakthrough on the counterintelligence front. It had served to confirm STONE's bona fides, as he had originally alerted the CIA to a Soviet source in the British Admiralty, and it had helped establish the authenticity of FOXTROT, the KGB walk-in from Geneva who had also indicated the existence of a mole betraying the Royal Navy's secrets.

142

If the case had been as simple as that, there would have been reason enough for some mutual backslapping. Vassall had volunteered a detailed confession and he would plead guilty when he appeared for sentencing at the Old Bailey later the following month. But there were still some unanswered questions. For example, why had Karpekov fled just as the Security Service had been closing in on Vassall? And was Vassall the only Soviet source in the Admiralty? STONE had mentioned seeing some NATO documents relating to the proposed expansion of the Clyde's two nuclear submarine bases, at Faslane and Holy Loch, but the clerk had been emphatic that he had never had access to classified atomic data. So did that mean there was another spy at large? MI5 was nervous, but not nearly as much as the Psalmists in Washington.

While the "D" Branch experts analyzed Vassall's statement and passed further questions to Superintendent Smith and his Special Branch detectives, McGee was preparing briefing papers for the Psalmists' political counterparts, the ELITE channel. The president's Intelligence Board met at 8:30 every morning in one of the red-brick "temporary" buildings in Foggy Bottom that had accommodated OSS during the war, and McGee had been assigned the task, with Bill Harvey, of drawing up the CIA's situation report on Cuba. Trouble was, he had little concrete to offer. Art Lundahl had processed the take from the latest U-2 flight, which had been completed over western Cuba the previous day, and there had seemed no change in the number of SAMs deployed. A further mission over the other end of the island, due early that same morning, had been scrubbed because of cloud conditions. That left McGee with just two reliable sources of intelligence: NSA's data and his two human sources—Ruano and Rolland.

McGee was sufficiently experienced to know that the NSA's product could be relied upon. Whatever criticisms could be made of SIGINT, he knew the Soviets would fight hard to avoid letting the United States eavesdrop on their communications. Thus, unlike fickle human sources, SIGINT was unlikely to be used as a conduit for deception. Furthermore, the NSA enjoyed unrivaled facilities for listening in on the Cubans and Russians. The Guantanamo base itself was vast, surrounded by a fortified perimeter that stretched nearly eighteen miles. Castro hated the continued American occupation of the strategic site but he was powerless to do anything much about it. There was a valid lease and, so long as successive administrations remembered to pay the rent, a legal basis for the presence. The only gesture left to Castro was his refusal to use any of the rental cash that was accumulating in a bank account.

In addition to the huge antenna field at Guantanamo, McGee suspected the NSA possessed other, equally sensitive methods of eavesdropping on the Soviet signal traffic. His evidence was the NSA's daily analysis of Russian telephone and cable transmissions, which the DIA had used to construct a local order-of-battle, complete with the full names and ranks of some of the key military personnel on the island. In fact, much of the raw material had been gathered by the *Oxford*, but McGee had never been indoctrinated into the detail of the NSA's clandestine collection program. His main preoccupation was what to make of Rolland's information. When combined with what he had relayed from Ruano, the Frenchman's data had been compelling: the sighting of a rocket "the length of a telegraph pole" heading for Guanajay. This was unquestionably an SA-2 Guideline, probably one of those photographed by Jim Schneider a week or so later. Then there was the Soviet takeover of a Cuban cement plant, and the NSA's identification of a major new communications center at Guanajay. The clincher had been Castro's reported interest in caving and his visit to the cavern under Gobemadora Hill. Bill Harvey had retrieved a volume from the CIA's enormous library that had seemed relevant: *Subterranean Cuba* by Antonio Nunez Jimenez listed eight hundred caves on the island, and it was hard to escape the conclusion that at least some of them were undergoing construction work of a kind that required SAM protection. A close look at Gobemadora or the famous Santo Tomas gallery near San Cristobal would have satisfied the Psalmists, but the last successful U-2 flight, flown by a U.S. Air Force pilot the previous Saturday, had revealed nothing out of the ordinary in terms of earthworks. What had proved disquieting, however, was the oddly trapezoidal configuration of the Guideline batteries.

This curiosity had been spotted first by a DIA photo analyst who had compared the shape of the SAM deployments in western Cuba with others in the Soviet Union. It had been his chilling discovery that they had exactly matched those at just one other location, at Plesetsk, six hundred miles north of Moscow and the only confirmed Soviet ICBM launchpad. According to ARNIKA, the monster-sized rockets at Plesetsk represented the Kremlin's complete arsenal of long-range nuclear delivery vehicles and, being liquid-fueled, were useless as a second-strike, retaliatory weapon. Since they required several hours of preparation before launch, their defense was regarded as a top priority, and the area had been ringed by SA-2 emplacements, all with a characteristic trapezoidal configuration.

The analysts had pondered the DIA's strange discovery, weighing the various possible explanations. McCone's favored scenario, that Khrushchev did indeed plan to deploy shorter-range IRBMs and MRBMs in Cuba, certainly made strategic sense to the extent that it would give Moscow a credible nuclear capability for the first time. But while the DIA accepted McCone's logic, its analysts had found it hard to contemplate the implications—the Kremlin leadership entrusting sophisticated hardware to a fledgling regime when it had previously balked at stationing atomic weaponry on the territory of Warsaw Pact stalwarts.

There was no denying the existence of the SAMs in Cuba, and besides, the Soviets had confirmed their deployment, though as a purely defensive measure. So the question remained, what was their real purpose? The location of the eight sites at the western extreme of the island had caused some comment among the Psalmists, for there were virtually no military installations at that end worth protecting. Why concentrate the Guidelines around San Cristobal and Guanajay when the vulnerable airfields of San Julian and Santa Clara were many miles away, and the naval base at Banes was at an even greater distance? Opinion at the CIA hardened around McCone's conviction that Khrushchev was a gambler, willing to risk high stakes to establish the Soviet Union as an authentic superpower, a fully-paid-up member of the nuclear club. In the DCI's view, Khrushchev had been forced into his position by the realization that the Soviet Union's technical inferiority had, to date, only been concealed from the West by propaganda, bluff, and old-fashioned deceit. Once NATO accurately gauged the Kremlin's true long-range capability, the myth would evaporate. The Soviet Union would stand exposed, naked in its relative weakness in this vital area. Under these circumstances, with the Pentagon producing accurate assessments of Soviet missile numbers for the first time, Khrushchev would be forced to restore the balance, even if the method used was potentially catastrophic. At stake was the safety of the *Rodina*, the motherland. And there could be no greater risk to a totalitarian regime, argued the Psalmists, than a recognition of its impotence. To be weak is one thing, to be known as weak is quite another. In terms of Soviet paranoia, and the state's institutionalized xenophobia, such a development was tantamount to political suicide.

Had Khrushchev been alerted to the change in the U.S.'s appreciation of the Soviet threat? Had word leaked from the policy committees and budget negotiators during the run-up to the appropriations debates? Or had the KGB discovered Penkovsky? If so, any future communications from him should be considered tainted, recommended McGee. But ARNIKA's value lay in his record. He had already made his contribution by dismissing the Kremlin's official ICBM production figures of 250 per annum since 1959 as fantasy and giving his own estimate of just a few dozen SS-6 Sapwoods as the true operational strength. What had prompted Khrushchev's move? According to the British, the Soviet buildup in Cuba had predated the summer, yet apart from one report from Penkovsky suggesting he had been placed under surveillance, there had been no clue in his messages to indicate that he had come under KGB control. However, as a precaution, McGee had counseled discretion and the CIA case officers in Moscow who routinely serviced ARNIKA's dead drops had been advised to be on their toes.

The Psalmists had gone back over the signs of escalating Soviet involvement in Cuba and had reexamined the evidence of nuclear hardware. The Watch Committee, which had met earlier than usual so the DCI could attend the President's Intelligence Board later in the morning, had listened intently while Art Lundahl expanded on the science of "crateology."

"Having monitored the movement of arms to Indonesia, we can give a fair estimation of what is being supplied, even if the material is shrouded or boxed." He pointed to an aerial photograph displayed on an easel beside the long table. "These are crates on the *Poltava*, photographed two days ago. They exactly match the dimensions of these ..." he deftly removed the illustration and replaced it with another black-and-white print, which proved to be Ilyushin-28 bombers, designated Beagles by NATO.

Lundahl returned to his seat to allow Bill Harvey to continue. "The DIA now reckons that up to thirty of these light bombers have already been delivered."

"Range?" asked General Carter.

"If they are the same models as those supplied to Egypt, about six hundred miles, and easily adapted for a nuclear payload," replied Harvey. "However, the SAMs have not been sited near any of the airfields where the Beagles might reasonably be expected to be dispersed. That suggests they will not be nuclear capable. In any event, Beagles are close to obsolete. They pose minimal threat to the United States."

The unnamed DIA representative took his opportunity. "The Indonesian situation is not really comparable to Cuba," he asserted. "The Soviet deliveries are mainly naval." He consulted his notes. "A Sverdlov-type light cruiser, the *Ordzhinikidze*, is the latest to be sent to Djakarta, along with several Whiskey-class diesel electrics, half a dozen destroyers and escorts, and some Komar-type missile boats." He looked up from his file. "*Komar* means mosquito in Russian, but don't let that mislead you. It is really one of our P-6s, built on a wooden hull and armed with two Styx missiles. It's a potent weapon, and the Cubans have got plenty."

"What about the missile?" asked Carter.

"Styx is a surface-to-surface naval weapon we first came across two years ago," replied the analyst. "It's about nineteen feet long, with a wingspan of about nine feet. It has a maximum range of around twelve nautical miles and is armed with a hefty eleven-hundred-pound warhead."

"How does it work?"

"It's fired at about half its range using Square Tie radar ... then an on-board terminal homer switches on and guides it for the final approach into the target."

"The Komar is the world's first guided-missile boat," interrupted Harvey, "but none is based near the SAMs."

"So what are the Guidelines protecting?" demanded the DDCI.

Harvey shook his head. "Nothing nuclear ... yet. The SAMs are deployed about as far from Guantanamo as is possible while still being in Cuba, which might mean the Soviets are anxious about being overheard in their new project, whatever it is. That, of course, is sheer conjecture."

"But no attempt has been made to camouflage the SAM batteries," added Lundahl. "There's no concealment whatsoever, although there's plenty of opportunity with all that tropical foliage. It's odd."

"Anything else new?" asked Carter, glancing at his watch.

"Only negatives," answered Harvey. "No special perimeter fencing, no elaborate bunkers, no KGB troops."

One of the Soviet Bloc analysts looked up sharply from his note-taking, so the veteran case officer elaborated.

"All nuclear weapons in the Soviet Union are kept in dedicated storage facilities and guarded by elite KGB detachments—they are easy to spot by their distinctive green epaulettes—but none have been seen in Cuba yet."

"So there are no nuclear warheads in Cuba," concluded Carter.

"That's our best guess. But the KGB *is* there in force, and it may be that they are supervising the construction of underground accommodations in existing caves. Preparatory acts certainly, but no atomic devices on site yet."

"It's essential we have more assets on the ground," said the DDCI with an air of frustration. Addressing Harvey he asked, "Bill, can you get your man back into Cuba?"

Harvey looked awkwardly at McGee and, after a moment's hesitation, nodded almost imperceptibly. It meant another mission for Rolland; would he take it?

Friday, 21 September 1962

U.S.S. *Oxford*

The BBC World Service broadcast at 2300 Greenwich Mean Time had been transmitted from the relay station on the British island colony of Antigua, and the news bulletin had concentrated on a report that a British Admiralty clerk had appeared before the chief metropolitan magistrate at Bow Street and been remanded to Brixton on a charge under the Official Secrets Act. Waters had listened to the news on a shortwave frequency shortly before going on shift for another eavesdropping session, and he had found it unremarkable. As the announcer had mentioned, this was the third major case in eighteen months, and some commentators had wondered about the apparent espionage epidemic. They had reminded the public of the Portland case the previous year, and that of George Blake, which had followed in May. Waters, however, had other things on his mind. The skipper had positioned the *Oxford* directly over the Cuban transatlantic telephone cable, and the RIMMER induction antenna, laid alongside, had given the intercept operators another opportunity to tap into the Russian communications. Fort Meade had supplied a breakdown of numbers assigned to Soviet military and diplomatic premises, and the surveillance had concentrated on key personnel deemed to be of interest to the NSA.

One of the individuals targeted for special attention was the new Soviet ambassador, the KGB officer named Shitov, who, perhaps for understandable reasons, used the name Aleksandr I. Alekseev. He was regarded as a priority target and the sophisticated on-board computer lit up like a Christmas tree whenever an embassy circuit was connected to a Moscow operator. But despite the

149

advanced technology dedicated to the operation, it had been sheer coincidence that Waters was on duty.

Waters listened in while Shitov conducted a brief and guarded conversation with someone in Moscow who appeared to be his son-in-law. As a reflex, Waters leaned over the console and punched the record button so the exchange could be taped, but instead of moving on to another call, or perhaps shifting to another signal source, he stayed on the line. His interest was piqued by the purpose of the call, which had been placed by Shitov. He had also listened to the BBC World Service bulletin, and he had heard something that prompted him to inquire as to the status of a person he referred to cryptically as "the captain."

Seasoned intercept operators the world over, whether they work for police forces or intelligence agencies, all aver that even if someone resorts to subterfuge to conceal their meaning, it is the tone of their voice that betrays them, not the words they have chosen. Awkward vocabulary and strange emphasis on unexpected words speaks volumes to those who make a profession out of monitoring telephone conversations. What struck Waters about Shitov's remarks was the implication that the person described in the BBC bulletin as an Admiralty clerk was obviously someone quite different to "the captain." However, once the KGB officer had been assured that "the captain" had been unaffected by recent events, he requested a complete suspension of all operations. The response from the Moscow end held Waters transfixed.

"That is impossible. For one thing, that mad Croat is fucking Katerina. She can't be put on ice."

More expletives followed, but whichever way Waters tried to interpret them, he could gain only one meaning. Shitov had heard about the arrest of Vassall on the World Service and had been anxious about the safety of a KGB source known as "the captain." Clearly, Shitov had been provided with enough information on the spy case by the BBC to make him believe that this other party was also in danger. The only deduction was that Shitov's man was also in the Admiralty, and possibly in a clerical position, even though his code name suggested a naval rank. Either way, it certainly looked to Waters as though the conversation amounted to evidence that there was another spy at work in the Admiralty in London. And what about the reference to "Katerina"? Since Shitov had wanted to protect her, too, it rather looked as though she might be vulnerable if the counterespionage authorities in England were about to go into overdrive.

It was not until near the end of his shift that Waters made up his mind about what he had heard. He was due to transmit a routine signal to GCHQ anyway, and he considered including a report on the intercept and his opinion of its meaning. It would, of course, be relayed through NSA channels and convention required the text to be disclosed to them in full. But what would Cheltenham's reaction be to news of yet another Soviet spy ring operating in London if it was to be conveyed by the Americans? Waters could imagine that such an indiscretion would not win him many friends. The only alternative was to get off the *Oxford* somehow and report directly, but he knew there was virtually no chance of pulling the ship off station until it was scheduled to be relieved, and that would not take place for another three weeks, by which time the shelf life of his snippet of intelligence may have expired.

Acknowledging that it would take little short of a crisis of national proportions to persuade the *Oxford*'s skipper to request a port call, Waters reluctantly took the expedient of inserting a KINGFISHER into the text of his signal to GCHQ. Rather like the deliberate errors included in messages from denied areas to confirm the authenticity of its content and the continued liberty of its author, Waters swallowed hard and used the word most feared by GCHQ personnel ... the one that indicated his station had come under hostile control. Waters wondered what his colleagues would make of it, but having made the decision, he passed the apparently innocuous situation report to the Comms Room for microwave transmission to the relay station. If the KINGFISHER procedure was spotted by the NSA, Waters hoped that he would be able to bluff his way out of a confrontation by labeling the signal as his eccentric sense of humor, but most operators would know that few professionals joke about such matters. Every organization had its own KINGFISHER arrangements, often called by other code names, and Waters had to hope that GCHQ would realize he had got into

151

difficulties and needed to be extracted urgently. Certainly, he thought grimly, this was one eventuality that no one had foreseen.

Cheltenham's response had been as fast as it had been impressive. Early on Sunday morning, Rusbridger had called Waters up to Commander Reilly's stateroom, where a message awaited him.

"It seems you are to be leaving us this afternoon," announced Reilly, handing Waters a signal flimsy. "You're wanted elsewhere, and you'll be collected by the U.S. Navy for onward delivery, I know not where."

Waters read the short message. He was to report immediately to SNOWI on H.M.S. *Malabar*, in person. "Who on earth is SNOWI?" he asked. "I've never heard of the H.M.S. *Malabar*. Can't be very big."

"Senior Naval Officer, West Indies. That's Royal Navy jargon for you. Let's see if we can find H.M.S. *Malabar*." Reilly leaned over to the bookshelf beside his desk and leafed through *Jane's Fighting Ships*. "*Malabar* doesn't get a mention. Can't help you there. Anyway, prepare yourself for the whaleboat at fourteen hundred." Waters was dismissed.

At the appointed hour Waters and Rusbridger watched from the fantail while the whaler was swung out on davits and lowered into the calm sea. The klaxon sounded, and the Englishman scanned the horizon for a ship.

"So where's the U.S. Navy?" he asked as he gazed through the binoculars.

Rusbridger tapped his shoulder and pointed to a tiny point twenty degrees over the horizon. "You're going out on a P-5 Marlin. Good luck."

Waters turned his attention to the shape in the binoculars and focused on an amphibious aircraft approaching from the northeast. He suppressed a low oath as he watched the plane circle to the north and then lose altitude for a landing into the wind.

"Have a good flight," smiled Rusbridger, as he realized that Waters had not anticipated the arrival of a flying boat. He then gave a short salute while Waters clambered down the casing and positioned himself in the stern of the whaleboat. "We couldn't make a sailor of you so we thought you'd like to try your hand as an aviator," called Rusbridger, grinning broadly. Waters looked distinctly uncomfortable as two of the *Oxford*'s crew rowed him toward the Marlin. The twin-engined plane settled on the surface in a tremendous cloud of spray a few hundred yards away and quickly decelerated. As it did so the bow dipped into the surf and the big radial props roared and feathered. As the whaler maneuvered toward the tail of the aircraft a hatch opened midships and a figure beckoned. As the boat came closer to the amphibian, Waters was impressed by the sheer size of the ugly plane. He judged the span of the gull wings to be more than a hundred feet, with a cockpit mounted high above the fuselage. The dominant feature, apart from the length of the brute, was the fat bulbous nose and a long tapered fin stretching aft beyond the tailfin. Two stabilizing wing floats were fitted on single pylons beneath the wings and extended into the sea, which lapped over them gently.

In a few moments the whaler was alongside the amphibian and Waters was climbing out of the bright sunshine into the cavernous interior, his duffel bag gripped tightly in his fist.

"Welcome aboard," said a young airman as he closed the hatch and secured it. "Go on up to the flight deck and see the skipper."

Waters made his way up the plane's long interior, past three crewmen hunched over instrument consoles, and then climbed a short ladder up to the flight deck. The pilot turned in his seat and gave him a broad grin. "Mr. Waters?"

"Good afternoon," Waters replied uncertainly. "Are you taking me to H.M.S. *Malabar*?"

"We certainly are," he replied. "Go below and make yourself comfortable. This will be a long flight. Next stop Bermuda."

"Bermuda," gasped Waters. "Is H.M.S. *Malabar* docked there?"

"You could say that. *Malabar*'s a shore station," said the pilot, as he made some adjustments to the fuel displacement, ready for takeoff. "We'll let your little boat get clear and then we'll be on our way. You just get acquainted with the crew and let them know if there's anything you need. We can oblige with just about anything, except signals. Radio silence while we're airborne, I'm afraid."

Waters nodded his understanding and, as the engine noise

153

increased, returned down the ladder to the operations deck where he introduced himself to another youthful crewman. "I'm Tom Waters," he said lamely.

"Come and sit in the jump seat by the radar operators," he said, handing him an intercom. "Plug this in overhead." He motioned to an instrument panel above his head. Waters followed his instructions and belted himself in behind the three operators.

"I'm Rudi, and I'm the tactical coordinator. Thanks for the diversion. This sure makes a change from flying patrol. We'll be your taxi anytime."

"I hadn't realized we were going to Bermuda," said Waters.

"It's no problem. We're based at Jacksonville but we regularly exchange with another squadron based at the Naval Air Station, Bermuda. It's a great place. You'll like it. Sorry we can't get you there sooner, but we have another mission to fly first."

The huge plane's twin Wright engines roared as the pilot pushed the throttles forward and the Marlin gathered speed. The amphibian sped across the sea and then, after what seemed an age, slowly lifted off the surface and gained altitude. Once they were aloft, Rudi switched his intercom to another channel and turned his attention to one of the radar screens. As he did so, the other jump seat beside Waters was occupied by another crewman who nodded hello.

"I'm Pete, the navigator. Nice to meet you. We're lifting you to Bermuda, right?"

"I hope so. I was half expecting a ship, not a plane."

"Don't worry about this crate," laughed Pete. "This is the navy's best. It flies as well as it floats."

"I believe you."

"It really does. One of our squadron once had to ditch in the Atlantic on one engine. He taxied more than two hundred miles, all the way to Mayport, Florida. It took him twenty-four hours, but he made it."

"What else does it do?" asked Waters.

"We're the most dangerous thing that ever happened to submarines," said the navigator. "The captain flies the plane, but while we're on patrol it's Rudi here who's in command. Our task is to find submarines and kill them. We're the best there is."

"Is that what the nose radome is for, and the pole on the tail?"

"You've got it. Let me give you the tour. Up front we have a five-foot-six search radar, so sensitive we can spot a target as small as a snorkel operating just above the surface. The cylindrical boom aft, the stinger, is the magnetic anomaly detector, which can take a fix on any large ferrous object, even one that's underwater. We carry a cargo of sonobuoys that we drop at regular intervals and then listen for submarines."

"And when you've found one?"

"Well, it depends on the circumstances. In a shooting war we are equipped with a combination of torpedoes, depth charge mines, and five-inch rockets, but right now we only have four torpedoes and some depth charges. But that doesn't mean we can't have a little fun occasionally."

"Like ..."

"Most of our sonobuoys are passive. We call 'em JEZEBEL, and when we drop them into the ocean the antenna component stays on the surface transmitting data while an acoustic device extends below to a predetermined depth. By logging the exact position of each buoy in the computer we can triangulate the location of any submarine approaching the pattern. Our on-board electronic wizardry, code named JULIE, can tell us the range, depth, speed, and heading of our target without it ever being aware that it's being tracked. We can let them know we have found them simply by dropping an active sonobuoy. This sends a signal underwater and will be heard by the sub. In a hostile environment, it would probably be the last thing the crew ever heard. As you can imagine, they don't like active sonar."

"Is there nothing a submarine can do?"

"Sure, there are countermeasures. They can respond in two ways. If they have any antiaircraft weapons they can surface and engage us, but most of the Soviet boats have had their guns removed to make them quieter underwater. Their only chance is to evade us, usually by diving deep and sending out noisemakers."

"How do they work?" Waters was getting a cram course in antisubmarine warfare.

"They're like decoys. The sub fires them through the stern tubes and at a preset distance they switch on to make a really loud, authentic, submarinelike noise to fool our sensors. A torpedo homing by sonar will be distracted from the real target and opt for the noisemaker—or so the theory goes. Meanwhile, the sub is making speed in the opposite direction. However, the experts are working on a discriminator to help our sonar distinguish between the real thing and the decoy. In the meantime, we have to settle for the three integrated displays here. It's a pretty foolproof system."

Waters smiled and said, "So the flying boat is the antidote to the submarine."

"It's the best. The U.S. Navy operates about forty Marlin P-5s, and we can fly low and slow for about twenty hours. There are patrol squadrons based at Norfolk, Jacksonville, and Bermuda, and we can cover the whole of the eastern seaboard. We operate at night, and there's a carbon arc searchlight on the starboard wingtip, which you may have seen. That generates 130 million candlepower and really lights up the sky. If we find an intruder who wants to play games, we can get rough. It's just a matter of placing an active sonar real close to the target. He surfaces real quick, but the brass doesn't like it. It's too aggressive and the Russians get upset."

Waters grew thoughtful and remained silent for a while. Then he said, "A month ago I was in Gibraltar, learning about SOSUS. Can you link up with the passive arrays?"

"SOSUS is classified, and I don't know much about it," replied Pete coyly. "Let's put it this way. We receive intelligence before we take off, and we're given a specific area to patrol. We are sometimes instructed on what to look for and where, with the exact coordinates, but they don't tell us how they came by the information. Once airborne, we maintain radio silence because if a sub is at periscope depth it will have a radar detector raised, and maybe a direction-finding mast to listen for radio traffic. We simply collect the data, and when we return home our computer can dump the accumulated data into the mainframe on the base."

"How often do you come across Soviet submarines?"

"It ain't difficult. We have about fifteen missile subs to monitor, and three long-range Novembers."

"Which pose the biggest threat?"

"The most modern is the new *Juliett.* I've never seen it, but it has four Shaddocks ... an antiship missile."

"Nuclear powered?"

"No. It's diesel electric, and like all the Soviets, it has to surface to fire its missiles."

Waters was surprised and asked, "*All* the missile submarines are surface-launched?"

"Yeah. There's a nuclear-powered Hotel and about a dozen diesel electric Golfs we watch for, and they're all armed with three Sarks each. They're huge missiles—nearly fifty feet long, liquid-fueled three-stage rockets with a range of 350 miles. A couple of old Zulus have been converted to carry a pair of Sarks, but I've never seen one. It's just an old 1944 vintage U-boat."

"So the Sark is the chief threat to the United States when it comes to nuclear weapons? If you can keep them out of range, they're relatively harmless?"

"Oh, no. All these fuckers are dangerous. Of course, the Shad-dock needs mid-course guidance so the firing platform has to stick around for twenty minutes or so after it has loosed one off, by which time we will have found it, but that's not much consolation to the folks on the ground two hundred miles away. And we take all the conventional subs seriously. They can just point a nuclear-tipped torpedo at the coast and pull the trigger. If you're on the receiving end it doesn't make a lot of difference whether your atomic device has arrived by air or sea. They can send a torpedo right up an estuary, no problem."

"But all of these subs have to get in quite close to be effective?"

"Sure. We don't let them past VP-45. That's the patrol squadron on Bermuda ... the front line, you could say. It ain't friendly to mess with us inside of six hundred miles from the beach. Any farther than that, and we're likely to lose our sense of humor. Now you sit back and enjoy the movie. I've got to do a little navigating if we're gonna be home for supper."

Waters switched his intercom to the operations channel and watched while the three search operators before him monitored the waves below. As they did so, he wondered about how his

KINGFISHER message had been received. Although he was apprehensive about how he would fare with the Royal Navy, his mind kept turning to the conversation he had overheard on the transatlantic telephone line. Had the KGB another spy in the Admiralty? And, more significantly, it was very alarming that the Red Navy should take so many risks to position missile-carrying submarines off the American coast when a few short-range weapons in Cuba would achieve the same advantage.

Southampton, Bermuda

Shortly after seven that evening the Marlin flew over Bermuda's Great Sound and landed on the calm water just as the clouds in the west were turning a dull orange red. The amphibian taxied to the quay of the U.S. Naval Air Station. After he disembarked, Waters was met by a British officer wearing the tropical white uniform of a lieutenant in the Royal Navy.

"Good evening, sir," he said. "Welcome to Bermuda. We're expected at Government House in half an hour." He motioned toward a small Austin. "Jump in."

Waters turned briefly to thank the Marlin's crew for the ride, and then climbed into the car.

"I've my passport here," said Waters pointing to his duffel bag. "Will it be needed?"

"Oh, no," replied the driver. "This is a British island. Actually, it's Britain's oldest colony. The Americans may run this base but technically they're our guests." He steered the vehicle around one of the seaplane hangars and gave a brief wave to the sentry as they exited the gate and turned left onto Harbour Road. "Ever been here before?"

"First time," replied Waters. "Where's H.M.S. *Malabar?*"

"That's the dockyard, in Somerset, at the other end of the island. My instructions are to get you straight to Government House, which is just the other side of town. It's not far, but the locals take the speed limit here very seriously."

"What happens at Government House?"

"Seat of power, really. The governor lives and works there."

"Who's that?"

"Major-General Sir Julian Gascoigne. Ex-Grenadier, commanded the Household Brigade. Been here for nearly three years. Won a DSO in the war. Much liked and respected."

"Thanks for the pen-portrait. My instructions were to report to SNOWI at *Malabar.* That caused a bit of mirth among the Americans."

"Don't worry about SNOWI. Anyway, he's off the island at the moment so you're spared Admiralty House. The governor also happens to be commander in chief in these parts. What he says goes."

The young naval officer guided the car along the picturesque north shore of the island. Across the harbor Waters could make out the city of Hamilton, all white roofs with buildings painted pastel shades, perched close to the sea. They then turned onto Front Street and made their way into town.

"Sorry I can't give you the scenic tour, but this is the quickest route to Langdon Hill," he commented as he swung the car off Front Street and up Court Street. "They call this back of town. The island is run by a group of families known as the forty thieves ... but they don't live here."

They continued past the brightly colored shops and houses, the pavements filled with evening strollers, mostly black. A few moments later the car left the urban sprawl behind and entered a residential district, the road was alive with small cottages and villas nestling in perfectly kept gardens. Then the car turned sharply right and into a private drive and slowed as it approached a police box, where a uniformed constable, complete with the distinctive tall helmet of the British forces, gave a crisp salute. The car continued up the steep drive, and then came to a halt under the portico of a large, square, ugly Victorian house. It rather resembled the kind of property a Surrey stockbroker might have built for himself at the turn of the century, thought Waters, who was grateful that much of the building was obscured by the rich foliage. As he stepped from the car a smartly dressed civilian in Bermuda shorts shook his hand.

"I'm the governor's ADC," he said, introducing himself. "I understand you're to see His Excellency's guests from Washington. Please follow me."

Waters followed the aide-de-camp across the entrance lobby and

159

down a long corridor to the right. There was an air of slightly faded splendor about the interior, the walls filled with mildewed prints. They walked briskly to the end of the passage, and then Waters was ushered into a large, high-ceilinged study. Once inside, he was immediately approached by two men, one of them in a white dinner jacket. The first he recognized immediately, Brigadier John Tiltman, the Special United Kingdom Liaison Officer at Washington, and GCHQ's representative in America. Tiltman was a legendary cryptographer who had run GCHQ's all-important Army Section throughout the war. Indeed, his service in GCHQ had stretched back to the early 1930s; he was one of GCHQ's last remaining cryptographers.

"Ah, Waters," he said with concern. "I am so pleased you're all right. You gave us quite a fright. May I introduce Harry Stone, from the Security Service?" The older man in evening dress strode across the room, his athletic build betraying his past as a rugby international who had played for Ireland.

"Good evening, Waters. I'm the Security Liaison Officer at our embassy in Washington. If you've got a problem with the Americans, I ought to know about it right away. You can be completely candid here. Perhaps you could do with a drink?"

"Thank you," replied Waters. "A whiskey and soda please. The U.S. Navy has dry ships, which is one item my director, Sir Clive Loehnis, omitted to mention in my briefing."

Stone moved over to a drinks trolley and poured the scotch. "I can't believe lack of alcohol was the cause of your SOS."

"No, indeed," replied Waters. He then went on to explain the substance of the conversation he had overheard between Shitov in Havana and Moscow. When he had finished his story, Stone looked thoughtful.

"I don't suppose you were able to bring the relevant intercept tape with you?" he asked.

"It would have been quite impossible. I thought I was taking enough of a risk invoking KINGFISHER."

"You certainly did the right thing in not sending this through regular channels. This would have done us a power of no good with our allies. Yet another spy scandal in London, as if there haven't been enough already. Just what we don't need. I rather agree with your interpretation. It looks as though Shitov thought his agent, 'the captain,' might have been Vassall. We'll have to check with the BBC to see exactly what was said in the broadcast."

"And what about 'Katerina'?" asked Tiltman.

"Sounds as if she's an active agent who's having an affair with her Soviet controller. Very unprofessional, but nothing surprises me these days. It's too late to send a signal tonight, but I'll send one first thing in the morning. Are you sure this Soviet described him as a 'fucking Croat,' and not a 'fucking Serb' or a 'fucking Slovene'?"

"I'm quite sure," confirmed Waters.

"Well, that will narrow the field considerably, if this character's a legal. There aren't any Croats at the Soviet embassy in London, for sure."

"Can you really be certain?" asked Tiltman.

"Oh, yes. Our order-of-battle people are meticulous. Every face is known in the embassy and trade delegation, and we make quite an effort to reconstruct the local *rezidentura*. Every name is analyzed, every passport photograph compared to those who have been posted elsewhere in the world. As a matter of fact, we rather pride ourselves on spotting the professionals among the rest. A Croatian would stick out like a sore thumb, unless he's attached to another Eastern bloc embassy or is an illegal."

"What are the chances?" asked Waters.

"Probably a satellite service, for my money. Illegals are at a premium after we captured Gordon Lonsdale last year. His identity would only be known to a very few people, yet this person seems to be known to Shitov, his son-in-law, and God knows who else as well. Too much circulation for an illegal in my view. I bet this Croat's a surrogate in one of the bloc embassies. Probably a well-established womanizer."

"Is it likely the Russians would be so indiscreet over such a sensitive matter?" asked Waters.

"Absolutely characteristic. They drink, they boast, they plot. That's your average First Chief Directorate profile. These are the elite. They are very career conscious, and although they are not corrupt by their terms, they survive on a system of favors. It's institutionalized. Let's suppose Shitov had a hand in recruiting the man he calls 'the captain.' His future will depend to some extent upon the progress of the case. If it's a flop, his file will be marked down. If 'the captain' is a success, Shitov can expect promotion. His own prospects are linked to the performance of his contacts and the plum jobs will be reserved for those with friends in the right places, and those who have maneuvered themselves through the organizational rivalries. Office politics in Moscow make American big business seem like rank amateurs."

"And is Shitov's son-in-law KGB, too?"

"Most likely. I'll see if we have anything on record, but the chances are that this conversation was part family, part business ... it's common enough. Our people in London will get on to this first thing Monday morning. I'm dining with H.E. tonight, but you can reach me at the Mid-Ocean Club during the rest of the weekend if anything else occurs to you."

Stone made a swift departure, leaving Tiltman and Waters alone.

"Congratulations. You've scored some Brownie points with MI5. Always useful."

"Did he come down from Washington specially?"

"He didn't, but I did. Bermuda has the best golf courses in the world, so Harry finds as many excuses to visit as he can. At the moment I understand he's supposed to be supervising a restructuring of the local Special Branch. The fact that he enjoys a semi-professional handicap on the links is entirely coincidental. Actually, it's not his fault. He simply doesn't have enough to do. He's been in Washington almost as long as I have ... must be eight years at least."

"And what am I to do? I really couldn't go back to that rust-bucket in the Caribbean. I have had quite enough sea."

"The director thought you might want a few days leave, depending upon how you had fared with the Americans, and I want to talk to you about what you've been up to."

"I haven't fallen out with them, don't get me wrong, Brigadier. But Cuba is the key to all the strange Soviet movements in the Atlantic over the summer. More than a hundred Russian ships have docked in Cuba over the past few months, and you would have to listen to the intercept tapes to believe the amount of military activity occurring on that island. I'm sure all the escalating commercial traffic has something to do with the submarines. Unfortunately, when I was on the *Oxford*, I was too isolated to get the big picture."

"Then perhaps Bermuda is the best place for you," replied Tiltman.

"How so? Bermuda looks tiny."

"It is, but it also happens to be one of the most strategically important locations in the Western Hemisphere. The Americans run antisubmarine operations from the Air Station Annex, where you landed, and from Kindley Field up at St. David's, which is a U.S. Air Force lend-lease base as well as a civil airport. The Operational Intelligence Centre there coordinates all the regional SIGINT. In addition, the Canadians manage the eastern seaboard's high-frequency direction-finding program at Daniel's Head in Somerset."

"Not forgetting Tudor Hill," interrupted Waters.

"You are well informed," agreed Tiltman. "Yes, all of NATO's latest static antisubmarine research terminates there. It's a listening post for this side of the Atlantic. If the Russians are up to anything in this ocean, this is where it will be monitored. I have arranged a reservation for you at the Hamilton Princess until Monday, but I'm sure it can be extended at this time of year. I'll talk to Cheltenham tomorrow to clear this with Sir Clive, but he'll be relieved to know that your KINGFISHER was not entirely serious. You enjoy yourself over the weekend; you've earned it. On Monday I'll take you up to Kindley Field to see what the latest is on the Soviets."

Texas; Thursday, 27 September 1962

John W. Fain looked out his office window in the Federal Building in Fort Worth and felt a little uneasy. Before him was a sheaf of papers from an unusual file, that of an American defector who had returned to the United States. Before Fain and his FBI partner, Tom Carter, even met the subject of their investigation, back in June, he had been intrigued by him. Here was a young man, not yet twenty-three years old, whose background had been quite conventional until his honorable discharge from the U.S. Marine Corps and his defection to Moscow. Fain had been assigned the dossier, known as a "301," as soon as news had filtered from the CIA in the Soviet capital that the man had turned up at the U.S. embassy and renounced his citizenship. Checks with the Domestic Intelligence Division had confirmed that the individual had served as a radar operator at a sensitive air force base overseas, at Atsugi, Japan, and had enjoyed access to classified material, including data about the U-2 spy plane. In April 1960, six months after the defection, Fain had interviewed the older brother, Robert, and the mother. They insisted they had not been in contact with him, apart from an initial exchange of letters from and to the Hotel Metropole, Moscow. Since then, their letters had been returned as "unknown at this address" by the Soviet postal authorities.

Fain had followed the case intermittently since then, and now, two and a half years later, he was worried. He and Carter had called the redefector into the FBI's field office for a routine debriefing in June, following his unexpected return to the United States with a Russian wife, and their conversation had lasted just over an hour. He had been a shallow young man, quite arrogant, and certainly unwilling to cooperate with the FBI. He had denied having made any intelligence connections during his stay in the Soviet Union, and had insisted that he had simply been a metalworker at a television factory in Minsk. Now he was living in a modest apartment on West 7th Street and working at a manufacturer of louvered windows. The meeting had ended on a note of hostility, with the ex-marine declining to undergo a polygraph test to verify his statement that he had not compromised any confidential information he had received while working in Japan. The matter would probably have rested there, and the 301 file consigned to the Records Division, if the man's Soviet-born wife, Marina, had not mailed a letter to the Soviet embassy in Washington within a few days of her husband's visit to the FBI field office. The letter, of course, had been intercepted and photographed, and had contained very little apart from her name, her new address in Fort Worth, and the number of her Soviet residency permit. What had caught the attention of the FBI, however, had been the fact that the envelope had been addressed to Vitali A. Gerasimov, a second secretary in the consular section and a suspected KGB officer. If Marina and her American husband were entirely innocent of espionage, why had she been in touch with a professional intelligence officer who had been known to try and recruit agents in the United States?

Gerasimov had not acknowledged the letter, but shortly afterward Marina had received a letter full of gossip from Ella Soboleva, who appeared to have been a girlfriend in Leningrad. The FBI had passed a photocopy to the CIA, which examined it and remarked that according to its computer, the return address on the envelope was that of Igor Pavel Sobolev, a senior officer of the KGB's First Chief Directorate who had until recently been working at the *rezidentura* in Vienna. Unfortunately, the computer had been unable to advise whether Ella was his wife or daughter, and what her relationship might have been with Marina.

Since June, Fain had met the redefector on only one occasion. Surveillance had shown that he had remained in his low-paid, unskilled job assembling doors and windows at Leslie Wedding in Fort Worth, but he had moved from his apartment to a slightly larger, furnished duplex in a shabby clapboard bungalow on Mercedes Street. At the end of August, Fain and Carter waited outside the Mercedes Street home, and upon his return from work, the two FBI agents had challenged the claim that the ex-marine had not given military secrets to the KGB. They did not mention the apparently innocent letter mailed to Gerasimov by Marina, or her correspondence with Ella Soboleva. This second interview lasted only a short time and had been conducted in Fain's car. The meeting had ended with the young man agreeing to report any contact initiated by the Soviets, but two days later the FBI in Washington reported an overtly innocuous request from Marina to the embassy for Russian newspapers and magazines. Since then, the FBI had maintained a loose rein on the 301, but now Fain was worried. His suspect had suddenly quit his job and had told his family that he had moved to Dallas. His wife and daughter were still living on Mercedes Street, and the FBI had discovered through a telephone tap that she had been provided with a post office box number in Dallas as a method of contacting him. Then, on Tuesday, she had been heard to say that her husband had taken temporary accommodation at the Carleton Boardinghouse in Dallas. Fain had immediately arranged for a discreet check to be made, but it had drawn a blank. The landlord of the dingy lodgings had no record of anyone answering the description of the young man.

Where had he gone? Why had he suddenly disappeared? Who had financed the move? Fain was anxious and he was now compiling his monthly report to the FBI's counterintelligence chief in Washington. Was Gerasimov the controller of an espionage network in the United States? What was the significance of the harmless letters to a girlfriend in Leningrad and to the Soviet embassy? Fain had none of the answers, but he could not have known that while he agonized over how to write up the mysterious vanishing act perpetrated by one Oswald, Lee Harvey, born 18 October 1939, FBI identifying number 327-925D, another important counterintelligence case was being concluded across the Atlantic.

The Boltons, London SW10;
Thursday, 27 September 1962

The interview had not been particularly painful, or very difficult. The Security Service interrogator, Tony Henley, had adopted the surname "Healey" to conceal his identity, and the middle-aged woman sitting opposite him had been both candid and contrite. It was teatime, and their empty cups and saucers were placed on the table between them. She was a senior civil servant in the Central Office of Information, and she had left her office early in order to meet her interrogator. Of course, she had wondered at first about the reason for his request. He had asked for an appointment to see her, at home, as soon as possible, and had explained that the matter was too urgent to be left to the weekend. He had also confirmed that her immediate superior had already been approached and had given his permission for her absence. As a rule, spies rarely realize they are under hostile observation, particularly if those undertaking the surveillance are skilled at their job. The MI5 watchers who had followed Barbara Fell home from her office in London's West End to her parents' home in Chelsea had included two of the teams that had trailed John Vassall so successfully just a few weeks earlier.

Their task had not been easy. Initially, once the message had been received from Harry Stone in Bermuda that there was a source known as Katerina being run by the KGB, the investigation had centered on the Soviet order-of-battle in London. Who was the "fucking Croat"? Certainly none of the KGB regulars fit the bill, so the Soviet Satellites section of the counterespionage branch had analyzed the Yugoslav embassy in Lexham Gardens and identified several Croatian names among the diplomatic personnel, including

Smiljan Pecjak, the press attaché who had been in London for some years. Surveillance on him quickly demonstrated that he was conducting an illicit affair with an attractive but older woman in her early fifties. It had not taken long to track her to her father's large mansion in an exclusive square, and identify her as a high flyer with the rank of assistant overseas controller. Aged fifty-four and unmarried, she had been in the civil service for twenty-three years, and her work had been rewarded with a coveted OBE. Her father, Sir Godfrey Fell, had spent most of his distinguished career in India and had retired to the Isle of Skye. Henley wondered what Sir Godfrey would have said if he had known his only daughter had taken as her lover a married man some fourteen years her junior.

The interrogation got off to a good start. Healey had denied being any relation of the Labour party politician Denis Healey, who had once been a Communist, and had taken the opportunity to bring the conversation around to the topic of contact with Eastern bloc Communists. This had allowed Barbara Fell to admit her long-standing affair with Pecjak, which, she said, had begun sometime in the spring of 1959. When Healey had raised the issue of classified documents, the atmosphere had changed, and after some skillful but gentle prompting, she had confessed to supplying her lover for the past seventeen months with copies of confidential Foreign Office briefing papers on Eastern Europe. Having obtained that admission, the MI5 officer had turned to other, more trivial matters, so as to put her at her ease. He had learned in his previous posting, while serving as MI5's Security Liaison Officer in Hong Kong, that it was important to let a suspect down gently, and to avoid ending a voluntary interrogation abruptly when someone had incriminated himself. Invariably in such cases, depression or panic set in, neither of which would be helpful when the police came to take a formal statement under caution. In ideal circumstances, the suspect would be made to think that the authorities were unlikely to take the offense very seriously. Underplaying its severity encouraged cooperation, or so he had been told by his recently retired predecessor.

As Henley walked through the early evening crowds toward the West Kensington underground station, he pondered the outcome of the case. If Miss Fell repeated her damaging remarks to a Special Branch detective, she would almost certainly be charged under the Official Secrets Act and convicted. Curiously, she had not asked him why he had called or how the Security Service had been so sure there was a leak. But even if she had asked, Henley would have been unable to tell her. He knew nothing of the background to the eavesdropping exercise off the coast of Cuba that had initiated the investigation. Henley was satisfied about the way the interrogation had concluded, and he was convinced Barbara Fell had been manipulated by Pecjak, but he was also aware of a growing uncertainty within the ranks of the counterespionage branch. He had interpreted the long faces on the fifth floor as a sign that the Yugoslav dimension to the case had been unwelcome, and perhaps had caused a reevaluation of Tito's supposed split from Khrushchev. In Henley's untutored view, the case had all the classic hallmarks of a false flag recruitment, with the naive Miss Fell succumbing to Pecjak's charms in the belief that he was himself an anti-Communist who needed her help and support, whereas in reality he had cynically exploited her for a purpose diametrically opposed to his stated motive.

Henley was too new in "D" Branch to participate in the high-level deliberations that had culminated in his briefing by the deputy director-general two days earlier. The entrapment of Vassall had been heralded as a triumph of elimination, and to some extent a vindication of STONE's bona fides. But what about the mysterious "captain" referred to by Shitov? Clearly the veteran KGB officer had been expressing concern about another mole in the Admiralty, one sufficiently prized for him to have been motivated to risking a breach of security by using a back channel to Moscow Center for reassurance. The logical explanation was that there was another, more valuable, source still at liberty. This realization had been kept to a small group of senior officers, on the express instructions of the director-general himself, Sir Roger Hollis. His motives could only be guessed at, but his subordinates suspected that MI5 would be unable to survive another spy scandal. Instead of initiating yet another investigation, Hollis had asked a single trusted officer to explore the possibility that Vassall had not acted alone in giving the Admiralty's secrets to the Russians. His instructions had been emphatic. The operation should not become more widely known, and under no circumstances should the Americans ever learn of it, in case their confidence was undermined. Instead, a message of thanks was passed to Sir Clive Loehnis, thanking GCHQ for its invaluable help in pinpointing Barbara Fell as an unwitting pawn of the KGB.

Bermuda; Monday, 1 October 1962

News of the commendation from Cheltenham reached Tom Waters as he sat in his bathrobe having breakfast on the balcony of the Hamilton Princess, overlooking the Great Sound. It was a glorious day with a fresh breeze blowing from the east, pushing the choppy sea into the harbor and making the rush-hour ferry skippers earn their pay as they maneuevred their crafts into the dock adjacent to the hotel. Waters had been on the island for just over a week and had fully recovered from the discomfort he had suffered aboard the *Oxford*. The message had been relayed by Brigadier Tiltman from Washington.

"This is not a secure line, so I will be brief," he opened. "That shit's lady friend has been arrested, and you have reason to celebrate. Get the picture?"

"I do," replied Waters. "Was he a Croat?"

"As a matter of fact he was. He's been PNG'd ... and I don't mean he is taking a trip to Papua New Guinea."

"Message received. Sounds as if he's destined for the salt mines. What are my instructions?"

"I guess you can stay put for the time being. Do something useful ... pay a visit to Cable and Wireless or Special Branch, use your talents. You've got a week's paid leave. Congratulations." Tiltman rang off.

Waters finished his breakfast and turned toward the bed, where a figure stirred under the sheets. He had met her the previous morning by the pool, and he had accepted her invitation to Sunday brunch, one of many American cultural exports endured by the Anglophile locals because it was good for business. The encounter could not have been more casual: she was a continuity girl on a BBC film crew extending her visit by an extra two days, and he was hungry for female company after the unrelenting masculinity of the U.S.S. *Oxford*. She was tall, good-looking with slightly angular features, and when she changed for an afternoon swim her bikini revealed her stunning figure. Waters could hardly take his eyes off her, and she had accepted his invitation to dinner at the exclusive Mid-Ocean Club, reservation and signing rights having been negotiated with an affable Harry Stone as a parting present upon his return to Washington.

During his years at GCHQ, Waters had enjoyed plenty of opportunities to get to know women. His own fiancée, an English nurse, had been killed in a car accident just outside Haifa in 1948 only a few months before the end of the Mandate, and since then his work had prevented him from developing a permanent relationship. Of course, there were plenty of single women among his colleagues, but he had endeavored to avoid mixing business with pleasure. He had only been partly successful, and he had been seeing a girl from the Diplomatic Wireless Service in Nicosia regularly but not seriously. They had taken a week off together to see Athens last year, and the relationship had lingered on, partly out of boredom. But Holly, from the deepest recesses of the BBC's Lime Grove studios, seemed like a live wire. She was full of energy, intensely ambitious, and keen to move from making travel programs. She had started at Television Centre as a typist and had talked her way into the studios as a lowly production assistant, but she was determined to go on a directing course. "It's the buzz," she had explained with a mischievous giggle. "I want to get into current affairs, if you know what I mean. Trouble is, so does everyone else. That's why my project is so important, and why I need your help."

At least she had been reasonably straightforward in stating her interest, conceded Waters to himself. He had told her that he had just come off a boat, and despite his natural discretion she had learned of his service connection, and in particular his somewhat tenuous link with H.M.S. *Malabar*, to which he was technically attached. Even though he hardly needed a cover story, he was instinctively reluctant to mention GCHQ, not least because outsiders rarely understood the organization's true function. Apparently Holly had been trying to extract some information from the Royal Navy about a retired seaman, but the staff at dockyard had been less than forthcoming. "All I need is his address. It's nothing secret," she had pleaded. "He's not listed in the telephone book and he's not replied to my letter to his post office box. But he's bound to be known to H.M.S. *Malabar*. He was a petty officer, a diver in Bermuda during the war, and now he lives here. They are just so uncooperative. I'm sure you could have a word with them. The diver's name is Jack Fishburn."

Waters had not been particularly sly about her seduction. She had been a willing partner, and he had agreed to help her, on condition she explain why she needed to trace the ex-diver. He had no illusions about the ease with which he had invited her back to his room the previous evening, and her motive in accepting. She had told her story during dinner.

"Jack Fishburn was one of several divers employed here during the war to check Allied ships for sabotage. He also worked on an armed tugboat that was used as an inshore escort for visiting convoys, guiding them through the reefs. But what I want to know about is a story concerning the *Queen Mary*. We did a program about her last year, and the captain told us that during the war she had been used as a troopship, taking American troops across the Atlantic."

"Nothing unusual about that," Waters had observed.

"Of course not, but according to the captain, in 1942 the *Queen Mary* was attacked by a French submarine, the *Surcouf*."

"French? Are you sure?"

"So the story goes. Anyway, the captain said that the incident had occurred off Bermuda, and the submarine had been chased away by a local escort. I did some digging here last week when I arrived with the film crew, and found that the incident was quite well known."

"What happened to the French sub?"

"Well, that's the key to it all. Apparently this was no simple matter of mistaken identity. The French submarine was a renegade, a Free French vessel that had been taken over by pro-Vichy mutineers. It deliberately attacked the *Queen Mary*. However, we probably won't ever know the full story because it disappeared soon afterward."

"That's extraordinary," agreed Waters. "It would make a marvelous documentary."

"It would, but there were no survivors, as far as we know. That's why I need Jack Fishburn in front of a camera to stand it all up. Practically everything about this submarine was extraordinary. Do you know, it's still in the *Guinness Book of Records* as the world's largest submarine?"

"A bit hard to lose then. How did it disappear?"

"It left Bermuda in February 1942 heading for Tahiti via the Panama Canal, but once over the horizon here, the *Surcouf* was never seen again."

"Wasn't it arrested or interned after the *Queen Mary* incident?"

"Evidently not. The whole story is weird, and very political. When the *Surcouf* first came to England after the outbreak of war the crew fired on the navy in Plymouth and killed several British seamen. The crew was changed after that incident, but the affair was hushed up so as not to upset de Gaulle. I think it was ordered to the Pacific to keep it out of the way. It even had a couple of British officers on board when it disappeared, and legend has it that they were very keen to disembark in Bermuda. However, the Admiralty ordered them back on board as liaison officers. It seems there was a fear that the French replacement crew were as unreliable as the first lot, and having been prevented from taking an active role in the liberation of the French islands of St. Pierre and Miquelon off the coast of Canada, some people thought the *Surcouf* intended to defect to the Vichy islands of Martinique and Guadeloupe in the Caribbean."

"Presumably all of this is documented?"

"Not really. I did some research in England, but that only demonstrated that the *Surcouf* was a fairly notorious submarine, even before the war."

"How so?"

"It was gigantic white elephant. It was armed with a couple of eight-inch guns that would have been more appropriate on a battle-ship, and it was so big that it even had a plane on board, inside a watertight hangar. However, nobody really trusted the *Surcouf* to return to the surface after it had submerged so it never operated fully as a submarine."

"Are there no official records of the *Surcouf*?"

"Well, there's a memorial at its original base, in Brest, which lists the names of the *Surcouf*'s 118 officers and seamen, but it doesn't mention the two British liaison officers. The Public Records Office in Chancery Lane has a few details from the con-temporary report of the boarding incident in July 1940 when the shooting occurred. There are also plenty of photographs on file, but no one knows what happened once the *Surcouf* left Bermuda for the last time. I'm hoping that Jack Fishburn will fill in a few of the details, if you can help me find him."

Waters thought over the proposition. It was certainly an intrigu-ing one. "What makes you think he knows more about the *Queen Mary* business?"

"Well, one of the rumors I've come across is that the *Surcouf* might have been sunk by our side, perhaps by a destroyer based here during the war. I've been told that the crew of one ship was dispersed after one incident in the Caribbean, and sworn to secrecy. Either the British or the Americans got fed up with the risk of a potential renegade. Anyway, since Fishburn was on one of the escorts here throughout 1941, he might be able to shed a little light on that aspect of the mystery."

"You think he might have known about it, or simply heard the gossip?" He wondered what harm there could be in tracing an ex-naval diver.

"Anything's possible. The important thing is to find him and see if he's willing to give an interview on film," said Holly with enthusiasm.

"And if he does agree?" Always cautious, Waters wanted to know what the outcome would be if Fishburn cooperated.

"Then I have a terrific story, and I can bring my own film crew back to Bermuda," she replied brightly.

Waters's decision to collaborate with Holly was borne partly out of a genuine interest in a remarkable footnote to history, but mainly because he enjoyed being with her. His mood, the climate, and the environment of the Hamilton Princess had conspired to throw them both together, and dinner in the luxurious surroundings of the Mid-Ocean Club up at Tucker's Town had, with a little help from some exotic cocktails and a bottle of chilled Pouilly Fume, made spending the rest of the night together the most natural thing in the world. It had been a wonderful evening, and in the taxi back to town his squeeze of her arm had been reciprocated warmly.

Now, after ten hours of relaxed lovemaking interspersed with light sleep, Waters watched as Holly regained consciousness and blinked at the sunlight flooding in from the balcony. He moved back into the room and perched on the bed beside her.

"I hope the telephone didn't wake you." She smiled and shook her head, adjusting to her surroundings as though she needed to be reminded where she was.

"The breakfast is delicious," Waters continued. "I didn't know what to order for you but I'll ring down for some more if you like. There's plenty of orange juice here though." He reached for the telephone, but his hand was intercepted by hers.

"Let's not make that call just yet," she said with a sleepy grin, drawing him toward her.

Monday, 1 October 1962

Hotel Nacional, Havana

Henri Rolland had woken up alone, and he was restless. He had not seen Celia, and he had been unable to get into the Hotel Havana Libre because it had been fully booked. So had his second choice, the Riviera, and so he had been obliged to settle for the Nacional. The ambassador had described it as "like Leningrad station ... ornate, drafty, and full of Russians," and from what he had seen in the last couple of days, the description was an accurate one.

The Frenchman had been briefed by McGee and Harvey before his departure, and on this occasion they had been quite candid about what they needed. This was not a matter of servicing an agent's dead-letter drop, although that, they had conceded, would be helpful. His principal task was to find evidence of KGB personnel and Soviet rocketry. Just a few days ago, Rolland mused, he had known practically nothing about missiles. Now, it seemed, he knew everything there was to know on the subject. But most importantly, he had been taught what to look for, and to recognize one kind of rocket from another. Since the information seemed like the very latest American intelligence on the subject of Soviet rocketry, Rolland had been eager to be taught. Much of the data had already been shipped back to *la piscine* in the embassy bag, and there could be little doubt of its authenticity or, indeed, its value. Indeed, Jack Maury, the CIA chief of Soviet Bloc Division, had been brought in to conduct the briefing.

According to Harvey, who had taken a private room in the Mayflower Hotel so Maury could give Rolland a general understanding of the subject, the missile gap was entirely bogus. The CIA officers had been reluctant to indocrinate the Frenchman so fully, but it was clear that this was the only way they were going to persuade him to return to Cuba so quickly. "The Soviets were wrestling with stone-age technology and a very limited inventory of weapons," said Harvey.

Maury continued the briefing. "We know of two kinds of missiles in Cuba at present. The first, the SA-2 Guideline, is the standard Soviet antiaircraft missile. It's big, and there's no mistaking its long, slim profile. Then there's the coastal defense Styx, which is essentially a subsonic, antiship missile of limited range. These are much smaller, about nineteen feet long, and have been fitted to the Komar-class patrol vessels delivered to Cuba. They can be seen operating from Banes and Mariel. In addition, there is a shore-based battery of them on the Isle of Pines and our SIGINT indicates there may also be a couple of other sites on the north coast, close to Mariel."

Harvey produced a photograph of a missile mounted on a six-wheeled truck taken during a Red Square parade. "It's a short, stubby brute not unlike the German V-1 doodlebug. The tailplane is quite similar, but imagine it with an integral engine instead of one mounted at the rear on a pylon. We're not too concerned about the Styx; it has only a limited range and poses no threat. Nor is it nuclear-capable. Also, its homing radar is primitive by our standards and easy to jam. Now we get to the big boys. We might expect to find two types of nuclear missiles in Cuba. One is a submarine missile, perhaps stored near a naval base to replenish Soviet submarines. I should emphasize we have no evidence that such a sophisticated facility for Soviet subs has been built, so recognition of this bird would constitute exactly that. The Shaddock is thirty-three feet long and just over three feet in diameter, and there are four deployed on a brand-new submarine designated *Juliett*, primarily in an antiship role. This is a significant threat because it has a range of about 250 miles and could be used against a coastal target. However, it has two serious disadvantages. Unlike our Polaris system, the *Juliett* has to come up to launch, and it must remain surfaced for the duration of the flight."

"Which amounts to suicide," observed Rolland.

"Exactly," agreed Maury. "We would hope to prevent it from coming too close to a target on land, and we would expect to neutralize its relay ship or aircraft rather swiftly. The *Juliett* is brand new. It was built at the Krasno Somovo inland yard in Gorky and it's diesel powered. We've monitored its progress carefully, and it's slow and noisy enough for us to keep it under fairly constant observation. Apart from the Shaddock, there is only one other kind of nuclear submarine–launched ballistic missile, the Sark. This a naval variant of the SS-4 Sandal, which I will be coming to in a moment. It's forty-eight feet long with a medium range of about a thousand miles, although some think this may be much lower, perhaps just a bit more than two hundred miles. Either way, it's a big, mean weapon."

"How many are there?" asked the Frenchman.

"We know of thirteen Golfs, and a single nuclear Hotel, that carry three Sarks each. They are quite easy to distinguish because the rocket is so large it has to be accommodated in an extension aft of the sail," replied Maury.

"And the Sandal?"

The chief of the Soviet Bloc hesitated. It went against the grain to discuss these topics with a foreign national. He liked the Frenchman's style of cross-examination even less. "The ground-launched version is rather bigger, being seventy-three feet long. It looks like a German V-2 rocket, which is really what it is, and is entirely mobile. The rocket is carried to a launch site on a huge transporter, and an erector then moves it into position. There are plenty of ancillary vehicles used to prepare the rocket, so we can expect to see fuel trucks, cherry pickers, oxidizer and propellant vehicles, support artillerymen, and all the rest of the paraphernalia. It's liquid-fueled and takes a long time to get ready for flight. A reload, for example, can't be achieved in under seven hours. Finally, we have the really big monster, the SS-5 intermediate range ballistic missile, known as the Serb. We estimate this to have a range of about two thousand miles although NATO analysts in Britain think it may be half that. In any case, it's big and requires a permanent concrete launchpad with flame deflectors. We would also expect to see the vehicle revetments, control bunkers, storage accommodation, and the like. That means big acreage with a perimeter fence guarded by KGB troops."

"But wouldn't you see that from the air?" asked Rolland.

Now Maury thought they were straying a little from Rolland's mission. He didn't blame him for trying to extract the maximum, but American reconnaissance capabilities were a little beyond his need to know. He hardly betrayed his unease as he answered. "Hopefully, if the camouflage is not too good, but part of the urgency of your mission is our relative blindness. Our last three reconnaissance flights had to be aborted because of poor visibility and the weather forecast for the Caribbean is plenty of cloud cover over the next couple of weeks. It wouldn't take long to build an IRBM facility, perhaps just ten days or so, which means we could be caught unawares."

"So any missile over thirty feet long is serious bad news," concluded Rolland, sensing he had pushed Maury to the limit.

Maury nodded. "Apart from the long thin SAM-2, any long bulky cylindrical object is a problem. A measurement will give us an idea of what it is."

"And you are not concerned about the aircraft?" queried Rolland, ever the professional.

"We know the Soviets have delivered MiG-21 Fishbeds and Ilyushin-28 Beagles. If you see any operational, let us know, but neither presents a threat. The Fishbed is really an interceptor, designed for dogfighting and equipped with cannon and heat-seeking Atoll missiles, so it has a very limited strategic role. As for the Beagle, it's nuclear-capable, but we regard it as obsolete. Good luck, and let's hope there's nothing to find down there."

Since his arrival in Cuba, Rolland had had plenty of time to consider what he had been told. Obviously the Americans suspected that nuclear missiles had been delivered to Cuba, but no mention had been made of the ten large shrouded objects, sixty feet long, seen on the deck of the *Kasimov*. Instead, the CIA had instructed the SDECE veteran to concentrate on the San Cristobal area, where there had been heavy SAM activity. The trouble was, Rolland had been confined to Havana; his attempts to travel farther afield had been met with frustration. There were no cars available

the Brits have already made an arrest inside their Admiralty. And according to STONE's scenario, the KGB was engaged in a highly secret operation that would have extraordinary significance for the balance of power in the world."

"But as I recall, STONE's proposition centered on disinformation. Whatever the KGB was planning, it was to be a bluff of some kind."

Miler leaped to the defense of the CI Staff's best source. "It may be that there is an element of disinformation involved, but I would not care to leave it to our political masters to work that out for themselves. It's the Agency's task to advise them of possible threats and give an objective evaluation of their probability. At that stage we can debate what is a credible danger and what's a sham."

"But the President already knows about the Soviet buildup in Cuba," Maury replied evenly. "He's been on national television telling everyone."

"Excuse me, but he didn't," retorted Miler. "He only spoke about an increase in defensive weaponry in Cuba. Nothing was said regarding the deployment of MRBMs and IRBMs within ninety miles of an undefended coast."

"But you have no evidence," insisted the operations chief. "You can't go to the White House and say that a KGB defector has given us a vague warning that might, or might not, have anything to do with recent events in Cuba. You'd be laughed out of court."

"For God's sake," McGee replied forcefully. "By the time we do have that evidence it'll be too late. Once those missiles have been deployed, the blackmail will have started."

"Then I suggest," said Dick Helms quietly from the side of the room where he had been listening to the heated exchange, "that you and Bill Harvey go and find them before they're operational."

TWA Flight 132 to Los Angeles; Monday, 15 October 1962

John A. McCone settled back into the first-class seat and squeezed Tylene's hand. They had only been married six weeks, and yet it seemed as though they had shared enough troubles together to last a lifetime. His first wife had died just after the President had appointed him DCI, and he had shared his grief with Tylene, whose husband had also recently died. Throughout their honeymoon at Cap Ferrat, the CIA's station chief in Paris, Al Ulmer, had been relaying messages about the latest developments in Cuba. He had a special interest in the island. When the President had asked him what he had wanted for a wedding present, McCone had not hesitated.

"A U-2 mission over Cuba, Mr. President," he had said.

Kennedy had smiled and granted him his wish. That had been at the end of August. Then, yesterday, news had come through that his stepson, Paul J. Pigott, had been killed in a car accident. Now they were flying to Los Angeles to accompany his body to the family home in Seattle for burial.

Less than a year ago, McCone had been chairman of the Atomic Energy Commission, and before that a highly successful business-man. His concerns had revolved around stock options, government contracts, takeovers, and the engineering industry. Now he was burdened with matters that had a global significance, and he was worried. Although he could say nothing to his wife, who was understandably distraught at the news of her son's death, he was preoccupied by the report of another flight that had been flown over the Caribbean the previous morning from McCoy Air Force Base, Orlando, Florida. In charge of the mission had been Major

Richard S. Heyser, one of the air force pilots indoctrinated into the secrets of the CIA's clandestine aerial reconnaissance program. This had been the first time Cuba had been overflown since 29 September, when cloud cover had obscured the Isle of Pines and had forced the mission to be aborted.

On this occasion, McCone had decided to take advantage of the favorable weather forecast and authorize two simultaneous overflights. Major Rudolf Anderson, also of the Strategic Air Command's 4080th Strategic Reconnaissance Wing, had been assigned the eastern end of the island, centering on Banes, while Heyser had swung over the Isle of Pines from the south and then taken a route across San Cristobal. Their U-2Es flew slightly higher into the stratosphere than the CIA's planes, and they had been modified to carry the very latest electronic countermeasures, which were designed to protect them from radar-guided SA-2 Guidelines. The sophisticated gadgetry did nothing to prevent the small, delta-winged Fishbeds from intercepting them, but both pilots were confident that no MiG could engage them successfully at maximum ceiling with only a pair of air-to-air missiles.

Once over the Cuban coast, the cameras on board both aircraft had started to function, taking hundreds of oblique photographs and using the vertical ports for the high-resolution stereoscopic imaging shots. Upon their return to Patrick Air Force Base near Cape Canaveral, Florida, the film was transferred straight to Art Lundahl's team in Washington, which had been on standby for the negatives. By the end of the day, 928 prints had been scrutinized and the first MRBM launchers found. In a clearing not far from San Cristobal, the photo interpreters identified seven missile transporters where, two weeks earlier, there had merely been clumps of trees. Now there were SS-4 Sandals, and the signs, unmistakable even from a height of thirteen miles, of intensive construction work.

Over the weekend, before the news of Heyser's flight had come in, McCone had studied a carefully constructed appraisal of the Cuban threat prepared by Leo McGee. It had traced the gradual escalation of Eastern bloc merchantmen plying the Atlantic, and pointed out that during the month of September sixty-six Russian cargo vessels had docked in Cuba. This had been a marked rise over the previous month's total of thirty-seven, and a dramatic increase on the average of fifteen a month during the first six months of the year. Then there were all the other circumstantial factors, the agent reports from Ruano and Rolland, the new Soviet signal nets detected by the NSA, and the influx of KGB personnel. There was also an interesting and perhaps unconnected curiosity from the CIA station in Moscow, which regularly eavesdropped on the radio-telephone traffic of the Kremlin's fleet of limousines. Apparently, Khrushchev was leaving his vacation retreat at Gagra, on Lake Ritsa, earlier than expected, and would be returning to the capital the following day.

In one respect, the news from the photointerpreters had not suprised McCone. He had been very conscious of the possible advantage to the Kremlin of deploying short-range nuclear weapons in the Caribbean and had advocated this as a possible scenario back in August so contingency plans could be prepared. At the time, of course, the Defense Intelligence Agency had been highly critical of the idea. Now the crucial issue was to amass all the evidence as quickly as possible, and that meant more overflights. The DCI had already drafted a request for immediate low-level reconnaissance sorties by air force McDonnell Voodoos and marine Crusaders. How many other sites were being built?

As McCone tried to comfort his wife on the flight, a new employee at the Jaggars-Chiles-Stovall Company of Dallas, Texas, punched in for work. He had been interviewed for a job in the photographic department the previous Tuesday and had been hired after a short interview. Although the company concentrated on photosetting advertisements, it enjoyed a lucrative contract from the Army Map Service to typeset its maps. At a rate of $1.35 an hour, six days a week, the Russian-speaking ex-marine translated place names in Cyrillic script for transposition onto classified U.S. government maps. He was a smartly dressed young man who, when pressed by colleagues for details of his background, mentioned having lived in the Soviet Union for a while after service with the marines in the Far East. Curiously, if anyone had tried to find Lee H. Oswald at the Dallas address he had given when he had been hired, they would not have found him. Instead of disclosing where he was living, he had given the address and telephone number of an acquaintance he had recently met, and hardly knew. But on this particular morning, after five days on the job, he had been switched to a new rush order that had just come in. There was nothing very unusual in the change, except that the place names for pasting onto the maps were Cuban, not Russian.

Bermuda; Wednesday, 17 October 1962

Thanks to Holly, Tom Waters had overstayed in Bermuda. He had been given a week's paid leave and had thoroughly enjoyed it. He had used Harry Stone's name at H.M.S. *Malabar* and obtained Jack Fishburn's address, which had helped cement his relationship with the BBC girl. As an economy measure, she had given up her room at the Hamilton Princess and moved into his. He had also been present at lunch at the Waterlot Inn near Southampton when Holly had used her feminine charms to pursue the story of the *Surcouf* with the retired Royal Navy diver. After two stiff gins, he had warmed to his subject.

"The *Surcouf* came to Bermuda twice, and on both occasions there was trouble. Word had spread about the behavior of the first crew, which had turned out to be pro-Nazi and had been interned. I think they ended up on the Isle of Man for most of the war. Then there was an incident of some kind in Canada, shortly before the St. Pierre operation. It seems the Allied authorities were not entirely confident about which side the new crew was on. Then there were the stories about the *Queen Mary*."

"But weren't you a witness to the attack on the *Queen Mary*?"

"I never saw the *Surcouf* attack the liner. It had all happened at dusk, so by the time we arrived on the scene it was dark. The *Queen* radioed that she had been shelled by a huge enemy submarine, and two days later we were ordered to escort the *Surcouf* into the Great Sound. We could put two and two together."

"How can you be so certain it was the *Surcouf* and not a U-boat?"

"The U-boats operated in packs and rarely attacked on the surface. This was a renegade and the Admiralty obviously knew it. I expect it had its own proof, but I wasn't privy to it. I just did my job."

"What did the Admiralty do?" asked Holly.

Fishburn took a deep breath. "It's a long time ago, and there's no harm in telling you now, but the orders to destroy the *Surcouf* came from Washington."

"The *Surcouf* was sunk by the Allies?" gasped Holly.

The diver nodded his head and took a sip from his pink gin. "By me, actually. I attached two limpet mines to the hull while in dock-yard the night before she sailed."

"You were ordered to?" asked Waters, amazed at the revelation.

"Of course," replied Fishburn, defensively. "This was an official operation, fully authorized."

"No regrets?" asked Holly quietly.

"None whatever. In a way, the *Surcouf*'s crew brought its fate upon itself."

Holly looked puzzled. "How so? I don't understand. Perhaps the submarine really did intend to go to Tahiti as ordered."

Fishburn pushed his glass of gin aside and started rearranging the plates and cruets on the table. "No chance. The limpets were timed to go off three days after she had left us. Let's say the salt shaker is the *Surcouf*." He moved two plates out of the way. "If she had really been heading for Panama, she would have headed for the Haiti channel and sailed past Jamaica." He moved the salt shaker through the gap between his empty wineglass and one of the plates. "But she didn't. Instead of negotiating the narrows off Guantanamo, she went south southeast, toward the Leeward Islands and Martinique. Accordingly, she was classified as an enemy vessel."

"So if she had kept to her proper course, she would have survived?" asked Waters, intrigued.

"Exactly," agreed Fishburn. "A signal would have been sent once she had been sighted off Cuba or Jamaica, alerting her to the existence of the explosive charges, or so I was told. Their removal would have been quite a simple matter."

"So the limpet mines were a sort of insurance policy, intended to eliminate the *Surcouf* if the crew misbehaved?" said Waters.

"I suppose so. It could also have been very effective as a raider. Can you imagine the havoc such a boat might have caused among the Atlantic convoys? She was a submersible cruiser, a very potent weapon."

"So what about all the rumors of her disappearance?" asked Holly.

"I've read them all. I think the skipper of an American cargo ship even convinced himself that he had run down the *Surcouf* off Cuba in the dark. It was all nonsense, of course. The fact is that the submarine would never have made it to the Panama Canal. There was clear evidence that the crew intended to make contact with Vichy forces in Martinique, and the decision was taken to stop her from joining the Axis. So the *Surcouf* headed south, and was never seen again."

Waters narrowed his eyes. "Do you know where she went down?"

"Not exactly. But it would not be difficult to calculate. The *Surcouf* made about fifteen knots on the surface and was making for the Lesser Antilles. I would calculate about 850 miles south of Bermuda, which would place her off Anguilla or Barbuda. Anyway, right at the top of the Leeward chain; a useful distance from the Vichy islands."

Fishburn's extraordinary tale had had a spellbinding effect on Holly, who had been scribbling notes throughout the lunch. By the end of the meeting she was more determined than ever to research the *Surcouf*'s story further, but Waters did not share her enthusiasm. "Why dredge all this up now?" he had asked. "It will only create bad feelings with the French, and de Gaulle is antagonistic enough anyway toward Macmillan as it is."

Holly had smiled sweetly, but she had been utterly committed to her story. "This is a little piece of history. And to the families of the *Surcouf*'s crew, quite an important one. Can't you see?" she pleaded. "This was an Allied ship, or was supposed to be, deliberately sunk by the Allies. It's a wonderful story and I'm going to make it. If I can just get some corroboration for Jack's version of events, we have headline material here."

"A little less of the 'we' if you please," replied Waters. "This is entirely your enterprise. I can't say I'm very struck by the idea. This was all a long time ago, and occasionally in war the unpalatable happens. It's best forgotten."

"No history would ever get written if everyone took that view. Or else it would all be Stalinist revisionism. This is the truth ... uncomfortable, yes ... but it really happened. It's our responsibility to get it recorded. Have you not thought of the two British liaison officers? Even if the French crew were renegades, what about them?"

Waters was unconvinced. "They were casualties of war, and I don't suppose their families will thank you for reminding them of an episode that ought to remain closed."

Holly and Waters had continued to debate the issue in the cab on their way back to Hamilton, and upon their return to the hotel there was a message from Brigadier Tiltman. Waters was to report to Kindley Field in the morning. Thus they enjoyed one remaining dinner and night together, and Holly hurried back to Shepherd's Bush. Waters promised to keep in touch with her from what he had discreetly referred to as "the communications department of the Foreign Office."

On the following day, Waters took a taxi up to St. David's Island and was met at the main gate to Kindley Field by a U.S. Air Force NCO who, having checked his identity, handed him a sealed envelope. Inside had been a message from his director, Sir Clive Loehnis, instructing him to make himself available to the Canadian Navy until further notice, or until the emergency was over. Having read it, he had turned to the American airman and inquired about the proximity of the Canadian Navy.

"This is it. Kindley Field is fifteen hundred acres of NATO base and I'm to take you to the Operations Intelligence Center. It's the classified accommodation at the other end of the main runway, by the NASA tracking station. Climb aboard, sir, and I'll give you a ride."

Driving on the left, the American airman guided the jeep through the builtup area of the base, and then turned onto one of the concrete aprons. Half a mile farther on, they approached a chain-link fence topped with barbed wire, and after a brief examination

191

of their passes at the gate, conducted by two armed guards, they came to a halt close to a large windowless block.

"This is the Ops Center. I don't have a clearance to go inside, but I guess you do. Enjoy your visit."

Waters swung himself off the jeep and, once through a tinted glass door, found himself in a small hallway under the scrutiny of another uniformed American airman who had been seated in a small booth. Having introduced himself and shown his identification, he was buzzed through two electronically controlled vault doors and into a large hangarlike room hung with maps and display panels, not unlike CAESAR in Gibraltar. It was a huge room, packed with electronic equipment and what looked like computer terminals. As he paused to admire the scene, his hand was shaken by a tall, suntanned officer in a pale blue shirt.

"Welcome to Canada," said Jim Torwood, introducing himself as the senior Canadian liaison officer, Bermuda. "Or at least this particular corner of the country. It's great to have you with us; I'm told you are an expert on Soviet surface ships."

Waters winced at the mention of expert. "I've been doing a study of the subject over the past few months," he admitted, "but I'm no expert. Merely a frustrated statistician who listens to the radio."

"Well, my information is that you are a qualified DF operator with an unrivaled knowledge of Soviet merchant fleet procedures and call signs. If that's true, you're the man we want right now."

"What's the emergency?" he asked. "I was supposed to be going back to England."

"You could say it's a small case of World War Three. Our American cousins have gone ape, but they won't tell us why yet. There's talk of mobilization, and this is no exercise. Our orders are to log every Soviet surface vessel and make contingency plans to deal with all submarines on the basis that they're hostile. I'm glad you were able to make the party."

National Photographic Interpretation Center, Friday, 19 October 1962

Art Lundahl had been at work continuously for the past six days, since Heyser's IDEALIST material had come up from Patrick Air Force Base for examination. Since then there had been an additional twenty U-2 overflights, and the news just got worse and worse. On Wednesday, two IRBM sites had been discovered, at Remedios and Guanajay. Then, the following afternoon, a U-2 pilot had reported the MiG-21s operational at Santa Clara, and his cameras had caught several Beagles in the process of assembly on the apron at Holguín. He had also pictured two MRBM clusters around Sagua la Grande.

The news of the IRBM sites had been the most devastating of all, because, according to the analysts, there was now a strong likelihood of a total of twenty-four MRBMs and sixteen IRBMs at nine separate sites—a development that, if correct, would increase the Soviet capacity to launch a land-based, first-strike nuclear salvo by 80 percent.

Quite apart from the strategic implications, the sheer quantity of weaponry that had suddenly appeared in Cuba in such a short space of time was overwhelming: five confirmed Styx coastal batteries, twenty-four SAM-2 sites, and MiG-21s deployed at three airfields, with Beagles confirmed at two more. Suddenly, Cuba had been transformed into an armed camp, bristling with sophisticated hardware and the infrastructure to support it. In an age when satellites, SIGINT, and the U-2 were supposed to make surprise impossible, the unthinkable had happened. Lundahl had every right to be depressed, but other Psalmists, with access to different parts of the equation were more worried. On this particular morning, Lundahl and McGee were exchanging confidences, aware that only a relative handful of people were in possession of all the facts. The compartmented category designated ELITE had been introduced for those indoctrinated into the political aspects of the situation. Neither man had any idea to whom the President would turn for advice, but they knew he would have to act fast if anything was to be done before all the nuclear missiles became operational. They also knew that elaborate measures had been taken to prevent word of the crisis from leaking out. Sir Hugh Stevenson, the chairman of the British Joint Intelligence Committee, had arrived in Washington for an Allied intelligence conference that had been planned months ago. Suddenly, just before his arrival at the Pentagon, the "E" Ring had been sealed off to prevent his team from straying too far, and perhaps noticing the camp beds that had been carried into the rooms of senior officers.

"There are some indications that the Russians realize that we have discovered at least one cluster of MRBMs. This morning prints show that some belated attempts are being made to camouflage the missile launchers," said Lundahl.

"I think we must assume they know," agreed McGee gloomily. "The day before yesterday they launched Cosmos 10 from the Tyuratam cosmodrome. According to the DIA, it's the first Soviet reconnaissance satellite, and it's taking pictures right across the southeastern United States."

"Is it transmitting them to earth stations or ejecting capsules of film for recovery?" asked Lundahl. Although he had access to highly classified data in his field, he was compartmented and therefore isolated from the latest Soviet developments.

"Neither," replied McGee. "Apparently the whole satellite will be deorbited and the film removed afterward."

"So the Soviets have no way of knowing what their cameras have picked up. It proves nothing," observed Lundahl.

McGee stroked his chin thoughtfully. "Then you think it's merely a coincidence that the very first Soviet satellite of its kind is launched into space now . . . and happens to be on an inclination that brings it over our most sensitive military establishments in the southwest once a day?"

Lundahl smiled. "Photointerpreters believe in coincidences. They have to, especially after they've examined a few miles of IDEALIST stereoscopic film."

"There's no such thing as a coincidence in the counterintelligence field," replied McGee easily. It was an axiom he often used, as did his CI Staff colleagues.

"Maybe," remarked the scientist. "But has it not occurred to you that satellite imagery has a dual role? As a clandestine means of collection it is unrivaled, which is why the NPIC exists. But it can also be a useful conduit once its existence has been disclosed."

"A means of deception?" queried McGee.

"Not necessarily, more a method of conveying a message that is bound to be received."

McGee thought for a few moments. "Perhaps we should give ELITE more credit than we have already," he observed. "There's a joint amphibious exercise called PHIBRIGLEX 62 under way off Puerto Rico at present. That would certainly look good on the satellited pictures."

"How big is it?"

"It's the usual annual jamboree. A big task force supported by carriers, destroyers, and troopships. Seventy-five hundred marines will storm ashore on Vieques Island and liberate it from a dictator called Ortsac."

"Castro spelled backwards?"

"It was planned a long time ago, but with enough muscle lined up for the Kremlin, it might make Khrushchev think twice."

"Frankly, I doubt it. That kind of subtlety doesn't show up on negatives. We can count tanks, aircraft, and ships, but we can't discern motivation. That's for you types."

"But the fact that the exercise is under way will be noticed. So will the mobilization."

"We've mobilized?" asked Lundahl, with surprise.

"Almost. The Pentagon has declared a status of DEFCON-three—which is just a whisker away from full mobilization—and that means major deployment of units the Russians will be interested in: the First Armored Division from Fort Hood, Texas, and the marines moving out from Camp Pendleton. If that doesn't scare the hell out of Khrushchev, nothing will."

But McGee had been only partly right. The 2nd Battalion, 1st

Marine Division, had indeed been transferred to the El Toro Marine Corps Air Station just south of Los Angeles in anticipation of a general mobilization, and artillery units equipped with Hawk and Nike missiles had been pulled into Florida and ordered to prepare their weapons for launch without the customary camouflage. The show of strength had also enhanced PHILBRIGLEX 62. Twenty destroyers had been attached to the exercise now converging on Roosevelt Roads, south of Puerto Rico, and the carrier *Essex* had been ordered to Guantanamo Bay, as was an airlift of troops. In addition, strike aircraft had been moved into the open and lined up at bases in Homestead, Jacksonville, and McDill. And for the benefit of the intercept antenna fields at Lourdes and atop the Soviet diplomatic missions in Washington and New York, General Thomas S. Power at the Strategic Air Command Headquarters at Offut Air Force Base near Omaha, Nebraska, had signaled all his bombers in plaintext to load full payloads and had put ninety Atlas and forty-six Titan ICBMs on full alert. As a final touch, B-47 bombers had been dispersed to forty civil airports around the country, with a special emphasis on those used by Eastern bloc airlines.

"What's your guess as to how this is going to turn out?" asked McGee. "It worries me that we're on the edge of a disastrous confrontation, yet hardly anyone knows what's really happening."

"That's what the ELITE channel is for. We supply the data; it's up to the politicians to make the tough decisions. There's much more to this business than even we know about."

"Such as?" asked McGee skeptically.

"We have no knowledge of the back channels being used by the Kremlin to communicate with the White House."

McGee suppressed a smile. Even if Washington's intelligence community had no inkling of unofficial contacts with the Soviet leadership, the CIA's Counterintelligence Staff monitored them with consummate skill. The most recent example had been a secret visit made by Khrushchev's son-in-law, Aleksei Adzhubei, to meet President Kennedy in late January.

"Are you trying to tell me something, Art?" asked McGee suspiciously.

"Not exactly," replied Lundahl unconvincingly. "But don't jump to any conclusions on this. Sure, the Russians have put missiles in Cuba. Okay, we can see about forty of them. But I haven't seen any warheads."

"Are you saying those SS-4s and SS-5s are unarmed?"

Lundahl nodded. "Don't ask me why, because I can't tell you. But based on our experience of warhead deployment in the Soviet Union, I have not seen anything from IDEALIST that even suggests the arrival of a single nuclear device."

"So this threat is not a nuclear one?" demanded McGee incredulously.

"Correct. Forty quite large holes in the ground, maybe, but emphatically no nuclear explosions. Of course, the warheads could be on their way as we speak."

Kindley Field, Bermuda;
Friday, 19 October 1962

Tom Waters sat hunched over the control console and took a triangulation on the *Bucharest*, a Soviet tanker moving west in mid-Atlantic. According to the computer it was a tanker, but that did not prevent it from coming under scrutiny. Earlier in the morning all the intercept staff had been given an object lesson in the dual role of most Soviet merchantmen. There had been numerous examples of apparently ordinary Russian cargo ships replenishing submarines of the Northern Fleet, and on this occasion the *Atrek* had been monitored south of the Azores. Its position was determined by the PUSHER circularly disposed high-frequency direction finding arrays at Daniel's Head operating in tandem with similar antenna fields at Lajes on Terceira Island in the Azores and at Stokksnes on Iceland. Whereas a regular vessel might have escaped further investigation, this one was automatically flagged for visual inspection, for the *Atrek* was no ordinary ship.

Built in 1955 at Rostock by the East Germans, the *Atrek* had been designed as a Kolomna-class freighter and then converted to a submarine support role. With five other, similar ships, she plied the world seeking submarines to replenish. With a range of 6,900 nautical miles at thirteen knots, she could cover long distances and her two forward five-ton cranes could transfer an impressive quantity of stores and armaments very quickly. Given the *Atrek*'s status, a maritime reconnaissance patrol had been despatched from Wideawake on Ascension to make an inspection. She was discovered almost motionless, with a November, a Zulu, three Golfs, and the sole *Juliett* on station at her stern. The sighting had been the cause of some celebration among the NATO operators,

198

but Waters had wondered why so many submarines had congregated. Although not exactly unprecedented, especially in the Pacific, such a large number of submarines in the same location was a remarkable event and an extraordinary breach of security. Not only was the entire group placing themselves at considerable risk, but they were actually compromising the safety of a substantial proportion of the entire Soviet submarine fleet. Waters had remembered some interesting figures he had learned during his visit to CAESAR. The entire Soviet submarine inventory was comprised of around 400 craft, of which 130 were of pre-1960 design and unsuitable for long-range deployment. Of the four Red Banner Fleets, the Northern Fleet took the lion's share of the submarines. Whereas the Northern Fleet only had 26 percent of the surface ships, it had roughly half the Soviet submarines, the remainder being spread between the Baltic, Black Sea, and Pacific commands.

More significantly, though, only about one-third of the submarine strength was ever available for operational deployment. The rest were either undergoing refits or working up their crews in training exercises. This meant that of the Northern Fleet's seven missile boats, only two or three were ever likely to be out in the Atlantic at any one time. Yet here were four, all in the same place, and on the surface. Waters knew that individual Soviet submarine commanders would have been extremely reluctant to rendezvous like this unless they had been given an exceptionally good motive for doing so. And as someone well versed in wireless intercept, he recognized there was really only one reason that made any sense: a verbal order that was of such importance that it could not be transmitted over the air on one of the regular schedules. For while Soviet submarines would routinely come close to the surface and raise an antenna to pick up fleet broadcasts, they would themselves maintain radio silence so as to avoid betraying their positions to NATO's ever vigilant PUSHER direction-finding scanners.

The knowledge that such an unusually high proportion of the Northern Fleet was conferring in mid-Atlantic did little to reassure Waters, who submitted a detailed report of his observations and returned to concentrate on the rest of the Soviet surface ships in his sector.

Langley, Virginia;
Saturday, 20 October 1962

It was late in the evening, and the DCI had spent most of the day with the President, who, according to the press, had succumbed to a cold. McCone and the other ELITE advisers had been smuggled into the White House through the tunnel from the Old Executive Office Building, and had left the same way after hearing Kennedy's decision. A naval blockade was to be imposed on Cuba and the announcement would be made Monday on national television.

From the Psalmists' point of view, the President had chosen a particular course of action, and it was their responsibility to direct all the latest intelligence to him so his strategy could be made to work. Having reached a decision, it was up to the CIA to ensure it received the best possible hearing from America's allies. Accordingly, two senior officers, Sherman Kent and Chester Cooper, had been selected to fly to Europe and brief President de Gaulle and Prime Minister Macmillan on the U.S. plan. Kent had been chosen to go to the Elysée because, although the irascible Frenchman understood English well enough, he pretended not to, and Kent, the head of the CIA's Office of National Estimates, spoke French like a native. Al Ulmer, the station chief in Paris, was a frequent visitor to the rue de Faubourg St.-Honoré and was highly regarded by de Gaulle; he had requested an audience late on Sunday evening, even though he had no idea of Kent's mission. The latter was now sitting opposite the DCI, taking notes in French, while General Carter and Leo McGee briefed him on the portfolio of enlarged black-and-white IDEALIST prints he was to show General de Gaulle.

Also present was Chester Cooper, who had only recently returned from a lengthy tour of duty at the CIA station in London.

He had arrived in Grosvenor Square in the late summer of 1955, in time to witness the trauma of Cyprus and Suez, and had made many friends within the local intelligence community. His instructions were to hitch a ride with Kent on the White House's Boeing 707 to a Strategic Air Command base in Berkshire, RAF Greenham Common, where he would be met by the U.S. ambassador, David Bruce. Together they would drive straight to 10 Downing Street where the prime minister had agreed to receive them. Meanwhile, the jet would fly on to Orly and then Cologne, so the third CIA messenger, R. Jack Smith, could see Chancellor Adenauer in Bonn. Smith was an Agency veteran and currently head of the Office of Current Intelligence under Ray Cline. The task of each sounded straightforward. They were to make a presentation of the photographic evidence compiled by Lundahl's NPIC and then explain the President's commitment to the imposition of a naval quarantine. They would be at liberty to answer any questions, but at the conclusion of each meeting it was to be made clear to each that this was not a consultation; it was notification of an issue that had already been decided. Accompanying the CIA personnel would be Dean Acheson, the former secretary of state, who would help Kent handle de Gaulle, and Walter Dowling, the U.S. ambassador to the Federal Republic, who happened to be in Georgia visiting his ailing mother. He had been recalled hastily to Washington. Equally inconvenient, the newly appointed ambassador to Paris, Charles Bohlen, had been discovered to be on a liner in mid-Atlantic, so Dean Acheson had been deputed to represent him in Paris and introduce Kent to the French president.

As for Canada, the U.S. ambassador, Livingston Merchant, had been tracked down to a football game at Princeton and, after a hasty summons from the White House, had been dispatched to Langley before explaining the situation to Prime Minister John Diefenbaker.

"Although nothing has been said in public yet," the DCI began, "we have every reason to believe the Soviets have been alerted to our discovery of their MRBM and IRBM launch sites in Cuba. On Wednesday, they put their first reconnaissance satellite into orbit. This morning, our time, they sent another, Cosmos 11. We must therefore assume a high degree of awareness on the part of the Russians in regard to our actions. We know only that the nuclear first-strike threat to our security is about to increase by a factor of 50 percent, based upon their current ICBM capability. On Monday, the President will declare an embargo on all deliveries of strategic weapons to Castro, effective at ten hundred hours our time on Tuesday. It will take considerable resolve to enforce it; General Carter will give you the rest."

The deputy DCI took over the role of lecturer. "This will be a naval and airborne blockade designed to achieve two objectives: first, to prevent further strategic materiel from reaching the island, and second, to apply pressure, backed by deadly force, on the Kremlin. If the Soviets challenge the quarantine we will require the cooperation of our allies. In practical terms, this will mean immediate support in three particular areas: from the Canadians, we will require access to their SIGINT and early warning bases; second, we will need Bermuda as a base of operations and consent to inspect all maritime traffic on charter from the U.K; and third, Cuba cannot be isolated from the air unless the French use their influence to deny refueling rights to Soviet aircraft in West Africa. In particular, we are concerned about Conakry, Dakar, and a few airfields in Morocco. If our sanctions are to be comprehensive, it is vital that we secure these transatlantic routes. It is up to you, gentlemen, to use all your persuasive powers to ensure our integrity."

The President was scheduled to leave Edwards Air Force Base early the following morning, and the operation went without a hitch. Prime Minister Macmillan had been enthralled by the slide show and had given his approval to the President's plan. Then the London station chief, Archie Roosevelt, had invited Labour opposition leader Hugh Gaitskell and his deputy, George Brown, to his magnificent home on the south side of Eaton Square and repeated the performance. Gaitskell had served in intelligence during the war, masterminding black propaganda, so he had an appreciation of the crisis, while Brown had been assiduously cultivated by Roosevelt since his arrival from the CIA station in Madrid. Both Gaitskell and Brown agreed to back Kennedy and help the government make this a nonpartisan issue. Over in Paris, Al Ulmer had ushered Sherman Kent into the president's ornate study and had pointed out each tiny missile trailer, erector, and fuel truck in the IDEALIST photos. By the time they had left, with de Gaulle's promise of support, they had gained the distinct impression that what had really influenced the president had been the technology required to take such detailed pictures from an altitude of thirteen miles.

But even if General de Gaulle had been sympathetic, and SDECE had promised to deliver Morocco's backing, its director, General Paul Grossin, had been less optimistic about President Ahmed Sékou Touré of Guinea, a fiercely independent ruler who valued his country's nonaligned status. The president of Senegal, Léopold Senghor, was reckoned to be more compliant, but special cables were transmitted to the CIA stations in each capital to do whatever was necessary to close the local airspace to Soviet traffic. However, by the time Ambassadors William Attwood and Philip Kaiser called upon their respective heads of state, substantial cash transfers had taken place in Zurich, and full support for the U.S. position had been secured—and paid for.

Having ensured that the air approaches to Cuba would be sealed off, and having promised an unexpectedly reluctant Diefenbaker that no Canadian ships or personnel would be involved in enforcing the blockade, the Psalmists were left with responsibility to advise the President about the surface craft and submarines likely to initiate a confrontation. This data came from Bermuda and, in the absence of any Canadian technicians at Kindley Field, from Tom Waters.

Kindley Field, Bermuda;
Monday, 22 October 1962

Despite the sudden withdrawal of the Canadians, the Intelligence Center had maintained an updated schedule of all Soviet shipping in the Atlantic, together with an estimate of exactly when they would approach the quarantine that had been established five hundred miles into the Atlantic. A line had been drawn on a map somewhere deep in the Pentagon, and Task Force 136, under the command of Admiral Ward, had been assigned to police it. Comprised of a sixty-three-ship surface fleet and an undisclosed number of hunter-killer submarines, the admiral had no shortage of resources at his disposal. All told, there were around thirty thousand American personnel deployed to detect and stop Soviet seaborne traffic to Cuba. And in order to emphasize the international nature of the perceived Soviet threat to the Western Hemisphere, warships from Venezuela, Argentina, and the Dominican Republic were integrated into the task force.

Despite all the frenetic naval activity along the eastern seaboard, the interest in Bermuda had initially been focused on a lone Soviet intruder, an Ilyushin-18, that had been spotted by a radar picket in the northern Atlantic heading south. Designated Coot by NATO, it was a low-wing, four-turboprop transport that had several variants, including a sophisticated maritime reconnaissance role complete with radomes and a magnetic anomaly detector boom, much like that on the P-5 Marlin. However, once fighters had been scrambled to make a visual check, the aircraft was confirmed as a 122-seat airliner bound for Rio de Janeiro to collect the body of the Soviet ambassador to Brazil who had drowned in a swimming accident some days earlier.

The panic over, at least temporarily, Waters returned to his task of assessing the Soviet surface threat. Having conducted a survey of all the NATO choke points and collated the intelligence from other sources, twenty-three Soviet ships seemed to be following a course to Cuba. Of these, the *Gagarin* and the *Komiles* were closest, with the tanker *Bucharest* not far behind, and eight more within fifteen hundred miles. The *Poltava* had already been logged as a likely missile carrier, and the *Bolshevik Sukhanov* was judged to be another good candidate. One to slip past the net was the *Leninsky Komsomol*, packed with Beagle bomber–sized crates on its deck. An extra spurt of speed at the last minute on Monday had allowed it to beat Tuesday's deadline of ten o'clock in the morning.

In addition to the twenty-three Soviet vessels, Waters was able to identify another group that were to give the diplomats and lawyers a few headaches. What would be the attitude of ships from other nations approaching the exclusion zone? The Intelligence Center used the huge, circularly disposed PUSHER direction-finding arrays on both sides of the Atlantic to isolate their transmissions and plot the exact position of each on an hourly basis. The President's declaration had been broadcast on all the marine channels and from the sudden escalation of wireless activity it was obvious that the masters of each vessel were hastily seeking instructions. Should they recognize an American demand to heave to and have their cargo spaces inspected for contraband? Some, it was clear, were unlikely to carry weapons or warheads, but the White House did not intend to discriminate against Eastern bloc carriers. Indeed, based on Waters's calculations, the first ship to reach the U.S. Navy's line would be a British freighter en route to Jamaica. Then there was the *Sirius*, a Greek tanker destined for Cuba, and the *Voelkerfreundschaft*, an East German liner carrying five hundred passengers. There were also two Soviet charters: a Swedish steamer bound for Cuba from Leningrad and, to complicate matters further, the *Marucla*, with Panamanian ownership, Lebanese registration, and a Greek skipper.

The communications of each were intercepted, with the PUSHER equipment constantly providing data on their speed and course.

205

Meanwhile, other intercept operators recorded the Morse and speech transmissions for analysis by intelligence personnel anxious to determine how each vessel would react when approached by a U.S. warship. Communications to the *Gagarin* and *Komiles* proved exceptionally interesting, for each was provided with a Soviet assessment of where the Americans had deployed their pickets, information apparently gleaned from Cosmos 10, which had been recovered on Sunday, having been replaced by Cosmos 11 on Saturday.

Perhaps of greater concern were the whereabouts and intentions of the *Atrek*'s flotilla of submarines. They had dispersed after their encounter with the American reconnaissance aircraft from Wideawake, and an intensive search was under way to find them and, according to orders straight from the White House, force them to the surface. The Zulu and the three Golfs presented little difficulty, as the former was a vintage craft, some ten years old, with noisy diesel electric engines—easy prey for CAESAR's listening arrays. Although some of the class had been converted to carry two Sark ballistic missiles, the arrangement had not proved a success and the program had been discontinued. The problem was that the Zulu's pedigree was essentially German, based upon a 1944 U-boat. And to be operated at its full range of 9,500 miles, its operating speed was reduced to about eight knots. Having three noise-generating shafts and insufficient space for modern sonar, the Zulu was regarded as easy meat by NATO's antisubmarine warfare strategists. The three Golfs were even slower and also boasted three clattering propeller drive shafts. Based on the old Foxtrots, which were of the same German origin as the Zulus, the Golf had simply been elongated by twenty-five feet to accommodate three Sark missiles in an extended fin. In every other respect the Golf looked and performed like a Foxtrot, with the same three diesel electric motors, the same number of torpedo tubes, and identical sonar equipment. Once again, the Golfs were quickly detected by aircraft in the Atlantic and forced to the surface.

While the *Juliett* was also a diesel electric and the same length as a Zulu, everything else about the boat was modern. It had only been commissioned in February, the first of the class, and was armed with four Shaddock missiles and ten torpedoes. It was also equipped with the very latest medium-frequency sonar, much of it stolen from the British. But what gave it an advantage was its speed, the twin shafts developing fourteen knots while submerged, which enabled the *Juliett* to accelerate away from the *Atrek* heading south and west, occasionally using merchantmen as cover for its escape. The fact that it managed to evade all attempts to track it brought consternation to the CAESAR operators, the U.S. Navy surface fleet, and the Pentagon. Although its four Shaddocks were primarily antiship weapons, its turbojet engine, backed by two solid fuel boosters, had a range of 250 nautical miles. To launch against a coastal target like Jacksonville or Miami Beach, the *Juliett* simply had to surface and fire, the mid-flight guidance being provided by another aircraft in the vicinity, or even a suitably equipped merchantman like the *Komiles*. The very prospect of this single submarine unaccounted for was enough to make the strategists blanch. But the Psalmists at Langley had another reason to be worried. They had been thrown into confusion by quite a different event. After six weeks of absolute silence, Colonel Oleg Penkovsky had made contact with his American case officer in Moscow and used a code word with a particular significance. It meant a surprise nuclear attack on the United States was imminent.

U.S. Embassy, Moscow;
Monday, 22 October 1962

Rodney Carlson had met ARNIKA only three times, at diplomatic receptions, but the original introduction had been made by Hugh Montgomery, the CIA case officer who had handled Penkovsky in tandem with Rory Chisholm at the British embassy. Carlson had been well briefed on the ARNIKA/RUPEE case, and he knew of the importance attached to it at every level in Washington and London. For the very first time, the West was gaining an insight into the Soviet strategic missile forces, the GRU, and the Kremlin. It was sheer gold in value, but something had happened to change all that. The Russian had not passed anything when they had last met, on 5 September; nor had he made any attempt to fill the ingenious dead-letter drop in the British embassy when he had visited there the following evening. The British had been unperturbed. They had regarded the rendezvous as an opportunity for his new SIS officer, Gervase Cowell, to take over from Rory Chisholm, who was returning to London at the end of his tour of duty. Ideally, Chisholm should have stayed to run the case, but his continued presence in Moscow would have attracted unwelcome attention.

Carlson was not as experienced as his predecessor, Hugh Montgomery, who had been in the CIA since leaving Harvard with a doctorate ten years ago, and had most recently been attached to the Athens station under diplomatic cover. Nevertheless, Carlson had realized the implications immediately when he had been telephoned at his apartment early in the morning and a Russian voice had given him the single emergency code word. Carlson could not swear that the person was Penkovsky, but there seemed little doubt. No one else knew the code word, and his home telephone number had not been given to any other Russians. This procedure was strictly a last resort, designed to prevent another Pearl Harbor, and Carlson was appalled. Without making any excuses to his wife, who knew of his clandestine role and had already found one hidden microphone in the apartment, he fled the building and drove to the embassy. There he drafted a flash cable to Langley and a note for hand delivery to the chief of station and the ambassador. Then he got back into his car and drove up Kutuzovsky Prospekt to check the lampposts for ARNIKA's telltale signal that his dead drop was ready to be emptied. This signal was an inconspicuous piece of black sticky-tape placed on the thirty-fifth lamppost, and it meant that a message had been left behind a radiator in the entrance hall of 5 Pushkin Street, but there was no tape to be seen. Perplexed and anxious, Carlson hurried back to the embassy and, later in the morning, assigned the task of making a second check to one of the CIA station's support team, Richard C. Jacob. Officially a clerk, Jacob was accustomed to such missions and began a lengthy countersurveillance routine to shake off any hostile observers.

In the meantime, Gervase Cowell had been startled to receive a strange telephone call. His arrangement with Penkovsky was standard tradecraft where most conversations with foreigners are intercepted and recorded. Two "silent calls," with the caller blowing into the mouthpiece three times and hanging up without saying a word, would initiate a predetermined emergency plan. However, ARNIKA had departed from the procedure and asked for Cowell by name. This was an extraordinary breach of security, as was his demand for an immediate meeting outside the Moscow State Circus. Perhaps it had been a veiled warning, for Penkovsky had added, "You know me. . . . You are my friend." Considering that "the friend" is a euphemism used by insiders to refer to the British Secret Intelligence Service, Penkovsky's mention of Cowell as his friend had a double meaning. But did it conceal a third significance, perhaps an intimation that he was no longer at liberty? Cowell had replaced the receiver with a lame excuse, and when he reached his office later in the morning, he filed a report detailing the occurrence. If ARNIKA was not already under arrest, his behavior over an open telephone line that was certain to be monitored would have compromised Cowell, and probably started a KGB investigation. It was to be some hours before Cowell's report reached Langley via London, by which time a furious debate had opened on what interpretation was to be placed on Penkovsky's extraordinary conduct.

21 Queen Anne's Gate, London; Tuesday, 23 October 1962

The news of Jacob's arrest in Moscow had come over the encrypted teleprinter in the communications room of the Secret Intelligence Service's main office at Broadway Buildings, which conveniently backed onto the period house that accommodated Sir Dick White. The news that the KGB had caught Jacob while attempting to empty one of ARNIKA's dead-letter drops was delivered straight to Harry Shergold, the desk officer in charge of the case, who copied it to his chief, Sir Dick, and the case officer responsible for handling Penkovsky's courier, Greville Wynne. Immediately recognizing the gravity of the situation, White called a case conference to discuss the implications. It was held in his paneled study on the second floor, overlooking the quiet cul-de-sac of Queen Anne's Gate. The three other participants—Harry Shergold, Oliver St. John, and Dickie Franks—had walked through the small courtyard that separated the rear of the two buildings.

Franks opened the meeting. "The Agency tells us that their man was detained yesterday while responding to Penkovsky's signal that one of his regular drops was ready for collection. The usual denied area countersurveillance measures were taken, and Jacob was considered clean when he approached Pushkin Street where the drop was located."

"Which implies a static operation on the site," observed St. John. As head of Soviet Operations, the news had been terribly disappointing, but he had more than a professional interest in the case. He knew, from personal experience, what it was like when agents are lost. His previous post had been as SIS head of station in Cairo, where his entire network had been rolled up by the local

Mukhabarat, the Egyptian security apparatus. Two of his best men had been executed, and several others were still in prison.

"Exactly. The KGB knew Jacob was coming and simply waited at the drop to pick him up. We must therefore assume our man has been rumbled, and presumably this is the explanation for the rather odd contact he made with Gervase in Moscow. He wanted to warn us that he was under suspicion."

"If not control," added White.

"That is something we shall have to consider, of course," replied Shergold. "But we must assume the operation has been terminated. The Americans are withdrawing Carlson straightaway, before he gets PNG'd."

"How much are we incriminated?" asked Franks.

"On the assumption that Penkovsky's activities have been monitored, we must accept that his last telephone contacts have been compromised and may even have been deliberate provocations manipulated by the Second Chief Directorate. That eliminates the Cowells. It may also put Ivor Rowsell at risk as well."

White asked for an explanation. As far as he knew, Rowsell had never been directly involved in the case. He was in Moscow as a backup, under embassy-driver cover.

"We had a dead-drop pickup procedure that involved Rowsell's apartment. His telephone was manned at exactly ten past nine every Monday evening. Two calls, one minute apart, with three blows into the mouthpiece was the signal. As you know, ARNIKA deviated from the established routine by calling Gervase direct and demanding a rendezvous. I'm afraid that was his way of saying good-bye."

"If he has blown that much, has he revealed the rest?" asked Franks, obviously anxious about his particular agent, the businessman who had acted as Penkovsky's courier. "Wynne is in Austria at the moment, and is about to go over into Hungary on one of his trade missions."

"He should be quite safe," said St. John. "A sudden cancellation at such short notice might attract attention to him and give the KGB a clue as to how long ARNIKA has been active for us. They are bound to know of Penkovsky's connection with Wynne, and it is only a matter of time before they investigate his possible involvement."

"You think they don't know already?" demanded White.

"Look at the problem logically," instructed St. John. A year younger than his chief, he was the only one in the room who had not gone to university. His background had been Sandhurst, the cavalry, and the Indian civil service; whereas White, Shergold, and Franks, the youngest, were all Oxford men. That did not intimidate him, nor deter him from openly speaking his mind in analyzing the case history. "We have run ARNIKA since early last year. The last time we actually saw him at liberty was at the embassy in Moscow on ..." he looked quizzically at his case officer, Franks.

"September sixth. He was supposed to spot Gervase by his tie-pin after a movie ... they were showing *A Taste of Honey.*"

"And since that single encounter last month we have had the telephone incident. He ignores the proper practice and calls Gervase. And instead of the usual signal he tries to engage him in a potentially incriminating conversation."

"And seeks to entrap him by demanding an unscheduled meeting," added White.

"Quite. But look how he did it. He might have stuck to the Monday evening arrangement. What would have happened then?"

"Gervase or his wife, Pamela, would have visited the grave of Sergei Yesenin in the Vaganovskoye Cemetery," replied Shergold.

"An ideal location for an ambush. But that didn't happen. Instead, Penkovsky used a formula that he knew would put us on our guard. I'll bet he did the same with the Americans," said St. John ruefully.

"I haven't had a chance to ask Kisevalter or McCoy yet," admitted Shergold, "but I'll do so as soon as I can."

"It looks to me as though Penkovsky has only told the KGB the barest minimum so far. He's on a short leash, and we should do nothing to undermine his position while he still has a chance," insisted St. John.

"Which means sending Wynne to Budapest," added Franks gloomily.

"Penkovsky is a skilled GRU officer," asserted Shergold confidently. "He's a professional and he knows the score. If he can satisfy the KGB with the expulsion of Jacob and the Cowells, he may be able to conceal the extent of his work for us."

"But that still leaves Wynne vulnerable," said Franks.

"It does," conceded St. John. "But look at the timing. The KGB knows that Wynne is due in Budapest shortly. The trade visit was announced long ago, and if they suspected his collaboration with Penkovsky, then surely they would have waited until he was also in their grasp before acting? The fact that Jacob was blown yesterday is an indication that Wynne is in the clear."

"So far. I wouldn't fancy his chances after Penkovsky has spent a week in the Lubyanka," replied Franks.

"This question of timing is critical," observed White. "Is it coincidental that Jacob should have been detained just as President Kennedy was about to announce a blockade on Cuba?"

"Well, it was certainly not in retaliation," murmured St. John. "Jacob had been arrested and released by the time the broadcast was made." Always sensitive to diplomatic protocol, the Soviets knew their own men in the West were vulnerable to harassment.

"But there may have been a leak," said White. "The CIA briefed the prime minister and the opposition on Sunday evening ... more than enough time to get the news back to Moscow." White had spent nearly twenty years in the Security Service before switching to SIS in 1956, so he was always sensitive to the possibility of unauthorized disclosure of classified information. It was not a quality that endeared him to his subordinates. "Oliver, can you start a preliminary inquest on the ARNIKA/RUPEE case? I also want an analysis from GCHQ of the London *rezidentura*'s traffic over the past forty-eight hours, and let's ask MI5 if any Soviets did anything unusual during the same period. Dickie, please brief your man in Austria and warn him not to do anything rash once he's over the frontier; Harry, we ought to arrange a joint meeting with the Agency and hear their views. Thank you, gentlemen ... and good luck."

Langley, Virginia;
Wednesday, 24 October 1962

The DCI's first appointment of the day in his modern office overlooking the woods of Virginia was the director's daily staff meeting, at which the chief of Current Intelligence briefed McCone on the events of the previous twenty-four hours. As Jack Smith was fond of remarking, "It's always midday somewhere, and someone always wants to tell us about it." His Office of Current Intelligence manned the Watch Office seven days a week, receiving cables and telegrams day and night from every corner of the globe. Sitting in a semicircle in front of the DCI's desk, with their backs to the large glass picture window made of bullet-proof glass, were Ray Cline, Leo McGee, and Smith.

For Smith, the previous two days had been astonishingly hectic. On Saturday evening he had been indoctrinated into the latest IDEALIST photointelligence. On Sunday morning he had flown to Greenham Common, and then on to Orly and Cologne, arriving late at night. After snatching some sleep at the residence of the deputy chief of mission in Bonn he had spent the day with Ambassador Dowling, preparing for their crucial meeting with the German chancellor. At six-thirty local time they were ushered into Adenauer's study; they completed their briefing in time to listen to the President's momentous broadcast announcing the blockade, which was relayed at midnight. At eleven the following morning he had caught a Lufthansa commercial flight from Cologne to New York, arriving back on American soil just fifty-four hours after he had left it. And instead of joining Ray Cline at the United Nations, where he had been assisting U.N. Ambassador Adlai Stevenson and others in the

ELITE channel, he flew down to Washington to man the Office of Current Intelligence.

"Apart from the fact that Adenauer couldn't believe my name really was Smith, the briefing went fine," Smith began. "He was very friendly and served us coffee and sandwiches. But he did want to know whether the missiles were hot. He actually used the term *cryogenic*. As I said in my cable, he was impressed by the clarity of the IDEALIST material and he'll support the White House."

The DCI nodded thoughtfully. "Ray, what's the situation in the Atlantic?"

Cline stroked his beard and consulted his notepad. "The latest word from Admiral Ward with the task force is that the *Gagarin* and the *Komiles* have stopped short of the five-hundred-mile limit."

McCone took off his glasses and rubbed his eyes. "Stopped as in stationary, or simply a change in course?"

"Dead in the water is what the *Essex* says," said Cline, glancing at a file on the table before him.

"So we've won this round?" asked the DCI.

"Maybe, maybe not," responded Cline. "The task force let through the British freighter and the Greek tanker *Sirius*. But worst of all, there's a Soviet submarine between the *Gagarin* and the *Komiles*. And the latest word from Bermuda is that the *Bucharest* has started moving again."

"The *Bucharest* is the tanker?" asked Smith.

Cline nodded. "The U.S.S. *Gearing* has been ordered to shadow and will intercept if it attempts to cross the line."

"Do we have an estimate for that?" asked McCone. He was desperately tired but he could not afford to spare any time. He needed to know when the crunch would come.

"Sometime tomorrow morning, if the *Bucharest*'s course and speed remain the same," replied Cline, having already made the necessary calculations. He was always exceptionally well briefed when he dealt with the DCI, who always demanded accuracy and had brought a businesslike discipline to the Agency.

McCone shook his head glumly as he heard the news. "Any other ships?"

"Two Soviet trawlers are being watched by a destroyer, the *J.R. Perry.* One of the trawlers has the other in tow, and they're headed for Havana." Cline, as ever, had the facts at his fingertips.

"No risk there?" asked McCone. He was addressing Smith.

"Much too small for any strategic cargo," replied the chief of Current Intelligence. "The British embassy in Havana will report their arrival." As he noticed a couple of heads turn in surprise, Smith elaborated. "The Brits have the crummiest chancery in town, the top two floors of a decrepit office block on the waterfront. But Her Britannic Majesty's ambassador has an office that happens to enjoy one of the best views in the country, right across the entrance to Havana harbor. Six are relaying details of every movement in and out."

"So there'll be no confrontation until tomorrow," insisted McCone.

"Guess not," responded Cline after exchanging glances with Smith. "But we have received a disturbing report from downtown. There was a reception at the Soviet embassy last night, planned some weeks ago. Anyway, one of the senior military staff, Lieutenant General Vladimir A. Dubovik, was heard to say that the Soviet ships had orders to proceed. He was emphatic they would not stop to be inspected."

"A bluff, perhaps?" suggested McGee.

"Possibly. We'll know tomorrow morning, or sooner if the *Gagarin* or *Komiles* responds to a signal from Moscow."

"What's going on in Cuba?" asked the DCI, polishing his glasses.

Smith left this to his subordinate. "There was a reconnaissance flight out of Cecil Field, Jacksonville, yesterday, which undertook a low-level flight across the island."

"Beneath the SAMs?" interrupted McCone.

"Very low altitude, and at high speed. I gather that at twelve hundred miles an hour these aircraft only remain in hostile airspace for four or five minutes. Too low for the Guidelines and too fast for the Czech antiaircraft batteries. Anyway, the bottom line is that the IRBM and MRBM sites show signs of being camouflaged."

"A little late in the day for that," remarked Smith.

"Anything else I should know about?" asked the DCI.

"Two other items," said McGee. "The British want a joint post-mortem on ARNIKA. I think it's in all our interests to pursue this as far as we can."

"Considering the contribution he has made, we must do everything to protect him. Do we know for sure he's in custody?" asked McCone. He had taken a close interest in Penkovsky from the start.

"Soviet Bloc hasn't risked too many drive-bys, but we don't think his lights went on last night," said McGee evenly, resisting the temptation to add a critical comment of his own, but he knew this was not the moment for recriminations. "We have to work on the basis that he is under interrogation and that he identified the dead drop where Jacob was arrested. On that basis I have already recommended that Bill Jones, Hugh Montgomery, and Rodney Carlson be flagged as known to the Soviets."

"And what about ARNIKA's last signal? Any views on that?" McCone asked. McGee was puzzled by the question. Penkovsky's final warning had come two days ago. Why would the DCI want a belated opinion when, presumably, he had already advised the White House of the imminent danger of a surprise Soviet attack? Then a thought came to him and he probed McCone.

"We have no way of judging the authenticity of the warning at present. Verification, of course, may come too late. How did the White House respond?"

McCone shifted awkwardly. "It's my decision on what gets fed into the ELITE channel, and when. Just make sure I'm the first to know of any developments on that front," he added brusquely. For McGee, the DCI's reply was a bombshell. It was clear McCone had not passed Penkovsky's warning on to the President. He was stunned but silent.

McGee paused for a moment to consider the implications. Kennedy had not been told that the CIA's star agent had warned of an imminent nuclear attack. Smith sensed the tension and broke in with his assessment. "The question of a surprise launch does not arise in Cuba, at least for the time being. The DIA is emphatic that the sites are not operational ... yet. There is also some doubt about warheads. In addition, the Beagle bombers are still in the assembly stage. The real worry of a first strike is either from mainland Russia or a submarine launch."

"Do you have the figures of Soviet submarines deployed in the Atlantic?" asked McCone quietly. He could see from McGee's expression that the counterintelligence expert had guessed the truth.

"The plots are being coordinated in Bermuda; at the last count we were missing a Juliett," replied Cline.

"How bad is that?" demanded McCone. He was a businessman, not a professional intelligence officer, and he liked to be reminded of the different types of Soviet submarines.

"The Juliett is a new class of long-range submarine," answered Cline. "It's diesel-powered and has four Shaddock nuclear missiles. If it can get close enough to launch against a coastal target, it would be enough to start a global conflict. That, of course, assumes the ELITE channel will retaliate against any nuclear strike in North America."

"Politics are not our business," said McCone, "but I take your point. How much significance do you attach to this single submarine?"

"It really depends on your standpoint," replied McGee evenly, his mind still churning from the realization that the DCI had deliberately withheld vital information from the President. "If Penkovsky's warning is authentic, then the sub has received orders to launch an attack. Perhaps an anticipated confrontation at sea will be the pretext."

"And the *Bucharest* is heading straight for the quarantine line," added Cline.

"Alternatively, this whole scenario may be a political objective and is part of the disinformation project STONE warned us of," said McGee. "Maybe Penkovsky was intended to bring us to this, and Khrushchev is playing a bizarre game to achieve a strategic advantage."

"Like gaining U.S. approval for the deployment of offensive weapons in Cuba?" suggested the DCI.

"Plus a few others, perhaps. Withdrawal of American Jupiters from Italy and Turkey? Or our Thor missiles from England?" added McGee.

"So everything hangs on this *Juliett*," concluded Cline.

"Then find it," demanded McCone. "Anything else?"

"London Station reports that Vassall was sentenced in London yesterday to eighteen years imprisonment," said McGee. "You'll recall that he was part of STONE's meal ticket ... the spy in the British Admiralty. He was arrested last month and he pleaded guilty. It's quite a feather in STONE's cap."

"Unless we find that *Juliett*," replied the DCI, "he won't even serve eighteen days."

"Make that eighteen hours," said Cline quietly.

The DCI looked somber and stroked his chin thoughtfully. "Very shortly I'll be going to see the President and he'll want to know what the PSALM advice is. As I understand it, and I want you gentlemen to correct me, we believe the quarantine will hold. Apart from the Canadians, who are lukewarm, NATO will give full cooperation. In addition, we have secured the West African air routes to Cuba." McCone looked around at the CIA officers assembled before him and they nodded in agreement. "That just leaves the sea," he continued, "and there the threat is twofold: a surface vessel deliberately forcing a passage or a submarine, the missing *Juliett*, initiating a launch."

"If we're contemplating possible confrontation scenarios," offered Smith, "I would be inclined to think in terms of an incident that the Kremlin could use as a pretext. Imagine if the *Bucharest* refuses to stop for one of our warships, and in consequence there is loss of life. This would be presented as aggression on the high seas, and it's possible the *Juliett*'s commander has orders to retaliate, either by sinking the U.S.S. *Gearing* or hitting the mainland."

"Which is in line with ARNIKA's warning," added McGee softly, looking pointedly at the DCI. He was wondering how McCone could be persuaded to tell the President the chilling news that Penkovsky believed a surprise nuclear attack to be imminent.

If McCone registered the edge to McGee's voice, he showed no outward sign of it. "So this speculation depends upon the reliability or otherwise of a single agent," concluded the DCI. "I need to know everything we have on him."

The DCI looked straight at McGee, and the counterintelligence officer shifted uneasily in his chair. Suddenly the issues had been blurred. A few weeks ago it had all been rather academic, depending upon the integrity of a single source working alone. Was he still kosher or had he come under hostile control? His business had been a kind of intellectual exercise that, at worst, would require the analysts to revise their assessment of Soviet missile strengths. Now, nothing was quite so easy. The DCI had deliberately suppressed a report directly affecting the nation's security, and only McGee seemed to have realized McCone's omission. If ARNIKA's doomsday message was true, the captain of a Soviet submarine might at this very moment be bringing four nuclear missiles into a state of readiness in preparation for a sneak attack. But if he was wrong, and the President responded badly, the implications were grotesque. This was, he thought, where you earned your dollar from the taxpayer, and young men grew old prematurely. The trouble was, he recollected, that at this particular minute the President had little idea of the gravity of the situation. He had to persuade McCone to reveal what he knew to the commander in chief.

"Penkovsky is an egomaniac," said McGee, immediately regretting the diagnosis. His mind was in turmoil, wrestling with how to present ARNIKA's case in the best light. This was, he recognized, a poor start. "That's not a pathological condition but more an explanation of his motive. Like almost every other supposedly ideologically pressured agent in history, he has a high regard for himself and contempt for his environment—that includes the system he works under, his family, his contemporaries. His actions, his original approach to us, are all explicable psychologically. He's not crazy. It's just that he has a talent that has gone unrecognized. He regards himself as a genius and is determined to express himself whatever the consequences."

"That is a devastating condemnation," protested Cline, who had a reputation for being loyal to his agents. "He may be shrewd ... he has to have such qualities in order to stay alive, but to portray him as some kind of selfish psychopath is intolerable."

"Let Leo have his say," replied the DCI. "I want to have it all. Too much depends on this for tact and diplomacy."

"ARNIKA isn't certifiable and Ray is quite right in some respects. The guy has guts ... more than his fair share. But he does conform to a type. He's working to a different agenda from everyone else. If you like, he's on a different wavelength, strange values."

"How can you say that?" demanded Cline angrily. "You're implicitly condemning every man who took a risk to save his country. Look at what he's given us. This guy deserves recognition not denigration."

"Exactly," answered McGee. "The hookers, the uniforms, the phony rank. It all adds up to achieving a status that is unattainable in his own society."

"Then you're talking about a psychotic," retorted Cline. "Not someone who has had plenty of opportunities to abandon his family and start afresh with a brand new bank account. He's committed, and not just some guy out for the main chance."

"Hold on," ordered the DCI. "What's all this about hookers and uniforms. Back up."

McGee explained, perhaps a little too uneasily. "Penkovsky has manifested several recognizable characteristics. It's not exactly a superiority complex but he's manipulative. He seeks power over women, and when he went to Paris last year Al Ulmer exhausted his little black book to find him willing companions. The girls had been screened, and ARNIKA turned out to have quite an appetite. I think even Al was a little shocked."

"Anything, er, odd in his sex?" asked McCone delicately.

"All quite normal," reassured McGee.

"So what's this with the uniforms then?"

"All very harmless. But it goes back to his desire for status, for acceptability if you will. We had to give him the uniform of a U.S. Army colonel. He's vulnerable, and the knowledge that he has a certain standing in the West is very important to his self-esteem. It gives him moral support in the early hours when his doubts emerge from the depths."

"Doubts?" asked Smith, surprised.

"We all have them," replied McGee. "Churchill called them 'Black Dog.' Try and remember, we didn't recruit Penkovsky. He recruited himself. He made the decision; he initiated the first approach. He wouldn't be human if he didn't lie awake at night wondering if he had really done the right thing ... betraying the *Rodina*, the motherland. It's a very Russian condition, bitterness mixed with hope. But for us that's an attractive quality because we know of his situation and he can't completely hide his feelings. He can deceive those around him, even his wife and daughter, but he would have difficulty with another emotional somersault."

"So he's psychologically conditioned to retain his loyalty to us?" probed the DCI.

"Yes," answered Smith. "But that's not necessarily the same as telling us the truth all the time. He may be prone to exaggeration, perhaps to enhance his standing with us."

"So, can we rely on his warning? Is he a martyr or is he suffering from a Samson complex, determined to bring the whole structure down with him?" demanded McCone.

This was the crux of the issue and McGee knew it. Was the GRU colonel a highly complex individual seeking to save the West, or a megalomaniac bent on self-destruction and maybe worse?

"If it were my call, I would need more evidence," replied Smith, finally breaking the silence. "Being an agent in hostile territory does strange things to one's perspective. We know he's been under intense pressure. He's very close to his family, despite his philandering in Paris, and he refused our last offer of a way out because his wife was pregnant, or so he said. I'm inclined to believe him. Touching candor combined with a stubborn streak."

"Have we ever known him to be wrong?" asked Cline. He had a talent for only asking questions he knew the answers to.

"We have no reason to disbelieve anything he has ever told us," said McGee forcefully. "The Brits sometimes questioned his ability to gain access to original documents, way outside his sphere of responsibility, but they all look good, even today. It has all checked out."

"What about corroboration? Have other sources verified his story?" asked the DCI.

"The technical stuff has been confirmed with the NSA. He's supplied a mass of data about missile capabilities, and it all seems to neatly dovetail with our telemetry intercepts. His value has been in the strategic field, and even the DIA has never found any fault with his product."

"What about the rest of his information?" pressed McCone.

"Well, the Brits have always beefed about his lack of specifics when it comes to the GRU order-of-battle," admitted McGee. "They wanted names, dates, and places of illegals, but Penkovsky hasn't been forthcoming. He's identified dozens of GRU professionals on embassy lists around the world, but he's yet to actually reveal a spy."

"And should we have expected him to?" asked Cline perceptively.

"Good question. I suppose we really don't know. Either the Russians really do maintain good security, and Penkovsky was sufficiently compartmented to be isolated from that kind of stuff, or there was a limit to the material he was prepared to feed us. The short answer is that we don't know. The GRU is pretty much a closed book to us. There hasn't been a GRU defector to the West since Grigori Tokaev went over to the British more than twelve years ago, and our last source, Piotr Popov, was caught three years ago. Almost everything we know about them comes from Penkovsky or Popov."

"So if he gave us nonsense about the GRU we wouldn't have the means to tell?" asked the DCI.

"It's not quite like that," replied McGee. "The Soviets would be unlikely to risk peddling anything that was obviously bogus in case we possessed the means to double check."

"But isn't the truth that we don't?" observed Smith. "Penkovsky could have told us anything about the GRU and we would have been obliged to accept it."

"Not entirely," said McGee cautiously. "There are external means, surveillance and so forth. The Soviets could never really be sure of the depth of our knowledge."

The DCI was nothing if not astute, and he detected that McGee was venturing onto difficult ground. The CIA's smooth operator was, uncharacteristically, at a disadvantage, but McCone couldn't put his finger on the reason for what he perceived to be McGee's evasion. "Let's be clear about this," he said sternly.

"This is not the moment to be coy. If you know anything germane to this discussion, spit it out. I want to be able to judge how much goes to the President. Jesus ... you know what's at stake here."

"I'm doing my best," replied McGee defensively. "This is a very gray area. We're talking about interpretations, nuances. It's not easy."

"We're talking about national security ... and getting through the next day or so. I need straight answers. Have we the means to verify ARNIKA's information? Yes or no?"

McGee hesitated and looked at the faces on either side of him, which returned his gaze. All had the very highest security clearances, and yet he still felt uneasy. "If the Soviets were controlling Penkovsky, using him as a disinformation agent, they might have used him in conjunction with a mole already inside the CIA. The spy could report back our reactions to his data, and keep him from exposing himself. That's one option."

"Unpalatable, I agree," murmured Smith. "Any evidence to back it up?"

"Testimony from STONE," said McGee. "He's convinced the KGB has planted a deep-cover spy in the Agency."

"But presumably he knows nothing about ARNIKA?" protested Cline.

"It would appear not. STONE has shown inquisitiveness about our windows into the KGB and GRU, but the greatest care has been taken not to reveal our knowledge, or ignorance, when formulating his questionnaires. He should have no reason to suspect an agent, or agents, within either organization on the basis of his interrogations." Almost as soon as he had completed the sentence McGee realized he had made a slip. The DCI seized upon it.

"Plural ... *agents*?" he asked softly.

"I was just coming to that," admitted McGee sheepishly. "There is another method of double-checking RUPEE, the counterintelligence aspects of Penkovsky's data. The FBI is running a walk-in GRU officer at the United Nations in New York. He's relatively low level but he's confirmed all the order-of-battle material supplied by Penkovsky relevant to the United States."

"Is this the super-secret source you've been so protective of?" asked the DCI.

McGee nodded. "It's really a question of legality. The Agency only found out about him because we put him under surveillance in Manhattan. Technically, that was illegal. We can't operate on our home turf."

"Are you saying the Counterintelligence Staff ran an operation against a Soviet at the United Nations, and then realized he was already working for the Bureau?" gasped McCone. "If so, I'm glad I didn't know."

"In a nutshell," agreed McGee.

"How did it happen? I want names ... the lot. And forget about the legal niceties here. We can deal with the inspector general later. Imagine you're talking to the President. You may have to before the day is over."

McGee shrugged his assent. "Penkovsky talent-spotted various GRU cronies as likely candidates for recruitment. One was the naval attaché in London, a man named Eugene Ivanov. MI5 has that in hand at the moment. He also recommended Dmitri Polyakov, who had done a short tour back in 1956 and was reappointed three years ago. He's now a major in the GRU."

"And you couldn't bear to hand him over to the FBI?" asked Smith, aware of what disclosure of the operation would do to the DCI's already strained relations with J. Edgar Hoover.

"It would have expanded the number of people indoctrinated into the case," said McGee in justification. "Sullivan over at the FBI wouldn't have authorized a recruitment operation without knowing the reliability of our information, and we thought Penkovsky quite vulnerable already without bringing more people into the circle. Frankly, we were dubious enough about the expedient of dividing his product into ARNIKA and RUPEE. As a method of protecting a single source, it stank."

"But you couldn't resist making a play for Polyakov," commented McCone.

"Who could refuse?" asked McGee rhetorically. "Ivanov looked good to the Brits. Hard drinking, hard whoring ... and married to the daughter of Aleksandr Gorkin, chairman of the Soviet Supreme

Court. He was a gift for a honeytrap. We thought we might try the same thing on Polyakov."

"What's the status of Ivanov now?" asked McCone.

"The operation has stalled, mainly because MI5 has run into difficulties with a middleman. They haven't given up hope yet."

"So you put this Polyakov under surveillance without consulting me," said the DCI.

"We followed him to a hotel on West 86th Street, and then spotted all the FBI types in the neighborhood. We backed off, and a little later the Bureau began circulating TOP HAT on a very limited basis. Major Dmitri Polyakov is TOP HAT ... QED."

"So the bottom line is that we do have an internal source to verify Penkovsky's authenticity," said Cline, rubbing his beard.

"You could say so," agreed McGee, "but an element of caution is still needed. Remember STONE's scenario. The KGB's disinformation department is engaged in a massive operation to dupe the West. It's a complex business with global implications. It might be farfetched, but it's not impossible that Penkovsky, Ivanov, and Polyakov are all instruments of a Machiavellian scheme—"

"Its purpose being ...?" interrupted McCone.

"Perhaps to establish each other's credentials," mused McGee. "Look at the chronology. Two years ago, Penkovsky appears on the scene and gives the West huge quantities of material ... unprecedented in our experience or, for that matter, that of the Brits. Much better than anything Popov ever gave us. He establishes his bona fides. Then STONE materializes to undermine his credibility. We exercise a degree of prudent skepticism about Penkovsky, and we are suddenly inundated with offers from inside the KGB."

"FOXTROT and SCOTCH," offered Cline. The DCI looked puzzled.

"FOXTROT is the KGB singleton who made a pitch in Geneva in June," explained McGee. "We sent Penkovsky's case officer to look him over. You'll have read Kisevalter's report. FOXTROT is Yuri Nosenko, son of the late Soviet minister for shipping and currently attached to the Second Chief Directorate. SCOTCH is in the same mold. His real name is Viktor Lessiovsky, U Thant's personal assistant at the United Nations and run by the Bureau in New York. So, after years of famine, we have achieved plenty. Of course, it could all be coincidence, but then again it might not."

"Are there any other risky operations that infringe the National Security Act you haven't told me about?" demanded McCone sternly.

"That's the lot," admitted McGee. "SCOTCH and TOP HAT are on the active list. FOXTROT is on hold. He went back to Moscow and said he'll let us know when he wants to make contact again. He was quite adamant about not wanting to defect. Very keen on his family ... shades of Penkovsky."

The DCI looked exasperated. "So what does this tell us about Penkovsky's reliability? Is this man to be trusted? Is the fact that other Soviets have volunteered their services to the West really significant? Isn't that the Agency's *raison d'être:* to attract and run like-minded professionals? If we deny Penkovsky, don't we negate our mission, our mandate?"

McGee was unsure whether the DCI was playing the devil's advocate or merely asking another of those rhetorical questions he favored. Either way, he felt obliged to answer. "Self-doubt comes with the territory. Part of my function is to think the unthinkable and check the obvious as well as the obscure. Human intelligence is like no other. It doesn't work in hundred percent certainties. Penkovsky could have been authentic from day one. I personally believe he was, and so does his case officer. But I also accept that as events have unfolded, we must assume that he has recently come under control. It would be very odd if he was still at liberty, given what happened to Jacob in Moscow on Monday." McGee realized he was thinking out loud, trying to clarify his thoughts on a subject that had tormented him for the past forty-eight hours. He realized the DCI wanted him to reach a conclusion, one that could be delivered to the President over the ELITE channel and be justified by history.

"My instinct is to accept Penkovsky's warning as genuine," said McGee boldly. "I feel reasonably confident that ARNIKA knew what he was doing when he gave the signal. It's my job to look under the rocks, but on this occasion I'd have to opt for a rational explanation. To accept a conspiracy theory in this context is too byzantine, even for my taste. My supposition is that ARNIKA knew he was under KGB surveillance and did his best to warn us. I also think he learned of Khrushchev's plans to launch a surprise attack on the United States. It's a warning that should be taken at face value."

"So unless the *Juliett* is found in the meantime, a confrontation with the *Bucharest* might precipitate a nuclear missile launch?"

"That's a reasonable assumption to make based on ARNIKA's signal," agreed McGee. "Someone ought to tell Admiral Ward not to be too heavy handed tomorrow morning."

Washington, D.C.; Thursday, 25 October 1962

At exactly midday, Joseph J. Gannon eased onto his perch on the fifth floor of the Philip Murray Building in downtown Washington. Unlike the rest of the people working on this floor, which accommodated the American Federation of Labor, he was punctual. The office in which he worked was occasionally borrowed from the AFL because it directly overlooked the Soviet embassy. Gannon was no union organizer. He was an FBI special agent attached to one of the foreign counterintelligence squads based at the Washington Field Office at 1900 Half Moon Street, SW. His particular unit, designated CI-4, was a group of fifteen specialists, mainly of Irish extraction like himself, who maintained surveillance on suspected KGB officers in the Soviet diplomatic community. Other CI sections handled the GRU, the KGB's elite Kontrazvedka personnel, and other Soviets of intelligence interest, but Gannon's target was Aleksandr S. Fomin. It had taken two years of steady observation to note that Fomin's status within the Soviet colony was greater than his supposed position of counselor. The FBI had been tipped off to his dual role by the British, who had noted his undiplomatic duties in 1948 when Fomin had been based in London. In reality, according to STONE, Fomin was Colonel Aleksandr S. Feklisov of the KGB and, as *rezident*, was second in standing only to the ambassador.

Fomin enjoyed a fairly regular routine. He would take an occasional weekend at the forty-acre Soviet enclave at Pioneer Point, near Centreville, Maryland, beside Chesapeake Bay and conveniently close to Annapolis. The remainder of his time was spent either at the embassy on 16th Street or at his apartment in River-

dale. As an experienced professional, he accepted that all his telephone calls were monitored, perhaps even those made from pay
phones on routes he used frequently, but it was information from
other Soviet bloc embassies that had initially revealed Fomin to
be rather more than a mere diplomatic functionary. The Czech
military attaché's cipher clerk had been negotiating his defection
and resettlement in the West, following the example of one of
his predecessors, Frantisek Tisler, and the FBI had given him a
questionnaire to test his bona fides. The FBI already knew the
answers to many of the questions, but the identification of the new
KGB *rezident* had been a "fishing expedition." It would not be
circulated to those on the Allied counterintelligence net as a true
bill until there had been further confirmation. This, fortuitously,
had come from STONE's comprehensive analysis of the KGB's
order-of-battle, together with a hint from FOXTROT, the KGB officer
in Geneva who had made an approach to the CIA early in June.
In addition, the FBI's latest hot case, a GRU major at the United
Nations on his second tour in the commercial capital of "the main
enemy," had come on line. Gannon only knew him as TOP HAT,
having been drafted into Manhattan at short notice to assist on a
countersurveillance mission. Most of the KGB types based at the
U.N. permanent mission, the consulate, and the other Soviet premises were well briefed and knew many of the FBI teams by sight.
So when a really heavy operation was under way, unknown faces
were brought in to man the observation posts.

Although Gannon was not a Psalmist, cleared for that particular
code-worded material, he knew there was a panic on. His brother-
in-law had been recalled from leave early and ordered to join his
unit of mechanized infantry at an obscure depot in Florida. There
had been other signs. The FBI's assistant director in charge of
foreign counterintelligence, William J. Sullivan, had cancelled vaca-
tions long overdue and imposed a new duty roster with unusual
emphasis on the KGB *rezidentura*. This was not the aggressive
harassment seen during the Berlin crisis, when every Soviet had
been tailed with an uncharacteristic lack of subtlety; this was blan-
ket coverage of an unprecedented intensity. Gannon, like his colleagues, assumed that this was just one of the ploys used to put

pressure on the Kremlin. Preventing the spooks from operating normally gave them a whole new perspective and soon made them feel uncomfortable. And when the KGB got edgy, the volume of telegrams back to Moscow Center rose dramatically.

Gannon accepted Fomin as a worthy adversary, another professional. He also had to admit that he was good at his job. He was not like some of the rather unpolished operators from the *rezidentura*, in their shiny, ill-fitting suits, who rarely took any security precautions and were delightfully indiscreet in their apartments—and even on the telephone after a few vodkas. But Fomin was the exception. He spoke good English and bought shirts from Brooks Brothers. His suits and shoes were expensive, and he often stripped down the interior of his Buick, in the privacy of the garage under his apartment building, apparently searching for hidden microphones and homing devices. Unlike more easily spotted KGB men, he maintained quite a rigid work schedule, one with an established pattern that could be monitored easily. He came and went at the same hour, a bureacratic hallmark shared by few in the First Chief Directorate, but he did have one habit that singled him out among his Foreign Ministry friends: He frequently engaged complete strangers in conversation, a maneuver deliberately designed to frustrate the Bureau. Even quite an unremarkable, everyday event such as discarding a newspaper could precipitate a time-consuming investigation, especially if it was left on the subway and pocketed by another straphanger. Fomin executed these diversions with studied nonchalance, apparently oblivious to the confusion his outwardly innocent behavior caused those watching him. Fomin had proved an especially challenging opponent because of his determination to mix with Georgetown society and cultivate contacts in the media. Even some quite well-traveled journalists had fallen for his self-confident, sophisticated charm and mistaken him for a Parisian.

Sullivan's pep talk to the troops had been full of the usual hyperbole—the importance of their assignment, the tense political situation that had followed the President's televised broadcast to the nation on Monday. But there were aspects to the current crisis that made it special. There had been an emergency evacuation exercise, designed to extract key federal employees from Washington to a predetermined rendezvous where they were to be transported in secret to protected locations. The contingency plans had been in existence for years, but they had not been tested before in a dress rehearsal. Nor, in Gannon's memory, had individual agents been instructed to watch particular Soviet chimneys for signs of documents being incinerated. That, of course, had been one of the telltale signs at the Japanese legation in December 1941 that, tragically, had passed unnoticed.

Gannon's morning shift had started with the chase teams passing control of Fomin over to him as he entered the embassy compound. He would remain in command, checking the outside telephone lines and photographing every visitor until his target moved outside, usually at lunchtime, invariably to fulfill an engagement that had been confirmed during an intercepted conversation. Today, Gannon knew, Fomin had a prepaid ticket for a Press Club luncheon where a NASA official would be making a presentation about the space program. Six special agents would cover his journey to and from the embassy, and three more were already at the Press Club checking the seating so he would always be in vision. It looked like a fairly normal day despite the rising temperature over Cuba. Gannon's anticipation of a quiet day was to be proved wrong by the first intercept.

"ABC Television," answered a disembodied voice on Gannon's intercept relay speaker.

"Mr. Scali, please," said Fomin.

"Who's calling?"

"Just say it's Sasha."

"Very well. One moment please." There was a moment's pause.

"Hi, Aleksandr. What can I do for you?" replied the familiar voice of the American Broadcasting Corporation's State Department correspondent.

"I need to talk to you," said Fomin. "Where can we meet?"

"Sure," said the newsman, with a trace of caution. "Let's have lunch." He liked Fomin but was wary of him.

"It must be today. This is urgent." There was an edge to Fomin's heavily accented voice.

"Not today. Don't you know there's a crisis in Washington?" Scali was deliberately baiting the Soviet so as to extract a clue as to the reason for his evident anxiety.

"I know. That's why I have to see you. It's urgent. Can we meet right now?"

Scali was obviously assessing the urgency of Fomin's call. "I can't. I'm just putting some copy to bed. How about after the lunchtime news? You say where."

"Very well. One-thirty? At the Occidental?"

"I'll be there," promised Scali. The connection was then broken.

For Gannon, this was an extraordinary development. Fomin was breaking his routine and making a last-minute lunch appointment at the famous meeting place next to the Willard Hotel. Furthermore, the Soviet had indicated what he wanted to talk about. Suddenly Gannon was on the telephone, giving clipped instructions over the scrambled circuit. When Scali and Fomin turned up at the Occidental, there would be a table prepared for them. It would also be wired for sound so the lunchtime conversation could be transmitted to an inconspicuous, unmarked panel truck parked directly outside. There, the voices would be recorded and, if required, relayed to the FBI's operations room. The necessary arrangements took less than an hour to implement. Later, when Fomin walked the eight or so blocks to the Willard, he was covered all the way, and when the two men met in the restaurant, their voices were clearly heard by Gannon.

"Our two countries are on a collision course," Fomin began abruptly. "That's why I had to see you."

"Well, look who put them there," replied Scali, intrigued by why a Soviet diplomat he had met only occasionally had sought him out.

"There will be terrible consequences," said the Soviet bleakly. "But there is a way out. You must suggest it in the State Department."

"Sure, there's a way out. Just get rid of those missiles," said Scali as he sipped his coffee.

"The missiles are not the issue here," Fomin protested.

"Well, that's interesting. The President says they are. Didn't you watch the broadcast?" Scali made no attempt to disguise the sarcasm.

"But he doesn't know the facts. You must tell him," said the Russian, becoming increasingly agitated.

"What facts?" Suddenly the newsman was interested.

"There is no nuclear threat from Cuba," insisted Fomin.

Scali was disappointed. He suspected that he was about to be peddled some worthless propaganda. "You don't call MRBMs and IRBMs a threat? I've seen the pictures."

"So have I," said the KGB officer. "The photos don't show warheads. There are none."

"Maybe so," said the journalist cautiously. "But that's the point of the blockade. These missiles can't be allowed to become operational. That's not just the administration's policy ... it's U.S. policy. I know that some close to the President would want him to go further. A full-scale invasion may be only hours away."

Fomin paused for a moment. "There will be a disaster tomorrow. American warships will try and board one of our ships. It's madness."

"Are you here to threaten?" asked Scali.

"I'm here because it is our responsibility to find a way out of this situation. I want to make a suggestion."

The television reporter was intrigued. "Go ahead. Does it have any authority?"

Fomin appeared to ignore the question. "It would be a tragic mistake to engineer a confrontation on the high seas. No Soviet vessel can be stopped legitimately. Instead, the United States must offer to make a trade ... the missiles in Cuba to be dismantled in exchange for the American missiles in Turkey and Italy. A fair bargain."

"Wait a moment," said Scali, catching his breath. "You're saying Khrushchev will withdraw the missiles in Cuba if the United States does the same in Turkey and Italy?"

"Precisely. But no boarding of ships."

"How can this work?" demanded Scali, thinking furiously. "If the rockets become operational the whole ball game changes. If the warheads slip past the blockade, Khrushchev could renege on the deal and be in an even stronger position."

235

Fomin wriggled in his seat. "This has nothing to do with the general secretary. He is a man of the past. The people you are talking to will honor our agreement."

"What people? Are you saying Khrushchev is no longer in control in the Kremlin?"

Fomin looked more awkward. "Be assured. Khrushchev will go. He is finished now. The situation in Cuba could be monitored by the United Nations."

"And Castro would agree to that?"

"In return for a pledge from the United States not to invade Cuba again, Castro will allow U.N. inspectors to supervise the removal of the missiles."

"So now it's no U.S. missiles in Turkey and Italy . . . and a nonaggression treaty with Castro?"

"That is the proposal. We must achieve this or there will be a catastrophe tomorrow."

"I don't understand," said Scali. "Why me? Why now? Why were the rockets sent to Cuba in the first place?"

"My friend, this is a complicated issue. Let us just accept the roles that we are given. This is a good compromise. Both sides get part of what they want. Let's leave it at that."

Scali was now very nervous. His initial excitement had given way to a hollow feeling in his stomach. "No way. I need to know who I'm dealing with here. You're asking for Kennedy to guarantee Castro's future, and for him to screw two of his NATO allies. In return, Cuba will return to the status quo and Khrushchev will disappear. No one will believe me."

Fomin was deadly earnest. "You know everyone in Washington. They will listen to you."

"I'm not so sure. And you still haven't answered a very fundamental question. Why now? This must have been planned months ago."

"There was a single motive for deploying our missiles in Cuba . . . parity. The only way we can achieve equality in strategic weapons with the United States is to place our shorter-range rockets closer to North America."

Scali had already worked out and accepted the logic behind the

Kremlin's strategy. It had been the sole topic of conversation in Washington for the past two days. "And they were spotted just in time?"

"No," answered Fomin, his calm restored now that he had seized Scali's attention. "The Politburo was only informed on Tuesday that the CIA had planted a spy in Moscow. He betrayed the relative weakness of our missiles. The KGB says that the CIA has known for the past eighteen months of the technical problems that have wrecked the Soviet strategic missile program."

"Who was this spy?" demanded Scali. He recognized another astonishing news story in the making.

"His name is Penkovsky. He told the Americans everything. He has been arrested and he has confessed."

"I've never heard of this guy," replied Scali evenly, making a mental note of the name. "But how can one man have precipitated all of this? It's not possible."

"Oh, yes, my friend. It has happened. Believe me. Ask your State Department about the incident in Moscow on Monday, when a CIA agent was caught red-handed. They will tell you."

Scali was not entirely persuaded. "But if this spy has revealed the Soviet weakness as you say, why are you suggesting a compromise? Nothing has really changed, apart from the KGB now knowing the depth of the CIA's knowledge."

"I told you it was a complex matter. Some elements backed Khrushchev's plan to compensate for the lack of progress in the development of a reliable Soviet intercontinental missile. The solution was deployment of our existing inventory in Cuba, which would either have given the Soviet Union strategic parity or a chance to negotiate the removal of similar NATO weapons in the equivalent countries in the Mediterranean. The idea was opposed by a powerful faction of opportunists who now realize that the traitor Penkovsky has jeopardized everything. The Americans have learned prematurely of the missiles in Cuba, and they know Moscow is impotent to launch a credible, first-strike attack. The certainty that the *Rodina* is vulnerable demands immediate action. Hence the confrontation tomorrow. We shall all regret it unless it can be averted."

"Are you saying that a group within the Politburo intends to use the blockade as a pretext to launch a preemptive strike against the United States?" asked Scali, ashen-faced. "How can this be possible? It's a strategy that's doomed."

Fomin shrugged. "The signs were there for all to see, but no one noticed. The Strategic Rocket Force was created by Khrushchev three years ago, an entirely new service. Then, just a few months ago, at least two senior officials were dismissed for opposing the Cuban scheme. General Golikov was the director of the Main Political Administration of the Armed Forces, and General Moskalenko was the deputy minister of defense and chief of the Strategic Rocket Force. Both advised against Khrushchev's desperate machinations and were dismissed. After that, there were only those left who sought to take matters a stage further."

"And these are the people who will risk a nuclear war on this issue?" challenged Scali.

For the first time, Fomin smiled. "Now, at last, I think you understand the situation. If you can make the Pentagon see sense, it will avert the unthinkable. For our part, we will isolate Khrushchev and his cronies."

Scali was thinking fast. This was not a news story, it was history. "I'll convey your message, and call you again."

"Don't call," said Fomin with urgency in his voice. "This is not something we can talk about. Let's arrange a meeting place now, close to the embassy."

"Very well. What about the coffee shop in the Statler?"

Fomin nodded in agreement. "Just let me know the time to meet and I will await your call. Timing is critical. Do not leave it too long."

Scali left the Occidental and took a cab to the State Department in search of Dean Rusk, but even before he had reached the entrance to the restaurant Gannon had arranged for a transcript of the recording to be typed up and passed to his assistant director. Gannon knew that back channels were exploited by diplomats on both sides as informal, deniable conduits, but this episode was more than a tentative approach to the U.S. government. It was the initiation of negotiations with an unknown group in the Kremlin, undoubtedly backed by the KGB to judge by Fomin's involvement, and the Soviets had chosen a newsman to deal with. Gannon was not sure why Fomin had selected Scali. Had he been an agent or sympathizer? Certainly neither had said or done anything to make one believe it. So, was it because Scali enjoyed good connections, which he undoubtedly did? Or was this part of a deception campaign to be perpetrated on the American media? He felt relieved that it was not his responsibility to decide. His task was to keep Fomin under observation, report on his contacts, and prepare suitable technical coverage at the Statler's coffee shop.

At twenty past seven the same evening Fomin walked out of the Soviet embassy, crossed the street to the Statler, and selected a table in the coffee shop that had just been vacated. He ordered a coffee; a few minutes later he was joined by Scali. If either man suspected that moments before his arrival Fomin's table had been occupied by two FBI special agents, and that most of the other customers were either their Bureau colleagues or CIA officers, neither showed any outward sign.

"Is the State Department willing to make a deal?" demanded Fomin impatiently. His voice was picked up clearly by the microphone concealed in the ashtray inches from his coffee cup.

"I think so," replied Scali. "But the offer will have to go through proper channels."

"Of course," said the Russian gravely. "The American embassy in Moscow will receive a letter in the usual way later tonight. But did you go right to the top? We have to know that."

Scali reassured him. "This has been cleared at the highest level. I can say no more than that. But one point was made to me: Once the bases in Cuba have been dismantled, there would have to be a promise not to replace them at a later date."

Fomin nodded enthusiastically. "I am sure that can be arranged. As a quid pro quo, would the White House agree to have the United Nations inspect certain military bases in Florida so no invasion could be launched?"

Scali looked doubtful. "You never mentioned that before. I think an extra condition would complicate matters. Let's not push our luck. I gather a guarantee for Castro's regime might be forthcoming. That's practically the same thing."

Fomin seemed to accept this and hurried off, muttering about the urgency of the situation. The encounter had lasted only a few moments, and as Scali rose to leave, he noticed that the Soviet was a heavy tipper. He had left the waitress a five-dollar bill for a thirty-cent check.

Kindley Field, Bermuda;
Thursday, 25 October 1962

It had been an odd kind of quarantine, Waters thought. Inside the map room he could see the route lines, marked in colored grease pencils on the huge Mercator projection of the western Atlantic. It was clear from the display that the *Bucharest* had been allowed through the U.S. Navy's line. And Waters knew, from having spent the past three hours hunched over the principal intercept desk, that the tanker had failed to stop when challenged by the U.S.S. *Gearing*. The Soviet skipper's declaration, over the marine frequency, that he was only carrying petroleum products had apparently been enough to satisfy the Americans. No boarding had taken place, and no threats had been issued. Yet the whole point of the blockade, reasoned Waters, was to inspect cargoes for contraband. His suspicions had been heightened by the treatment afforded to the *Coolangaata*, a Swedish freighter under Soviet charter. That, too, had failed to stop, in defiance of the President's broadcast and in spite of the presence of twenty-five destroyers, two cruisers, and an aircraft carrier. Waters had been sufficiently puzzled by the lack of American action to raise the issue with Jim Torwood, who had continued to command the Ops Center regardless of his prime minister's instructions.

"Why are we going to all this trouble to monitor the merchant traffic destined for Cuba if Task Force 136 isn't enforcing the blockade?" asked Waters.

"Our task is to feed in the intelligence," replied the Canadian. "It's up to the ELITE channel to call the shots."

"Ours is not to reason why?"

"It's a little weird, I agree," said Torwood, "but maybe the *Bucharest*'s cargo has been verified already."

"And the *Coolangaata*, too?" Waters was unconvinced.

"Okay. I take your point. But let me put it this way: Would you like to order a ship to stop, and then stop yourself, if you knew there was a hostile submarine in the area, armed with at least ten torpedoes."

"The missing *Juliett*?" suggested Waters.

"I just talked to the liaison officer at Tudor Hill," confided Torwood. "There's a real panic on about it. The skipper is an experienced professional and he's made his craft disappear. There's no trace of the *Juliett* anywhere."

"Why can't CAESAR pick it up?" asked Waters. "I was told in Gibraltar that the SOSUS arrays are extraordinarily sensitive and can hear a Soviet diesel engine hundreds of miles away." It seemed illogical to the radioman that with so much technology applied to finding a single submarine it could disappear. It made him uneasy at a moment when there was already too much to worry about.

"Sure they can," confirmed Torwood with a trace of admiration in his voice. "But this guy has been using all the surface naval activity to cover his movements. There are around sixty warships working the quarantine line under Cruise Condition Three, which is no lights visible and only limited communications. Look at our wall map: nineteen Soviet vessels, six Easteren bloc, and twenty-three Soviet charters, together with the other nationalities ... three Greek, two British, one Spaniard, and an Italian. Each one is an opportunity for an enterprising submarine captain determined to avoid being located, especially when the U.S. Navy is thrashing around at a flank speed of twenty-seven knots. That generates a lot of noise."

"But they're sure to catch him eventually, aren't they?" asked Waters, betraying his mounting anxiety.

"That's what they thought at Tudor Hill yesterday, and the day before that," said the naval officer, studying the wall map. The unspoken fear on Waters's face had reached him. "Now they're not so sure. They know he's closed the SOSUS field between here and the Bahamas, but now he's gone quiet. It doesn't look good. As long as he's on the loose, Washington is reluctant to get tough with a Russian ship."

"Which is why they let the *Bucharest* through," murmured Waters thoughtfully. He knew there was a single renegade Soviet on the loose, and he was acutely aware of what was at stake.

"Probably. I guess they knew what the tanker was carrying, and the same went for the Swede, but the *Marucla* is different."

"The Soviet charter?" Waters concentrated on the trace of red grease pencil that tracked the ship across the Atlantic.

"Yeah. It left Riga on 3 October and should reach the limit tomorrow evening," said Torwood, leafing through a sheaf of tele-printer paper that represented the latest recorded track data of each vessel. "Naval Intelligence says it's a good candidate for car-rying strategic materiel, so the Americans have got to stop it. If they don't, the blockade will lose its credibility and the missiles already in position will be that much closer to an operational sta-tus. Washington may have been able to fudge the *Bucharest* and the *Coolangaata*, but this one will be the crunch." Although as a Canadian Torwood was supposed to be detached from this opera-tion, he found it impossible to stand aside. He felt a professional pride in the skills being exercised in the Ops Center, and a deep chill at the way events were unfolding.

"Which means there's less than twenty-four hours in which to find the *Juliett*," added Waters, wondering if others had reached the same conclusion. Did Washington really understand what was happening out here, he wondered.

"That's why they're tearing their hair out at Tudor Hill. They don't have a clue," agreed Torwood.

The two men lapsed into silence. So much depended on locating the *Juliett*, but they felt powerless to help the search. There was a vast expanse of ocean and the Soviet had all the advantages. "Just how easy is it to hide a submarine?" asked Waters, moving his finger across the Caribbean, squinting at the tiny print identi-fying some of the more exotic islands.

"There are two options," replied Torwood. He was a professional naval officer and had attended all the NATO staff courses on anti-submarine warfare. He had also spent time at sea on a Canadian destroyer, but his knowledge was strictly theoretical. The ship on which he had served as communications officer had limped into Halifax with engine trouble before it had played its intended part in a NATO exercise off Nova Scotia. Nor had he encountered any potentially hostile contacts while showing the flag in Haiti. He was sensitive to the widely held view in Britain and the United States that Canadians don't take their navy seriously, and he had heard the joke about Canadian ships being vulnerable to rust-seeking missiles too often. He was determined to demonstrate his professionalism. "If it's moving it can keep close to the thermoclines and use passive sonar to avoid detection. It can also exploit the 'noise shadows' of surface ships and, as a last resort, use noisemakers as decoys to distract the hunters. If it's immobile, it's a question of taking refuge at depth, and keeping very quiet."

"And that will defeat sonar?" asked Waters thoughtfully.

"Eliminating the source sound will prevent the passive arrays from locking onto a target, but the sheer bulk of the submarine still presents a handsome profile for active sonar and the magnetic anomaly detectors," said the Canadian, as though he was reading from a textbook. He knew them all well enough; he could easily conceal his lack of practical experience.

"So what's the antidote?" demanded Waters. He felt there had to be a logical solution to the puzzle, just as there always was in the radio world. Signals weren't transmitted accidentally. There was a purpose, meaning, and source for them all. Identifying them had been his life.

"Perhaps sheltering under a geological structure, an overhang to shield the craft from surface sonar, or behind an existing ferrous mass," speculated the Canadian. Now he was venturing into a more difficult area.

"What's that?" asked Waters, surprised.

"It might be an outcrop of iron ore, or nodules on the ocean floor, or even a shipwreck. They all give a positive return on an anomaly detector, maybe strong enough to shield a submarine."

"Is that likely?" Waters was evidently determined to pursue the issue.

"Difficult to say," countered Torwood, increasingly uncertain of his ground. He knew the theory, but was all this really happening now, he wondered. "It depends on the amount of homework done by an individual submarine commander. These sites would have to be surveyed well in advance, and it would take great skill to exploit a topographical feature, particularly if the skipper was denied the use of sonar to maneuver his boat."

"So if the *Juliett* is trying to lie doggo, it must have planned the exercise well in advance?"

"That's a fair deduction, if the submarine has any chance of survival in a shooting war. Contingency arrangements would have been made long ago, all part and parcel of modern underwater warfare."

"And would the Americans as well as the Russians have surveyed convenient spots where submarines could sit without being noticed?"

"Of course. Both sides take enormous trouble to map out the contours of the sea bottom, and the plots of wrecks are openly available to anyone buying a chart."

"Then ... where is the *Juliett*?"

"Beats me. The U.S. Navy has deployed all its resources, and the air force is flying round the clock. All for a single, solitary Red. If it wasn't so deadly serious, it would be comic. We're talking about millions of dollars being spent every hour to trace a lone Soviet operating in Uncle Sam's backyard. Furthermore, they have the advantage of not needing to maintain real wartime conditions."

"The Americans, how so?"

"Everything is weighted in their favor. They're on home turf, and there is no surface threat within a hundred miles. Even the underwater threat has been reduced to a minimum—a new, untried diesel. They enjoy overwhelming numerical superiority and they can use active sonar to their heart's content, without risk. That's what the *Juliett* is pitched against. It hardly stands a chance."

"But it does, provided it can lie low for the next day or so," asserted Waters.

Torwood shook his head vigorously. "Not so, we may be working to that time scale, but the Russian skipper isn't. He has no idea what's going on in the outside world. He can't communicate with

Murmansk, or even one of the merchantmen close by. If he did, we would nail him instantly. He's blind and dumb. He can't use his active sonar for fear of alerting us, and he can't signal base. Either way, he's dead. If he surfaces, we'll spot him, and the merest hint of him using his radar will bring us running. There's no question about this; he got his orders from the *Atrek*, and he has no viable means of sending a signal."

"But can he receive without danger," observed Waters. He was thinking aloud, and his mind was racing. Perhaps the solution lay in signals, and he could make a contribution here, after all.

"It's not exactly foolproof. He can either float a buoy on the surface or raise an aerial, but both are vulnerable to aircraft. Alternatively, he can trail an antenna from his stern, but there are hazards to that, too."

"Such as?" wondered Waters. An idea was forming in his mind but he had not specialized in submarine communications. He knew some of the background but not the full story. It was another one of those compartmented secret topics that only specially indoctrinated personnel could study.

"He'll only catch the signal at a shallow depth, so he'll be susceptible to detection from infrared, magnetic anomaly, and, in this weather, visual identification in the clear sea," explained Torwood. "Just take my word for it, no commander is going to risk his boat and crew by coming near to the surface except at night."

"Then he can't send or receive," concluded Waters. He was trying to visualize the Soviet submarine commander, get a feel for his isolation.

"Not without the risk of compromising his mission," remarked Torwood. "Standard procedure would call for him to listen at predetermined times, but the Red Banner headquarters would not expect an acknowledgment until the sub was safely back inside the Soviet territorial limit."

"So the Soviets will be transmitting on a regular schedule?"

"Yes, but that doesn't help us. The *Juliett* probably comes to periscope depth after dark and uses its snorkel to recharge its batteries. No doubt it raises a radio mast at the same time."

"Which would be virtually impossible to spot at night?" Waters was racking his brains. He was trying to get inside the head of a Russian who now, more than any time in the past, was feeling the loneliness of command.

"If a reconnaissance aircraft happened to be in the area it might catch the snorkel on radar, or have it show up on the MAD ... if the operator was paying attention," added the Canadian. "A positive return on either would lead to a sonar sweep, and the submarine's detection."

"Considering the importance of its mission, would the *Juliett* risk all that?" asked Waters. Why would the Soviet jeopardize his mission?

"It would have no choice. The diesel electric design of submarines is not only of World War Two vintage, it's really an arrangement for what is essentially a surface vessel to spend a limited time underwater. Sure, the *Atrek* will have refueled and replenished the *Juliett*, so it's not constrained by other factors, but it still has to run its diesels to top up the batteries for the electric motor."

"Which, presumably, is a noisy undertaking and susceptible to passive sonar." Waters tried another tack.

Torwood nodded in agreement. "The submarine commander will choose his spot carefully, well away from any known SOSUS arrays, and he'll use his electronic countermeasures to avoid being caught by one of our airborne maritime patrols."

"The *Juliett*'s ECM will be a radar detector?"

"Naval Intelligence reports that the *Juliett* has a standard ECM mast that combines a radar detector and a direction-finder. I have a file on the *Juliett* here, somewhere," said Torwood as he rummaged through the papers strewn across a long trestle table. "If any ship or aircraft approaches displaying radar, the ECM will give enough warning for the submarine to go deep. It will also advise where the threat is coming from, so the skipper can steer away from that quadrant."

"According to your scenario, then, there is very little chance of finding the *Juliett* unless one of our aircraft comes across it by accident, and the commander is quite careless." Waters was deliberately narrowing all the options open to the Soviet.

"And judging by his performance so far, the evidence suggests the very opposite," said Torwood. The more he thought about the *Juliett*, the more he had to admire what its commander had accomplished.

"Which in turn suggests that if the *Marucla* is fired upon, the *Juliett* will receive an order to retaliate the next time it tunes in to Moscow."

Torwood nodded. "That's about the size of it. If the *Marucla* continues on her present course and speed, she will be challenged to stop around dusk tomorrow, leaving plenty of time for the *Juliett* to raise its antenna under cover of darkness, get the launch command, surface, and fire its missiles."

Waters pondered the conundrum. "The Shaddock only has a range of a couple of hundred miles, so that considerably reduces the amount of ocean it has to operate in. Since we know the *Juliett*'s maximum speed submerged, we should be able to determine roughly where it is."

"That's all very well," Torwood pointed out, "but you're talking about thousands of square miles to search. It's a tall order, especially when you consider that all the *Juliett* has to do is keep still and silent."

"But if the *Juliett*'s commander knows the entire U.S. Navy is out searching for him, he's not going to park anywhere, is he? He'll want security. He won't just choose any old spot to bed down ... he'll want a measure of protection from sonar and the anomaly detectors."

"I agree," replied Torwood, "but his choice is quite small. The ferrous sites are known to both sides, and they will be checked regularly. So will the shipwrecks. They have all been surveyed and, as you would expect, most occur along the coral reefs and would be too shallow to offer any comfort to something the size of a Juliett class. That leaves a geological formation, known only to the Russians and not to the Americans, under which a submarine can hide. It's just too improbable ... imagine trying to maneuver the boat into position ... blind and without one's normal active navigational aids. It would be impossible, especially if the exercise had to be repeated every night when the sub goes up for air."

"And what if the Soviets knew of a deep-water wreck, in the right area, that was unknown to the Americans?"

Torwood shook his head. "Very improbable. The United States has spent years conducting oceanographic research for precisely this reason. They would be bound to have surveyed most of the wrecks, and anyway, the Russians wouldn't want to risk using a location that *might* be known to the Americans."

"But supposing the Soviets could be *sure* a particular site was undiscovered?" pressed Waters. An idea had occurred to him and he needed to eliminate all the options.

"I don't really see how they could ever be confident of a negative like that without access to the U.S. Navy's classified survey of magnetic anomalies in the region. Without that, there'd be too much risk involved. Anyway, what are you driving at?"

"Bear with me for a moment," pleaded Waters. "Just suppose for a second that the Russians knew a particular wreck had not been found. Wouldn't they be attracted to it?"

"Not necessarily. An old wreck, like that of a U-boat victim from the last war, might just as easily be discovered in an intensive search with anomaly detectors as an operational submarine. Its profile, or return on the MAD computer, would be compared with others already logged into the memory. There is a world of difference between the signal of a big cargo vessel, with flat hull plates, and the relatively long, rounded, slim lines of a submarine. The MAD computer can discriminate between the two in a matter of seconds. And in today's conditions, close to a shooting war, any new find would be subjected to a sonar scan just to make sure there was no sub nestling close to whatever remained of the superstructure. In short, even an undiscovered wreck on the seabed would not be a sufficient guarantee of no interference from the searchers. Sorry, but there goes your theory. Unfortunately, we are still no further ahead."

"On the contrary," replied Waters triumphantly, "I think I know exactly where the *Juliett* is hiding."

Waters had offered two reasons why he should be excused temporarily from the Operational Intelligence Center on Kindley Field, and both had been accepted. The first was that he needed a break from the stifling atmosphere of the windowless building, and the second was that much of his work had been completed. The *Marucla* had been settled upon as the first Soviet to be stopped and inspected and that event was, by the latest calculations, still some hours away. The task of monitoring the movements of the remaining suspect ships was a routine affair, easily mastered by the other intercept operators manning the banks of DF consoles. It had been the vague hope from Waters that he might be able to give a clue to the missing *Juliett*'s location that had persuaded Torwood to lend Waters his car and driver for a quick visit down to Southampton. He had also supplied him with the other items Waters had requested: a chart of the eastern Caribbean, a ruler, compass and dividers, and the weather reports for the area for a particular three-day period in February 1942. Just under two hours later, he was back at Torwood's desk in the OTC, having spread the chart in front of the Canadian.

"As they say in the buried treasure movies, X marks the spot," announced Waters. "Or if not the exact spot, then I'll bet the *Juliett* is along this line." He traced a route on the chart, north of the tiny British possession of Anguilla.

"We can certainly pass it on," answered Torwood skeptically, "but what on earth makes you think this is where the sub is?"

"Let me explain my idea first," said Waters. "You mentioned that if the Americans came across a new shipwreck while searching for the *Juliett*, the magnetic anomaly detectors would instantly discriminate between the large mass of a ship and the much smaller return from a submarine?"

"Correct."

"Then tell me what would happen if, say, a P-6 maritime patrol aircraft came across the wreck of a really enormous submarine?"

"But that makes no sense," protested Torwood. "There may be a few U-boats left down in the Caribbean, but their locations would be well known. And anyway, they would not be significantly different in size from a Juliett."

"I'm not talking about an old U-boat," explained Waters. "I'm thinking of a monster of a submarine ... a submersible cruiser."

"Was there such a thing?"

"There was indeed, the *Surcouf*. It was lost with all hands in February 1942, right about here," he said, tapping the chart.

"If it's so big, how come the wreck hasn't been found?" Torwood was intrigued but unconvinced. Nevertheless, he was willing to hear what his English subordinate had to say.

"Because," answered Waters, "quite simply, nobody really knew where to look. The *Surcouf* was a renegade French submarine, of enormous dimensions. It was big enough to have an aircraft hangar on the stern and a gun turret mounted on the foredeck sufficiently large to do justice to a surface cruiser. It left Bermuda on 17 February 1942 with orders to sail to Tahiti via the Panama Canal; once she cleared the reef off Dockyard she was never seen again. The alarm was raised only when she failed to turn up at the canal, and according to my contact who has researched the incident for the BBC, the search backtracked on the *Surcouf*'s supposed route from Bermuda via Jamaica."

"Then why was no trace found?" demanded Torwood. He knew that even in wartime the air-sea rescue searches had been intensive.

"Because the *Surcouf* was way off its proper course when it sank," explained Waters. "It is my belief that it never intended to go to Tahiti. In fact, it was headed to Vichy-held Martinique when it went down and, just to add to the confusion, an American freighter reported having struck something at night, and it was assumed that this had been the *Surcouf*'s fate."

"And what makes you think it wasn't?" asked Torwood as his gaze moved back to the converging lines on the wall map. The urgency of the situation was increasing by the moment, and he needed to be persuaded.

Waters realized he was going to have to justify his proposition, however outlandish it sounded. "The BBC found a retired naval diver, still living here in Bermuda, in Southampton in fact, who swears he sabotaged the *Surcouf* just before she left Dockyard."

"And that's who you've been to see?" The Canadian could scarcely conceal his disappointment. Bloody Waters was basing his hypothesis on the memory of some ancient mariner.

"Right." Waters was unapologetic. "I needed to know the exact timing of the charge attached to the *Surcouf*, and the time she slipped her moorings. We know that she was unable to submerge, and we can estimate her speed, which, if Martinique really was her destination, would place her about here on the chart, rather to the north of Anguilla."

"What makes you think the wreck of the *Surcouf* has never been discovered, at least by the Americans?" Torwood knew he was going to have difficulty with something so improbable. His initial reaction was that he had never heard of the *Surcouf*, but then, before he said anything, he tried to remember whether there hadn't been talk of some monstrous French wartime submarine when he had been up in Halifax.

"Because the whole case was, and is, a great cause célèbre," continued Waters, "one of the great unsolved mysteries of the last war, if you like. Finding the *Surcouf* would be like finding the *Titanic* ... headline news, at least in France. Also, the site would be declared an official war grave by the French government and placed out of bounds to divers. None of those things have happened because only a handful of people actually knew what had happened to the *Surcouf*, and they had their reasons for keeping quiet."

"And you think the Russians found it?" suggested Torwood. Now he thought he did remember something about the *Surcouf*. Hadn't it liberated the Vichy islands of St. Pierre and Miquelon, off the St. Lawrence?

"That's my guess," agreed Waters, concentrating hard on the chart, oblivious to Torwood's change in heart. "Perhaps they stumbled across it while looking for suitable boltholes in the Caribbean, or possible a Soviet mole learned of the affair and gave the information to the KGB so it could be used to its advantage. Exactly how they found it doesn't matter. It's a question of whether, if I'm right, they have used it to conceal the *Juliett*."

"I admit it's an intriguing solution ..." Torwood was warming to the idea. "A rather daring double bluff to hide a relatively small submarine right beside a really huge one. The return on the MAD would be much too big for the *Juliett*, and that's the data the computer would spit out. A sonar scan would show one big submarine, not two."

"And you'll note that the course I've drawn on the chart, a straight line from Bermuda to Martinique, would take the *Surcouf* very close to the *Juliett*'s operating area, based on the Shaddock's range of 250 nautical miles, with an additional allowance for the distance the sub could cover submerged, at fourteen knots."

"Quite a coincidence." Torwood was impressed.

"Maybe. But look at it from the Soviet point of view. They locate this huge wreck and identify it. That wouldn't be too difficult because the *Surcouf* was absolutely unique. There could be no mistaking it for another submarine, or even a warship. She was utterly distinctive. Then consider that, rather unusually, they could be certain that the site had not been discovered by the Americans, because of the *Surcouf*'s notoriety. Such a find would be big news. From the *Juliett*'s standpoint, the wreck must be very attractive ... certainly offering more hope than keeping on the move while the U.S. Navy deploys an entire fleet just overhead. And let's look at the worst-case scenario: The *Surcouf* shows up on the screen of a hostile maritime patrol aircraft. Unless divers go down to carry out a visual inspection, or a really intensive sonar survey is conducted, the smaller *Juliett* is likely to escape discovery. And in combat conditions neither option is really likely. Once a ship or plane had satisfied itself that the *Juliett* was not an active threat, it would hurry on to continue the search pattern, leaving the submarine to shelter in the wreck's sonar and MAD shadow."

"If your thesis is correct we'd better get these coordinates to Jacksonville straightaway," murmured Torwood, poring over the chart and calculating the longitude, "before it's too late."

Epilogue

With no publicity whatever, the Soviet Union's sole Juliett-class missile boat was forced to the surface in the eastern Caribbean in the early hours of Friday, 26 October 1962. The operation had been conducted by a squadron of P-6 maritime reconnaissance aircraft working with a flotilla of five destroyers led by the U.S.S. *Wasp*. During the same morning the East German liner *Voelkerfreundschaft* was allowed through the quarantine line without inspection. However, when the *Marucla* approached at seven o'clock the same evening, it was ordered to heave to by the U.S.S. *John R. Pierce* and the U.S.S. *Joseph P. Kennedy, Jr.* The *Marucla*'s captain, Georgios Condorigos, agreed to a boarding request, and declared his cargo to be sulphur, newsprint rolls, twelve Soviet-built trucks, and some assorted spare parts.

Satisfied there was no contraband aboard, the captain of the U.S.S. *John R. Pierce*, Nicolas M. Mikhalevsky, allowed the *Marucla* to proceed; it got under way at about nine o'clock without incident. Ironically, Mikhalevsky was himself of Russian origin, having been born in Sevnica, Yugoslavia, to a family of Russian refugees from St. Petersburg. As the *Marucla* steamed away into the darkness, Mikhalevsky received orders to stop and search another Soviet vessel, the *Grozny*, a tanker carrying ammonia destined for the nickel refinery at Nicaro.

The rest of the world became aware that the Cuban missile crisis had ended the following day, Saturday, when it was announced that in an exchange of letters with President Kennedy, Nikita Khrushchev had agreed to the immediate withdrawal of all Soviet bombers, IRBMs, and MRBMs from Cuba. The fact that Kennedy had secretly promised to dismantle the thirty Jupiter IRBMs in Italy, the fifteen in Turkey, and the sixty Thor IRBMs in Britain— a decision bitterly opposed by NATO's General Lauris Norstad— was undisclosed. Nor was any mention made of the President's undertaking not to subvert Castro's regime. In the eyes of many, the world had only just stepped back from the brink of a nuclear exchange. By Monday afternoon, U.N. General Secretary U Thant had arrived in Cuba, accompanied by his special assistant, Viktor Lessiovsky, to mediate with Castro.

He was followed on Friday, 2 November, by Foreign Minister Anastas I. Mikoyan, who flew to Havana, via New York, to persuade Castro to accept the Soviet withdrawal and supervise the dismantling of the missile bases and the crating of the Beagles. This proved to be one of the most difficult tasks of his long career, and Castro did not give his consent to the removal of the bombers until 19 November. The United States monitored these events through the *Oxford*, still on station in the Caribbean, which successfully intercepted much of Mikoyan's signal traffic, including a rather poignant telegram informing him of the death of his wife. Instead of returning to Moscow for the funeral, Mikoyan chose to stay in Cuba to complete his assignment. A fleet of forty-four Soviet merchantmen, led by the *Bratsk, Divnogorsk*, and *Metallurg Anosov*, arrived to remove the offending weapons, and the ships obligingly uncovered their cargos so they could be inspected on their voyage home by American photoreconnaissance aircraft. The blockade was eventually lifted after just twenty-seven days, when the last of the Ilyushin-28s was carried back across the Atlantic. The weaponry accumulated over so many months, and brought to Cuba by no less than 167 ships, was removed in less than two weeks.

The conclusion of the crisis was not, however, without incident. Shortly before Khrushchev's final letter arrived at the White House, confirming terms of the settlement, a U-2 aircraft on a routine HASP mission from Elieson Air Force Base in Alaska lost its bearings and accidentally strayed over the Chukotsk Peninsula, provoking a major air defense alert in the Soviet Union. U.S. and Soviet fighters were scrambled simultaneously, and the errant plane was escorted safely back to American airspace without any shots fired. Perhaps coincidentally, the FBI reported that the Soviet embassy in Washington had begun to burn its archives at about the same time.

The final episode, for the Psalmists, was marked by the tragic loss of Major Rudolf Anderson on Saturday, 27 October, shot down with his U-2 over eastern Cuba just after dawn. Aged thirty-five, Anderson was an experienced fighter pilot who had flown classified reconnaissance missions in Super Sabres throughout Korea and the Far East. In 1955 he had returned from overseas and, as a Psalmist, had been stationed at Laughlin Air Force Base at Del Rio, Texas. The holder of the Distinguished Flying Cross with two oakleaf clusters, Anderson's objective had been to photograph uncrated Ilyushin-28s at San Julian, and overfly Banes, but his plane had been hit by a SA-2 Guideline. A secret Soviet inquiry was subsequently held into the incident, and it was determined that the surface-to-air missile had been fired on orders from General Igor D. Statsenko, without authority from Moscow.

In the aftermath of the crisis, Generals Moskalenko and Golikov were restored to their posts, and in October 1964, two years after these events, Nikita Khrushchev was the victim of a Kremlin coup.

The one unexplained aspect to the entire affair, which remains a mystery to this day, was the role played by the young American defector, the ex-marine who successfully evaded the FBI's surveillance in mid-October 1962. Soon after the crisis he reemerged and, still working at Jaggars-Chiles-Stovall, moved into a new ground-floor apartment on Elsbeth Street, in the Oakcliff district of Dallas. A year later, on 27 September 1963, he made two visits to the Soviet embassy in Mexico City and was interviewed on both occasions by Valeri V. Kostikov, a known KGB officer under diplomatic cover. He had given up his job and was keen to travel to Moscow via Havana. He also called by telephone, and went to the Cuban embassy twice. All of this had been routinely monitored by the local CIA station, headed by Winston Scott, a veteran who had been in Mexico since 1956. Three days later the young man returned to Texas, apparently without the visas he had applied for and, on 10 October 1963, the FBI in Washington received a copy of Scott's report from Mexico.

The young man had been positively identified by the CIA and the FBI, but again he managed to drop from view, this time by finding a room in North Beckley Street in Dallas and taking a menial job in the Texas Book Depository, where he was working on the morning of 22 November 1963.

Postscript

Colonel Oleg Penkovsky was sentenced to death after a short trial, and on 16 May 1963 it was announced that he had been shot by a firing squad.

George Kisevalter, the brilliant CIA case officer who ran Penkovsky and FOXTROT, has now retired from the CIA and lives in McLean, Virginia.

STONE still lives under an assumed name in the United States. He initially bought a farm in upstate New York but, after the tragic death of his daughter from a drug overdose, Anatoli and Svetlana moved to Florida.

FOXTROT defected to the CIA in February 1964 and was revealed as Yuri Nosenko, but he never succeeded in persuading his critics that he was not a KGB plant. He underwent 292 interrogations during a period of three and a half years of solitary confinement. He was rewarded with a consultancy post with the CIA.

Viktor Lessiovsky, U Thant's special assistant, rose to the rank of colonel in the KGB in spite of his eventual identification as the FBI's source code named FEDORA. He died in Moscow some years ago, as did General Dmitri Polyakov, who was known to the American intelligence community as TOP HAT.

Bill Harvey, the swashbuckling CIA officer, was subsequently appointed chief of station in Rome; he died of a heart attack in June 1976.

Henri Rolland remained in the United States after he had been summoned back to Paris by his SDECE chief. He now lives at Lighthouse Point, Florida.

Fifteen Soviet Juliett-class submarines are still in service with the Northern, Pacific, Black Sea, and Baltic Fleets. Considered very successful by the Soviets, the first was decommissioned in 1984.

Sir Clive Loehnis continues to watch cricket and divides his time between his home, just off Eaton Square, and White's Club.

Celia Sanchez died of cancer in 1984. Her house on 23rd Street remains untouched, as a shrine, and it is rumored that Castro occasionally spends the night there alone.

Leo McGee remained STONE's staunch supporter but was isolated and forced into retirement when he refused to endorse a CIA report confirming FOXTROT's bona fides.

John Vassall was paroled from prison in 1972 and, having changed his name, works as a clerk in a solicitor's office in London.

Barbara Fell served a two-year sentence at Holloway and Askham Grange open prison; she married a blind former colleague upon her release. Now a widow, she still lives in her father's house in Kensington.

Tom Waters took early retirement from GCHQ and now lives with Holly in Withington, Gloucestershire.